BROMHEAD'S WAR

Vietnam GZ Thriller Series
Book Thirty

Eric Helm

SAPERE
BOOKS

BROMHEAD'S WAR

Published by Sapere Books.

24 Trafalgar Road, Ilkley, LS29 8HH

saperebooks.com

ISBN: 978-0-85495-691-3

PROLOGUE

General Vo Nguyen Giap stood under the harsh tropical sun and watched as a division of the People's Army of Vietnam passed in review. He wasn't worried about a surprise attack by American or South Vietnamese aircraft. They rarely penetrated this deep into North Vietnam and this close to Laos. These were young men who would be taking the fight to the South Vietnamese and their allies, the Americans. These soldiers would prove the resolve of the Vietnamese in their war against imperialism. The fight had been long, beginning with the Chinese, the French, the Japanese, the French again and now the Americans with their coalition from many Asian and European countries, not to mention the Australians.

Giap was uncomfortable in his heavy dress uniform and wished that he didn't have to participate in these ceremonies. They were necessary for the families of the soldiers who were leaving home, maybe for good, and for the soldiers themselves. It was a show that reinforced the idea that this war was necessary and even if he wasn't going south with them, they had his complete support.

When the parade ended, Giap moved to the microphone and told them of the long struggle ahead of them. He said that it was worth any price that had to be paid because the result would be a free and unified Vietnam. An autonomous country that would be a glowing beacon of Communism for the world to see and admire. He didn't mention that he, and those at the top of the political structure in Hanoi, would enjoy freedoms and benefits that those at the bottom of that structure would never know.

As he finished, a flight of MiG-23 fighters flew low over them, trailing colored smoke that represented the North Vietnamese flag. Giap didn't tell the soldiers on the parade ground that the pilots were Soviets, and the aircraft were from the Soviet Union. Such knowledge might cause the soldiers to question their ability to carry out the war themselves. It was a Vietnamese struggle against the imperialism of the West. It was better that the soldiers believed that they were taking on almost the whole world by themselves. That was supposed to instill pride in them.

Three hours later, Giap met with the commanders of the various units about to begin the long march into the south. They would follow the Ho Chi Minh Trail as far as they could, but would march beyond the southern terminus, to a point in Cambodia that was due west of Saigon, the ultimate target. It was a long march and only part of it would be made in trucks and other vehicles. Much of it would be on foot as they carried the necessary supplies with them.

The officers were all sitting around a large, highly polished table that held a silver tea service. Giap was at the head of the table, looking at the four colonels who would be leading the various components of the division south. They were all combat veterans who had distinguished themselves in the past. This was the last meeting before they climbed into their jeeps to take their soldiers south.

Giap pointed at Tri Minh Nguyen, the oldest and most senior among the colonels. He was now wearing the style of uniform he would wear for the next several months. It was going to be his last combat command because of his age. Upon successful completion, he would return to Hanoi as a hero, promoted to general and then retired. If he failed, his name would be stricken from all records, his accomplishments erased, and he would be forgotten by all.

Nguyen was small with leather-like skin and dark eyes. A scar started at the corner of his mouth and continued down to his neck. The wound would have been fatal if it had been an inch further round, where it would have severed the carotid artery. What his fellow soldiers didn't know was that he had been wounded in a knife fight with an outraged husband, and not battling the puppet soldiers of the South.

"Do you understand the importance of your role in the plan?" Giap asked.

"Yes, comrade. I am to destroy the American camp that blocks our route to Saigon. When it has been overrun, the next wave will enter the south to carry out the drive to Saigon." He grinned broadly, as if to say that his task would be a simple one. Those in the camp would flee at the first sign of trouble.

"You will hold that base, and all the equipment captured there, for as long as necessary. You will execute all the puppet soldiers you capture, interrogate any American soldiers captured and then send them north for internment."

"If they are wounded in the fight?"

"If they are unable to travel north, they will then unfortunately die of their wounds. We will return the remains, if that is convenient. If not, they will be disposed of according to your orders."

Giap looked around to be sure they all understood the order. "South Vietnamese prisoners will be executed, their families, if on the camp, will be rounded up for reeducation. All military-age males will be executed. Women and children will be sent away to tell what happens to those who take up arms against us. Young women will be offered the opportunity to serve in any of several capacities. Is that understood?"

All the colonels nodded and Nguyen said, "Yes, General."

"We have been over this plan many times. You have all studied the terrain, the photographs of the camp and the other intelligence gathered by our allies, the Viet Cong. There is no need to cover the strategy and the plan again." With his foot, he searched under the table for a button that activated a buzzer in another room.

"Before you go, we will have a final meal together."

As he said it, the door opened, and several young women entered carrying plates of food. They were not dressed in traditional Vietnamese clothes but looked more like they were about to go swimming somewhere in the decadent West. All had long, black hair, deep brown eyes, and long legs. There was one woman for each of the colonels and two serving General Giap, proving that rank had its privileges.

They were followed by a young soldier, dressed as a waiter in a fancy Western restaurant, who carried a bottle of imported wine. He first showed the label to General Giap and when the general nodded, he poured a small amount into his glass. Giap picked it up, swirled the wine around and then tasted it. Satisfied, Giap said, "Please serve the colonels."

Ten kilometers away, the lower ranking officers and the enlisted men of the division were dining in large tents erected under the cover of the jungle for the purpose. They were eating from metal trays that held food that had been prepared quickly by Army cooks. It wasn't the best cuisine, but it did keep the soldiers from hunger. They were eating in shifts and had to carry their own trays to the tables. They were drinking colored water that was cool at best and had a chemical taste.

Finished with their meal, they were herded into a holding area where there were trucks waiting for them. They sat on the ground, trying to find a little shade. They had their equipment with them and were provided with unit ammo and squad equipment for them to carry to the south, as well as food and water. Their officers and NCOs circulated among them, looking and listening for signs of discontent. Such anti-government thoughts would be stamped out quickly. There would be no dissention in the ranks.

The soldiers had no role, except to wait. If they tried to sleep, there was an officer of NCO to wake them. They were not allowed to relax too much. They couldn't move around because they had been split into the loads assigned to a specific truck. When it was time to depart, they would be right where they needed to be and ready to go.

Giap, having finished eating, realized it was time for departure. It would take twenty or thirty minutes for the colonels to join their units. He stood, held up his wine glass. As the colonels stood and raised their glasses, Giap said, "To the success of our mission and the fall of Saigon, and to our soldiers who will make this happen."

The colonels repeated the toast, and they all drank.

"Colonel Nguyen, you will be the tip of the spear. You will engage the enemy first. You will remove the main obstacle to our route to Saigon. Good luck to you. I will meet with you when you return."

Colonel Nguyen came to attention and saluted Giap. "Thank you, sir. We will not fail."

CHAPTER 1

South Vietnam was considered a mature theater. In military terms this meant that the United States Army had been engaged in combat operations long enough that the supply lines, which initially had carried only that equipment and supplies necessary to sustain those operations, now had room for what might be considered comfort items. There were American television stations operating through the Armed Forces Vietnam Network, known by the letters AFVN. Hootches, that once had slowly rotating ceiling fans for cooling, now had air conditioning. The PX was filled with comfort items that would seem ridiculous to the average GI from World War Two. No one needed a fur coat in the topics, but these could be found. New cars could be purchased there as well, and nearly everyone returned to the World with a killer stereo ordered through the PX system.

Captain Jonathan Bromhead, United States Army Special Forces, who had served one tour as the executive officer of a Green Beret A Team, was on his second tour, this time as the team commander. He was sitting in the air-conditioned team house that held a refrigerator that contained a case of beer, but more importantly, a case of Pepsi, and in the freezer were two half gallons of ice cream. Bromhead had been thinking about that ice cream for about an hour but was resisting the urge to eat some of it, wanting to save it for desert.

Bromhead was a little young to be a team leader. The tropical sun had turned his skin a deep brown, hiding the freckles that made him look even younger than he was. Like his fellow soldiers, he was trim without seeming to be skinny, strong, and in other circumstances would have been considered an expert in unarmed combat.

He heard a noise at the door and glanced in that direction. Sergeant First Class Sully Smith entered and let the door bang shut. He was wearing tiger-striped fatigues that were sweat-stained and mud-caked. He carried his M-16 by holding onto the pistol grip. He still wore his web gear, though the pistol belt was unfastened and hanging loose.

Smith leaned his rifle against the wall and then saw Bromhead. He said, "Afternoon, Captain."

"How'd the patrol go?" Bromhead set the book he had been reading face down on the table, so that he didn't lose his place.

"We'll hold a debrief in thirty. Gave the patrol time to relax, clean up a bit and do whatever they needed to do." Smith hesitated and then asked, "Is it too early for a beer?"

Bromhead grinned at the sergeant. "Are you on duty?"

Smith had reached the refrigerator but hadn't opened the door. He said, "Technically, yes."

"Do I detect a but in that answer?"

"Yes, sir. But I've been on patrol for three days and only had warm water to drink. I'm dehydrated and I believe that I deserve something better than water."

"I'm not sure that beer is the best thing to rehydrate," said Bromhead. He thought for a moment, wondering if he should mention that Smith was a senior NCO and had an obligation to lead by example. Did he think that the other members of the patrol should have a beer?

Smith opened the refrigerator and took out a can of beer. "If there is no objection, sir."

"Sully, you're old enough and senior enough to make that decision without commentary from me."

Smith hesitated and then put the beer back. Instead, he took out a Pepsi and sat down at the table with Bromhead. "There is enough cold beer that I can give one to each member of the patrol. It was a good patrol. They deserve a reward."

"Did you see anything?"

"No, sir. We didn't see much of anything. Saw the farmers in their rice fields but I'm not sure that they saw us. They didn't seem to be concerned about anything except the rice. We saw no sign of recent VC activity though we did find an old AK. Looked as if it had been dropped a couple of years ago. That was before the ambush."

Smith then popped the top of the Pepsi and took a long pull. "That certainly is what I needed. Well, almost."

"I'd ask you about that, but I'll wait for the debriefing. Think about any recommendations you have for the next patrol?"

"Certainly." Smith paused and then said, "We should move to the south and west, toward the Cambodian border. I think that if we push in that direction, we'll have a better chance of finding the enemy."

"Without crossing the border."

"Goes without saying, Captain. Just move parallel to it to see if we can find signs of infiltration and then follow those."

Bromhead rubbed his chin for a moment, thinking about what Smith had said. Infiltration from the Ho Chi Minh Trail was a problem, but Bromhead thought they were too far south and too far from the border to make such a patrol feasible. Logistical support would be difficult and if they ran into a large force of either VC or NVA, reinforcement or extraction would be problematic unless they had helicopters on standby, which wasn't completely out of the question.

"Do you think that's a good idea, given our overall mission?"

Smith grinned. "Isn't one of our missions is to seek out and destroy the enemy's capability to wage war wherever it might be."

"Unless it's on the other side of the border, but let's talk about this after the debriefing," said Bromhead.

First Lieutenant James Carson had joined the team late, after the previous lieutenant had been evacuated with a bleeding ulcer. Bromhead hadn't believed the diagnosis at first, but it had been confirmed, first by the team medic and later by the doctors at the evac hospital. The word was that he would be treated in the States and might not return to the team. Bromhead hadn't been happy about having a replacement. It was like throwing an unknown into the mix. The new officer hadn't trained with the men on the team, who had been together for months before they had deployed.

Carson was fully qualified. He had been at the top of his class at Camp Mackall, had gone through Army Reserves Officers' Training Corps in college, been commissioned and attended the Infantry Officers' Basic Course. He'd seen a call for officers with language skills and had applied. He hadn't expected to find himself in the Special Forces, but that's what happened. The ironic thing was that he was fluent in Greek, which didn't help him in Vietnam. Sometimes the Army just got things wrong, forcing a square peg into a round hole.

Carson was a young man, barely twenty-five. When he arrived in Vietnam, he began a campaign to grow a mustache but failed. He was now clean shaven, but his skin was tanned a deep brown. Although he looked skinny, he was as strong as any man on the team. Unlike many of the other soldiers, Carson had been through school and military training nearly all his life. Normally, a Special Forces officer will have worked his way up, through the ranks, or had served on active duty for a couple of yours. But the Vietnam War had changed that situation.

Carson walked into the team house and saw Bromhead sitting at a table. The captain was just sitting there, as if worn out from a long day in the field, though he hadn't left the camp in a couple of weeks.

"Sully's patrol is back," said Bromhead.

"I saw him. We're going to have a debriefing after he gets the strikers settled. I was going to find you to sit in."

Carson walked to the refrigerator, opened the door and hung onto it as he studied the contents. "Too early for a beer?"

"If you have completed your assigned tasks and we don't expect an enemy assault tonight, then knock yourself out."

Carson reached for a beer, hesitated, and then grabbed a soft drink. As he shut the door, he said, "Must set a good example for the men."

Smith reentered the team house and asked, "Set a good example by doing what?"

Carson held up the can. "This is not a beer."

"Captain, are we now authorized a beer?" asked Smith.

"Sully, we've had that conversation. I suggest you take your lead from Lieutenant Carson."

Smith took a swig of his Pepsi. "I've invited Lieutenant Nguyen to join us here."

"He's a good man," said Bromhead.

"Yes, sir. I think it's because he earned the rank rather than buy it."

Nguyen walked in. He was dressed in a clean and pressed tiger-striped uniform. He looked as if he was ready to report to a general rather than attend a debriefing in the team house. Like most of the Vietnamese, he was a small man but who was as tough as they came. There was a scar on his face from a knife fight in which the opponent had not survived. He didn't talk about it, and no one knew the details of the fight.

"Please excuse the delay, sir. I was ensuring that the soldiers were taking care of their equipment, especially their weapons, before they relaxed."

Bromhead grinned but only because his English was so precise. Nguyen had been educated in the United States, but Bromhead suspected he was something of a polyglot. He seemed to speak French and Chinese. The multinational nature of Vietnam during both the Second World War and later, as the colonial empires began to collapse, had some interesting language skills.

"Grab the beverage of your choice and sit down."

They waited for several minutes as the rest of the patrol began to filter in. Some of them carried their own beverages and a few took theirs from the refrigerator. Only two selected a beer. None of the officers mentioned that. They all figured that the soldiers had earned the beer if they wanted it.

When everyone was seated, Bromhead spoke. "This is the informal after-action report. Sully, you and Lieutenant Nguyen will prepare a formal document later for me to file with Nha Trang. For now, I just want to know what happened while you were wandering around in the jungle for the last three days."

"Yes, sir. We left the camp about two hours before sunup. I thought we'd be able to get into the jungle before anyone saw us leave the camp, if someone was watching. I saw and heard nothing to suggest that we weren't successful."

Smith began to stand, but Bromhead waved him down into his chair. Smith cleared his throat and began the narrative. He said that he had taken the point, but only to get the patrol through the wire and across the open area that they thought of as the killing field. The patrol carefully followed him so that they didn't trip any of the booby traps or flares that were set around to alert the camp of someone trying to sneak through the wire at night.

He was tempted to sprint across the open ground but in the dark, it would be easy to trip and break a bone. The patrol looked like shadows concealed by the darkness. Speed wasn't as important as silent movement. And even if they did make noise, here, near the camp, it wasn't as important as it would be later, deeper in the jungle.

They reached the tree line and entered. Smith avoided both the farmer's paths and animal trails. The enemy would anticipate them following a trail. To avoid an ambush or booby traps, he stayed away from the trails. It was more difficult to move through the jungle without making any noise that way, but was safer, if safer was the right word.

An hour later, they came to a place where the jungle thinned slightly. The ground was level and overhead, rather than triple-canopy jungle, was an umbrella of bright stars. Smith didn't recognize any constellations. There was just a smattering of stars scattered around.

Without orders, the patrol formed a circle, with each of the strikers facing outward. They could see the man on either side of them. This was a security feature that would prevent anyone from slipping up on them undetected. They were to relax for a few minutes and drink a little water. Smith didn't like for them to smoke, mainly because the enemy would be able to smell the cigarettes, not to mention seeing the match flame. Smokers didn't realize how far that odor could carry or how bright a match could be in the semi-darkness of the jungle.

As the sun came up, the jungle came alive. The monkeys started chattering at one another and then the birds took flight, chirping wildly. Dark shapes turned gray and finally colorful as the sun climbed higher. It made patrolling easier and reduced the chance of an ambush. The sun didn't erase it completely, just made it more difficult for the enemy.

Using hand signals, Smith got the patrol moving again, but he was no longer on point. One of the senior strikers, who was a careful man and aware of the danger of being on point, now had that job. They still avoided the trails, pushing through the jungle as quietly as they could. It had been relatively cool, at least for the tropical environment, but soon became warmer. The humidity was sapping their strength and after ninety minutes, Smith called for another halt.

This time, they rested with half the patrol on alert for thirty minutes, and the other half resting. Smith sat in the middle of the circle with Nguyen, but they didn't speak. Smith was eating from a can of peaches. He knew he shouldn't be eating them that early in the patrol, but he couldn't resist. He'd be sorry later in the day and when they halted for the night, he'd wished he still had them. Canned fruit was a welcome break from what was in many of the C-ration boxes.

Finished with his breakfast, he took a position on the perimeter. He wasn't leading by example, and it wasn't long before those who had been at rest replaced the others.

One of the strikers lit a cigarette. Before Smith could react, Nguyen had taken the butt from the striker and crushed it out. There was a whispered conversation. Smith knew the striker was being told that the cigarette smoke could identify their position. He was surprised by the incident, but then small packs of cigarettes were included in some of the C-rat boxes.

The rest of the day was spent moving through the jungle, looking for signs of the enemy, signs of new bunkers near clearings, signs of increased activity, but they found nothing.

The farmers were in their paddies, and some women worked beside them. The patrol saw a youngster leading a water buffalo along a rice paddy dike. Smith didn't think the child saw them and if he did, he ignored them.

The night passed quietly. The only noise was from the animals and insects. At one point, Smith was sure that he heard a snake moving through the rotting vegetation. He didn't worry about it. Most snakes avoided humans and as long as he didn't step on it by accident, he would be fine. While they were resting for the night, they set up as an ambush. Smith didn't expect they would encounter the enemy — or rather the enemy wouldn't encounter them — but he wanted to be ready. They had seen no sign of the VC or any NVA, although they had heard an artillery strike in the distance and occasionally heard helicopters overhead. Once they heard one flying low, but it was gone in a minute. They didn't see it and there was still no sign of the enemy.

That came the next day. It was near noon and the point walked right by the enemy soldier. An instant later, another VC fired a round, giving away their location. Without a command from Smith, the strikers charged the suspected ambush. They moved, firing on full auto, screaming as they attacked. The intention was to distract the VC, to frighten them and keep the enemy from shooting back. That broke the ambush, with the VC scattering, rather than holding their positions.

Smith saw one of the men, dressed in the khaki of the NVA. He hadn't opened fire but was trying to clear his weapon. His AK-47 had jammed. The man didn't take cover and seemed oblivious to what was happening around him. He was just kneeling there, concentrating on clearing his weapon. Smith fired from the hip. The three rounds stitched across the man's chest, knocking him over. He didn't move, but Smith keep an eye on him until he was close enough to see the man was dead. Smith grabbed the man's weapon, not as a souvenir, but to prevent the enemy from reclaiming it.

The firing increased until it was nearly one long, drawn-out explosion. To Smith it sounded like M-16s. He thought he heard an AK-47 firing, but that was cut short. The shooting continued, but he wasn't sure that any of the enemy were still engaged. He knew the threat had been eliminated.

Smith moved with the rest of the patrol. They'd overrun the ambush. There were several dead VC and one wearing the khaki of the NVA. One of the strikers was picking up the weapons while two others searched the bodies. The others were beginning a pursuit of the enemy.

"Call back your men, Lieutenant."

Nguyen glanced at Smith and then issued an order in Vietnamese. Most of the strikers stopped in place. One knelt and fired a long burst, emptying his magazine into the jungle. The man stood up and began walking deeper into the jungle. Nguyen called him back. Smith would remind him later about fire discipline.

They quickly searched the dead, taking anything of intelligence value, any papers, maps or wallets, and picking up the weapons. There were four dead and two wounded. He stopped the strikers from killing the wounded, but he had no plans to take them prisoner. They'd slow his patrol down and the wounds looked to be fatal. It might have been kinder just to shoot them in the head, but Smith stopped that.

Once they had gathered up everything that might be of value, they moved out. They were no longer worried about making noise. The short firefight had announced their presence in the area. Now it was important to get away from the ambush site.

That also ended the patrol. The enemy would know they were in the area. Now the imperative was to return to their camp.

"We didn't take a direct route back here," said Smith. "We did move faster though. I didn't want to get caught by a larger force chasing us. But then, I saw no evidence of a pursuit."

"You get anything of intelligence value?" asked Carson.

"No, sir. They had very little on them. I noticed they were a mixture of NVA and VC. Most of them were VC and I don't think they were very well trained. That was why someone fired prematurely. Had that not happened, we might have taken some casualties. Lieutenant Nguyen has taught his strikers well."

"You brought in the weapons?"

"Yes, sir. Looking for a souvenir?"

"You can't take an automatic weapon home legally," said Carson.

Smith couldn't help but grin. "Well, sir, maybe you can't, but I can."

Bromhead interrupted. "We don't need to expose all our secrets here. We'll let Lieutenant Carson in on those secrets later."

"Yes, sir."

"Is there anything else?"

Smith thought for a moment and then said, "I think the makeup of the ambush is important. NVA are in the area and are in contact with the VC. They're working together."

"That would be expected."

"Yes, sir. I just thought the fact there were NVA in that ambush, working with VC who were poorly trained, might be important. It might suggest something is being planned for the near future. I mean, they haven't really been able to overrun a

Special Forces camp except for Lang Vei a couple of years ago. I wondered if they might try to do that again, for propaganda purposes. Quite the propaganda success if they could overrun another camp. It would inspire young Vietnamese men to join them and it would look bad in the papers."

"Lang Vei was a special camp. Close to the border, and the NVA had tanks. I don't think the locals will have tanks."

"Yes, sir."

"We're getting off our purpose here. Lieutenant Nguyen, do you have anything you want to add?"

"Our strikers responded very professionally. I'd like to do something for them. To reward them for their professionalism and their valor."

"What do you have in mind?"

"A week's leave. Trip to Saigon, or their homes, as appropriate."

"That's something for your commander to approve. Get the after-action written and I'll speak with him. We'll get something worked out, but we can't send all of them to Saigon at once."

"Yes, sir. Thank you, sir."

"If there is nothing else?"

"No, sir," said Smith.

"Then I suggest we break up. Beer is still in the refrigerator for those who are of a mind."

As Smith stood, he asked, "Are you going to let B Team know about the contact?"

Bromhead shook his head. "Not about the contact, but I will mention your concern with the NVA working so closely with the local VC."

CHAPTER 2

Army Special Forces Major, MacKenzie K. Gerber, pulled the cover sheet off the map set up on an artist's easel. It was tucked in a corner of the operations bunker that was made of sandbagged walls and covered by thick wooden planks and several layers of sandbags. There was a desk nearby, two chairs that had seen better days and a fan aimed at the desks in an attempt to keep the occupants cool. The noise of the fan was annoying and the cooling effect minimal.

On the map was a plastic overlay marked by red grease pencil designating enemy locations. For those who didn't understand the Army symbology, it looked as if the Viet Cong and the North Vietnamese Army controlled the area from just inside Cambodia into South Vietnam around the Parrot's Beak and the Angel Wing areas. These were west of and slightly south of Tay Ninh.

On the paper map, under the plastic overlay, were the blue markings of the American and the South Vietnamese Army locations. To the outside observer, it looked as if those locations were surrounded by the enemy. The truth was that most of the enemy were suspected locations of headquarters that had few soldiers assigned to them. The theory was that if they were ordered into action, they would activate civilian units that operated as more of a civilian defense force or a national guard than a regular combat unit. They would gather at the headquarters to receive their orders, but the American forces operated in the area without any real concern about the enemy. They rarely came into contact with one another.

Gerber, like most of the others around him, knew that the situation wasn't as bad as it looked, but it was still somewhat disturbing. Sometimes he thought about calling artillery down on one of those headquarters just to see what would happen. He believed they would just destroy some empty bunkers and little else.

Special Forces Sergeant Major, Anthony B. Fetterman approached. He was over forty, had served in World War Two as a paratrooper, but had been in the Special Forces for most of his career. He liked to say that he was related to the cavalry officer, Captain William Fetterman, who had bragged that with eighty men he could ride through the entire Sioux Nation. He had his chance in December 1866 and failed. Not a single man with him survived the battle.

Fetterman was holding a can of Pepsi, but he wasn't drinking from it. He took a seat and waited for Gerber to say something.

"Looks bad for Johnny," said Gerber.

"We agreed that since he is now a captain and he has his own A-Team, that maybe we should refer to him as John or Captain."

"Sometimes, Sergeant Major, you are annoying."

"Yes, sir, but I'm right. You have said that yourself."

Changing the subject, Gerber asked, "You see anything on the map of interest?"

"When was the last update."

"The Intel NCO said about nine this morning. He used the latest from MACV and the local intel guy, so the data are current."

"Changes from the last time?"

"Nothing significant that I can see. The twenty-fifth made some contact here," said Gerber, pointing to an area just south of Tay Ninh City. "Lasted about thirty minutes and the VC withdrew. They found half a dozen bodies and two weapons. There were blood trails that they followed, but they were headed into Cambodia."

"Surprised they left the weapons."

"Yeah, I had the same thought," said Gerber. "They were probably pressed by the soldiers."

"Why are we interested in this?"

Gerber pulled the sheet back, covering the map. "I was just trying to figure out where the next push would be. If there was something that might tell us what they're going to do They've been quiet too long and that always makes me suspicious."

"And have you figured it out?"

"I certainly have, Sergeant Major. Have you?"

"I only had a quick look at the map, but it seemed there were a couple of areas in which the concentration of enemy soldiers has increased, especially just over the border in Cambodia. Looks like that increase is in the Parrot's Beak and the Angel's Wing south of Tay Ninh."

"Were you able to determine the size of those units?"

Fetterman took a drink from his Pepsi and then squeezed the can. "I suspect more than a regiment but no more than three."

"Yeah, that's what I thought too."

"We going to take a look? It seemed that the largest concentration was around John's camp."

Gerber stretched, raising his hands over his head. "I didn't see anything that would suggest an attack on his camp. If they did hit it, I don't think they have sufficient numbers to overrun it unless they begin to pull in the local VC and I saw no intel that suggested a sudden decrease in the numbers of young farmers."

Fetterman took a deep breath. "So, we're not going to look for ourselves?"

Gerber sat down in one of the wooden chairs. "I was thinking that maybe we should go talk to the intelligence puke to see what he can tell us about the activity in that area."

"Intelligence puke?"

"Tony, he's a straight leg with four months in-country. I don't think he's acclimated to the situation, but he probably has access to the raw data that will tell us something. I want to see that raw data."

"Why not talk to Captain Bromhead?"

"Because I get the feeling he resents us showing up all the time. He takes it as a sign that he needs our help to run his team. He doesn't get that we just enjoy getting into the field and his is a good camp."

"Which means we're not going out in the field?"

"I thought we'd talk to the intelligence guy and then maybe whistle up a helicopter so that we could conduct an aerial recon. Something about midafternoon and home before the grunts drink all the beer."

"Are we authorized to do that?"

"That's the nice thing about being a field grade officer. Most of the time no one challenges you because everyone assumes that we field grade officers know what we're doing and we have the authorization to do it. And we get to move to the head of the line in the club so that we get a cold beer."

Gerber and Fetterman were seated in the cargo compartment of a UH-1H Huey Helicopter. Gerber was on one side and Fetterman on the other so that both were in position to get a good look at the ground. They had flown southwest of Tay Ninh, over relatively open ground. They were looking for signs of increased enemy activity, but they weren't seeing much. Gerber had noticed that many of the farmers refused to look up at the helicopter. It was almost as if they were afraid that looking would draw hostile fire or give away a vital piece of intelligence.

Gerber keyed the intercom and asked, "Can we get closer to the border and farther to the south?"

"Yes, sir. How close to the border?"

"I don't want to put us in jeopardy by getting too close. I want to see the terrain along the border."

The helicopter subtly changed direction. Gerber wondered if the pilot was making gentle turns for fear of making those in the back sick or if there was no reason to make a sharper change of direction. Using the intercom, he said, "You don't need to worry about us back here. We've been flying in helicopters quite a bit."

There were just two clicks over the intercom, telling Gerber that the pilot understood, but the turn didn't steepen.

Gerber leaned to the right and touched Fetterman on the arm. He raised an eyebrow in question. Fetterman shook his head, a big grin on his face.

The open land was filled with rice paddies and sporadic clumps of trees, signifying a cluster of hootches where the farmers lived. There were not more than four or five of the hootches in the cluster, a pen or two for water buffalo, and low fences. Sometimes there was smoke from a cooking fire. Oddly, there were few people around, but it was getting late in the day. The farmers had headed home. It was strange to see no people outside, but it was not strange enough to cause any anxiety.

"Should we head back?" asked Fetterman.

"I'm not sure, Tony. If there has been a regimental build up, I would expect to see more activity. I would expect to see people out to make the scene look more natural. This is a little suspicious."

"They would have heard us coming from a long way off and had time to get under cover."

There was a sudden ripping sound. Gerber thought it was from the left, but he couldn't see anything below.

"We're taking fire," said the pilot. "Out about our eleven o'clock. Single weapon."

The crew chief spun his door gun to the right. He opened fire in short bursts. The tracers seemed to fall short of the enemy.

Over the intercom, the aircraft commander said, "You're not coming close to that guy."

"No, sir. Just wanted to keep his head down."

"I didn't see anything," said Gerber.

"Line of tracers that were too far away to do any damage."

"Can you come around?"

"Yes, sir, but my inclination is to turn tail. We're a single ship."

"What about artillery? Can you call in artillery?"

"Yes, sir, but I hate to do that. We don't know what we're facing, and it might be just one guy surrounded by a bunch of noncombatants. Maybe women and children."

"We've taken enemy fire," said Gerber. "We need to respond."

"Was this what you were looking for?"

"Can you fly in the direction of the enemy fire?"

"Yes, sir, but I'm climbing to three thousand feet. Keeps us way out of effective small arms range."

"Fine with me."

"You think this is an indication of one of those regiments?" asked Fetterman, shouting over the noise in the back of the helicopter.

"I don't know. Could be, but I would expect more people shooting at us if there was a regiment around."

They were near a finger of jungle that reached down from the north and expanded to the west, into Cambodia. They flew over what looked like an enemy installation, meaning a few low bunkers, no real above-ground structures, and no sign of farmers. Gerber saw no evidence of recent activity.

As they flew over, three more weapons fired up at them. The tracers didn't come close. Gerber said, "Not very disciplined."

"I think we might have found what we were looking for."

To the pilot, he asked, "Can you call in artillery?"

"I can try. If they've got a fire mission, they'd have to complete that first."

"How long can we stay over the target?"

"About an hour but we'd have to refuel at Tay Ninh."

The aircraft commander keyed the mic. "Tay Ninh arty. Tay Ninh arty. This is Ranger two one. I have a fire mission southwest of Tay Ninh."

"Ranger two one, confirm enemy."

"Roger. We have taken fire from four to six automatic weapons. They are concealed in a tree line. I have seen no civilians in the area."

"Ranger two one, say location."

He provided the grid coordinates and said that he was orbiting to the northwest of the enemy position. He thought that would keep him out of the gun target lines.

Gerber said, "I don't think those were the correct coordinates."

"Sir, I am sure about them."

"Ranger two one, one round smoke. Shot over."

"Shot out."

To those in the aircraft, he said, "Let me know if you see the round impact."

"Got it," said the crew chief. "About ten o'clock."

Over the radio, the aircraft commander said, "Left fifty, add one fifty."

"Shot over."

"Shot out."

An instant later there was an explosion at the edge of the tree line. "Add fifty and fire for effect."

The tree line erupted in clouds of brown-gray smoke. The arty was both high explosive that detonated among the trees and rounds that were clouds of smoke fifty feet above the trees, shredding them with white-hot shrapnel. The high-explosive rounds were designed to take out the bunkers and the other rounds were anti-personnel.

"Are we going to be able to assess the damage?" Gerber asked.

"Depends."

"Last rounds on the way. Tubes clear."

"Ranger two one, roger."

They watched as the last of the artillery rounds fell. Smoke was rising from the impact site. They descended toward the area, but this time took no fire. From fifteen hundred feet and looking down into the trees, there wasn't much to look at. There were the remains of a single bunker that had taken a direct hit, leaving a smoking crater, but they couldn't see if there were any bodies in or around it.

"Can we fly lower?"

"Not a good idea, sir. We shouldn't be orbiting here. We're giving the VC a chance to take a few more shots at us. We should be getting clear of the area, but I'll get with our intel guy to report them. Might get a patrol out, but it'll be in the morning."

"I've seen enough," said Fetterman.

"Let's head back to the barn," said Gerber.

They climbed to two thousand feet and headed toward Tay Ninh to refuel. The AC provided Tay Ninh arty with the after-action information but could only say that one bunker had been destroyed and there was no body count. It was not an impressive outcome.

The Long Range Reconnaissance Patrol, known as LRRP, was designed for that specific purpose, that is a long patrol. They were sent out for several days or weeks to search for enemy activity. Their mission was not to engage the enemy, just to spot the enemy and report on their location. Others, at a higher level, could then decide on the best way to engage and to eliminate the enemy. LRRPs were the very definition of a sneak and peek mission.

Sergeant First Class Henry Kincaid was sitting in the dayroom, his feet up on a chair, watching the afternoon programming on Armed Forces Vietnam, AFVN, television. It was the programming that had been aired the evening before, but Kincaid didn't care. He was just interested in the background noise it created. It sometimes reminded him of home, and he could forget where he was and what he was doing. He could even forget the heat and humidity for a short time while sitting where a fan could blow on him.

The company commander, Captain Richard Hackett, walked in and sat down next to Kincaid. "You haven't been drinking, have you?"

Kincaid looked at his watch. "Too early in the day. But then, there's nothing on the schedule until Tuesday, and I'm off duty, so it wouldn't be against regulations to have a beer."

"Wanna bet?"

"No, sir. You apparently know something that I do not."

"Helicopter took some fire near the border south of Tay Ninh. Pilot called in artillery about an hour ago. We need to find out what happened, and I thought of you."

Grinning, Kincaid said, "They called in artillery after somebody shot at them. Mission accomplished."

"I'm not in the mood for this. Get your team together. There'll be a chopper on the pad in about thirty minutes. You can get a current briefing from the Intel Officer. You're to be back by dusk. We just need to get someone in there on the ground to see what they hit. Minimum equipment but a full load of ammo."

"That's not the way we operate, sir."

"It is when the order comes down from Brigade. Somebody has his panties in a bunch. I suspect there might be something more to this. If nothing else, we do have our orders."

Kincaid closed his eyes, as if preparing himself for an argument. "Yes, sir." He pushed himself up and turned off the television. He then asked, "If I'd had a beer, would I have caught this?"

Now it was Hackett's turn to grin. "Not if I could find Hendrickson, but he's very good at hiding on his days off. You're too easy to find."

"Punished for doing the right thing?"

"Virtue is its own reward, Sergeant. Intel is waiting. Pilot has been briefed. You'll have to walk about four or five klicks. Chopper will put down in four or five open areas so that Charlie won't know where you got off, or if anyone got off."

"I often wonder if that trick fools anyone."

"Gives the pilots a chance to practice their landings. I'll meet you in operations."

Kincaid found his team waiting at the helipad. They didn't carry much. Just weapons, canteens, first aid kits, radios and a few grenades. Since they weren't going to remain in the field after dark, they didn't bother with some of the other equipment they'd normally carry. The helicopter was not there.

"You guys know what's going on?"

Sergeant Virgil Hilts said, "We're going for a short walk in the woods and then come home for dinner."

"Yeah. Looking for recent enemy activity. I'm told that a company is on standby in case we fuck up and get seen. Other than that, we just look at the impact site from an artillery strike a couple of hours ago."

"That's not our job."

"I'll make a note of that, and you can tell the Brigade commander when we get back. I'm sure he'll be interested in your analysis."

"No thanks."

"Any other questions?"

Sergeant Miles Woods said, "Sure. How do I get out of this chicken outfit?"

Kincaid shook his head. "What happened to you guys? Lose at poker or something?"

"This is not the kind of thing we do."

"I am aware of that, but I say again, the brigade commander has authorized this mission so we will happily comply with our orders unless you have orders from the division that countermands what we have."

The helicopter approached and as the pilot leveled the skids to touch down, he stirred up a cloud of dust that threatened to blind everyone. Kincaid turned his back and shut his eyes. An instant later the helicopter was on the ground and the dust dissipated.

Kincaid scrambled into the rear of the aircraft and crouched between the pilot's seats. The aircraft commander pushed the mic out so that it could pick up anything Kincaid said. The pilot keyed the mic and heard Kincaid's words.

"You know where we're going?"

The pilot shouted, "I was briefed by Ops. We make five landings and you guys are gone on the third. That's closest to the impact site."

"Roger that." Kincaid moved back and sat on the troop seat. He set the butt of his weapon on the cargo compartment floor, the barrel pointed straight up. The theory was if the weapon discharged, for any reason, the bullet would do the least damage, unless it happened to hit the main rotor. Unlike the regular infantry units, there was no red, plastic cover on the flash suppressor. LRRPs were considered professionals and didn't require that reminder.

The helicopter lifted to a hover, spun around and then the nose dipped and they began a rapid climb out. Kincaid looked at the soldiers with him, but they seemed relaxed. It was a short mission and since they were to avoid contact, the odds were that they would be back by dinner.

Outside, the landscape changed from nearly endless rice paddies to a wooded area that looked more like a forest than it did a jungle. More like a patch of trees in the Midwest. Once beyond that, there was the occasional hootch and sometimes a small cluster of them. There was smoke coming from some of the clusters, suggesting the Vietnamese were beginning their evening meals.

One of the door gunners tapped him on the shoulder and yelled, "First LZ coming up."

The helicopter banked and began a steep descent. There was a small opening in the trees. They didn't touch down; they hovered briefly and then climbed back out. They reached altitude and turned. Looking through the windshield, Kincaid saw the spread of the jungle and knew that this was the thick, triple canopy that extended deep into Cambodia. They wouldn't have to work their way through that.

They made a pass into a second LZ, climbed out and headed to the third. Kincaid made sure that he had a round chambered. He leaned forward and shouted, "Coming up on three." He held up three fingers.

They lined up in the cargo compartment doors, two on each side. As the aircraft hovered three feet above the ground, they all jumped out. When the helicopter began to climb again, they ran to the nearest trees and then spread out. There was no sign that anyone was around them. They had gotten in without being detected. At least that was what Kincaid hoped.

Using hand signals, Kincaid pointed in the direction he wanted them to patrol. Woods took the point and pushed his way deeper into the jungle. He moved quietly, choosing the route carefully, avoiding trails. He looked right and left, trying to spot any tripwires or landmines. He didn't expect to find anything. They were too far away from any military base and the VC didn't use booby traps in areas where it was more likely that the locals would trip them rather than American soldiers.

They had been traveling for about an hour when Woods stopped and held up a balled fist. The rest of the team knelt.

They were covering all directions of approach. They didn't know why Woods had stopped.

There was a slight breeze that rattled the leaves and the chirping of a bird. Insects buzzed around them. Kincaid concentrated on the noise. He thought he heard voices but couldn't make out what they were saying. They sounded like Vietnamese, which made sense given their location.

Woods slipped back to him, put his lips close to Kincaid's ear and whispered, "Vietnamese. I think they're NVA."

"Why?"

"Better noise discipline than the VC."

"Close?"

"Twenty-five yards? Maybe a little more."

"We need to get a count."

Woods nodded and started to move back to the point. Kincaid grabbed his arm and pulled him back. Kincaid then moved forward. He wanted to see the enemy for himself.

He hadn't crawled very far when he caught a whiff of smoke. The enemy was very good at concealing their fires. If he could smell the smoke, it told him they were close. It also told him that they were fearless. They didn't expect American soldiers and if they were found, they believed they could defeat the Americans. It meant they felt safe in the area because of their numbers.

Kincaid had wanted to see them. Their uniforms and equipment would identify them, but he didn't want to push his luck. He had found what he had been sent to find. He had located a sizable concentration of enemy soldiers near the area where the artillery rounds had landed. His job now was to withdraw without the enemy finding him. It was to their advantage to disappear back into the jungle.

Slowly, he fell back, being extra careful with his movements. He didn't believe that a snapping twig, or a slight rustling of a bush would alert the enemy soldiers, but Kincaid wasn't one to take chances that weren't necessary. Once back, he signaled his soldiers to follow him. Silently, slowly, carefully, they moved back the way they came.

After they had moved a klick, Kincaid believed they were far enough away from the enemy concentration. He took a knee and let the others join him. They were in enemy territory, which meant they weren't safe. Of course, in the field, they were never safe. There could be roving patrols or listening posts or another large concentration of the enemy that they hadn't spotted. He took out the radio and whispered, "Border Team Three ready for pick up at LZ Delta in 20 mikes."

He didn't wait for confirmation. He switched off the radio and then pointed to the southeast. Woods nodded and took the point. The others fell in behind him, spreading out in case of an ambush. Kincaid was now at the rear of the patrol, the one position he really hated.

As they reached the clearing that was LZ Delta, they halted again. Kincaid moved to the forward position. Across the landing zone was no sign of the enemy. Nothing looked out of the ordinary. The animals were making noise, and the birds were wheeling overhead. Nothing had disturbed them for an hour or more.

Kincaid used the radio again and said, "Three in position."

"Three, can you pop smoke?"

Kincaid pulled out a smoke grenade and pulled the pin. He held the spoon in place and threw the grenade out, near the middle of the LZ. He still hadn't heard the helicopter.

"ID red."

"Roger."

"Inbound."

They didn't hear the helicopter until it was nearly on top of them. It dropped out of the sky rapidly. It barely cleared the trees, dropped lower and flared out. It came to a hover at the far end of the LZ. Kincaid and his team sprinted through the knee-high grass. They reached the helicopter and jumped into the cargo compartment. Before they could get settled, the helicopter spun around and began a rapid climb. At the last minute, there was the chattering of an enemy machine gun. None of the rounds struck the aircraft and Kincaid's team fired nothing in return. Kincaid didn't attempt to call in artillery. He just marked the map with the locations of the enemy forces.

Fetterman, sitting behind the wheel of a jeep, looked at his watch. "They're late."

Gerber, who had been sitting with his eyes closed and trying not to think of everything that might have gone wrong, said, "Patience is a virtue, Sergeant Major."

"You say that, but I'm not sure you believe it."

"At the moment, all we know is that a chopper was dispatched to pick up the team. At the moment, they are heading back. Therefore, at the moment, there is nothing we can do other than wait. I have opted for patience."

"It strikes me," said Fetterman, "we could have been waiting in the air-conditioned comfort of the operations bunker or one of the clubs rather than sitting out here in the weather."

Gerber opened his eyes. "There. That's probably the chopper."

Fetterman looked at his watch again. "We've been here for five minutes."

"You have a hot date or something?"

Fetterman finally grinned. "Nope. I just like to point out that some people have no sense of time."

"Maybe they're just trying to be fashionably late. Maybe they have a sense of style."

The helicopter approached slowly, flared out, stirring up a cloud of dust and settled to the pad. Four soldiers jumped out, ducked unnecessarily and moved off the pad. When they were clear, the helicopter turned and lifted off.

As the noise of the turbine and the pounding of the rotors faded, Gerber called, "Sergeant. Over here."

One of the men walked over toward the jeep, saw Gerber, but didn't salute. Various protocols prohibited saluting in the field or on the flight line. Saluting only served to identify the officers for the enemy snipers. None of that really applied in the middle of the large base camp. Gerber didn't care about some of the military customs, especially in the field.

"Yes, sir?"

"I need to know what you found out."

"Yes, sir. I don't know you, sir, and I'm not sure how highly classified the information might be. I can't tell you much of anything."

"I can rectify that problem by telling you that I ordered the reconnaissance and that I know you were out near the border looking for the enemy. We were worried about a high concentration of the enemy near the border that haven't been detected and that might endanger several of our camps."

Kincaid hesitated for a moment, saw the Special Forces patch and the Green Beret, and said, "Yes, sir. We didn't get too close to the enemy, but we did find the enemy in the area feeling confident enough to fire on our helicopter as we lifted off."

Gerber handed Kincaid a map that had been folded so that the area near the border was exposed. "Can you show me where?"

"Yes, sir. But wouldn't this be better handled in operations?"

"Possibly, but I don't want to sit through a proper debriefing. I just need the preliminaries so that I might alert some of my teams. They're the ones who need the information."

"Yes, sir." Kincaid studied the map and then pointed. "We found the enemy here, but I don't have numbers. What we saw was about a platoon, but it could have been more. My job was not to get the numbers. Just the location. I can just say they were confident enough that they weren't worried about noise discipline, and they had started some fires. We exfiltrated to this point where the chopper picked us up. Took some fire as we lifted off from an RPD machine gun. One gun and it missed by quite a bit."

"Thank you, Sergeant. Can we offer you a lift somewhere?"

"Be sort of crowded."

"You don't have much in the way of equipment and I think we can squeeze everyone in."

Kincaid waved to the other three members of his team. "Hop in. We have a ride."

CHAPTER 3

Chief Warrant Officer Three (CW3) Wayne Cornett was one of those rare Army aviators who was dual qualified in fixed-wing and rotary-wing aircraft. He was qualified in almost every Army helicopter except for the Sikorsky CH-54 Skycrane. He held multi-engine ratings in fixed-wing aircraft and although checked out in several four-engine airplanes, he was qualified only in those with two engines.

Cornett was older than most of the helicopter pilots in Vietnam. He was just under six feet tall, stocky, with a hairline in fast retreat. He was clean shaven and had built up a deep tan from his months in Vietnam. Under normal circumstances, he would have been assigned to a headquarters working in Operations or as an aviation advisor to the commanding officer. He hadn't wanted that. He wanted to be out, in the field, with the youngsters who were coming directly from flight school to combat assignments in Vietnam. He thought he could save lives that way. Of course, the brass had a different idea for him.

He had a previous tour in Vietnam as a Chinook pilot but hadn't liked the assignment. He felt like an aerial truck driver hauling equipment and supplies around Three Corps and sometimes south into Four Corps. Now, he was more of a taxi driver, hauling the brass around South Vietnam in a specially equipped Huey and sometimes in a Chinook. It was a relatively safe job, not like those flying combat assaults in Hueys on a daily basis. He was rarely taken under fire, and that was by small arms that didn't have the range to reach him at four or five thousand feet.

Cornett knew about flying combat assaults in D-model Huey helicopters because, during TET of 1968, nearly all the helicopter pilots were tapped to join the air assault units. Every Army flight school student who was learning to fly helicopters or transitioning into helicopters had been qualified in the Hueys before graduation. It meant, simply, that every Army helicopter pilot knew how to fly the Huey.

Given the number of missions being flown, and the fact that "blade time" wasn't an issue, many of the pilots who weren't normally called on to fly combat assault found themselves as copilots flying combat assault. Cornett was driven to the flightline in a truck with a half dozen other pilots drafted for the day's missions.

The driver turned around and yelled, "Cornett. This is you."

Cornett grabbed his helmet and chicken plate and dropped to the ground. He walked up to the aircraft, saw the pilot already there and said, "I guess I'm your peter pilot."

The man looked up and said, "Give me a hand here."

"Okay." Cornett put his equipment in the cargo compartment. "I'm Cornett."

"Davis."

Cornett followed Davis, the aircraft commander, around the helicopter as they peered into various access doors. Davis climbed up on top of the aircraft to examine the rotor head. Cornett remained on the ground.

When that was finished, and before they climbed into the cockpit, Davis asked, "How long have you been in-country?"

Cornett shrugged, as if embarrassed, and said, "Eight months. You?"

"Six. You flown combat assaults?"

"No. I usually fly Shithooks. We fly support —"

"I know what they do. You know where the evac hospitals are?"

"Around here? Twelfth Evac is at Cu Chi. Doesn't Dau Tieng have some sort of aid station?"

"Yeah. If it's closest that is where you should go if the wound isn't bad, or if you don't think the wounded guy will survive the flight to one of the evac hospitals. Depends on the situation."

Cornett stared at the man, who looked to be a refugee from high school. He wanted to ask the guy how old he was, but Cornett was only twenty-two himself. He wasn't exactly an old soldier but having been in Vietnam for eight months made him a veteran.

"You know what we're doing?"

Davis said, "All I know is that we're supposed to be ready to launch if the word comes down and don't worry, the word will come down. I think that nearly everyone who has any time in helicopters has been drafted for this duty. Lots of flying time available."

"I already have my four hours for the month." He meant that according to regulations, to be eligible for flight pay, he needed to log just four hours. In Vietnam, nearly every pilot had his four hours on the first of the month; many qualified before noon.

They climbed into the cockpit, strapped in, and then sat quietly for a few minutes. The door guns had been mounted, and both the crew chief and the door gunner were sitting in the cargo compartment. Cornett reached down and pulled a paperback out his pocket. He didn't like to be bored, and he didn't like sitting around. He always had a paperback with him because on a normal day, there were stretches of time when they were sitting on the ground, waiting for someone to call for them to launch the next mission. He figured he had qualified for an Air Medal while sitting on the ground at flight idle.

One of the aircraft sitting near the runway began to wind up and Davis said, "That's us."

Behind them both the door gunner and the crew chief yelled, "Clear."

Davis reached down and pulled the trigger under the collective to start the turbine. He watched the gauges as the engine RPM and then the rotor RPM climbed. As soon as they were at full RPM, Davis keyed the mic. "Chalk Five is up."

"Roger, Five."

Cornett had not heard a call for a commo check. Of course, it could be SOP with the unit.

In minutes all the aircraft had made the commo check. Lead said that he was moving to the runway. Davis watched the other aircraft and then picked up to a three-foot hover. The rotor wash blew around the loose dust, creating a cloud that nearly obscured everything. As they reached the runway, that cloud dissipated, and they set down.

"Lead, you're down with ten."

Unnecessarily, Davis said, "That was Trail telling Lead the flight was assembled."

Cornett looked around. A line of soldiers was approaching the runway and began separating themselves into loads of ten soldiers for each. That was a change from the normal eight for a combat assault. They climbed into the aircraft.

"Lead, you're loaded."

Cornett turned his head. The soldiers were sitting on the red troop seat at the rear of the cargo compartment, on the floor, two sitting braced against the armor seats of the pilots, and the others sitting near the cargo compartment doors. None of them had red covers on the flash suppressor on their weapons.

One man held an M-79 grenade launcher as if it was a big shotgun.

"Lead's on the go."

A moment later, Cornett heard, "You're off with ten."

They climbed to fifteen hundred feet and then began a large circling loop, as if in a crowded traffic pattern. They finally turned toward Saigon. They flew over a small village and took some fire. One of the door gunners returned it and the gunships dived on a hootch, raking it with machine-gun fire. No one shot at the gunships.

Normally, as they approached Tan Son Nhut from the west, helicopters were required to low-level for several miles. It kept the helicopters from fouling the airplane traffic from the airfield. This time they remained at altitude.

"Lead, you are cleared to land on the approach end of the active runway."

Gun lead approached the flight, did a one eighty, and began to dive toward the runway. As he passed over the end of the runway, the door gunner threw a smoke grenade.

"ID red."

"Land fifty meters beyond the smoke."

"Roger."

"Chalk Eight taking fire on the right."

"Nine taking fire on the right."

"Seven, losing RPM. Be landing in the smoke."

"Lead, make a go around."

Cornett was sitting straight up, his hands lightly resting on the controls just in case he had to suddenly take over. He'd never been that close to the enemy. By the time a Chinook was called in, there was little enemy fire, if any. He'd taken a few hits in the body of the aircraft, but there was no real damage, and no one had been hit. The bullet holes were quickly patched at the end of the day.

Lead rolled over and began a climb out. As he did, the gunships rolled in, using their miniguns to suppress the enemy fire. It slowed as the helicopters climbed out. They raked a small ten-by-ten building that was painted in a checkerboard pattern.

"Lead, I have trail covered. You are out with eight."

"Lead, go around and come back in on the same heading, landing in the same spot."

"Roger."

Cornett turned his attention to the ground outside the cockpit. There were several buildings off to one side. Some of the fire was coming from there but the gunships neutralized it, first with miniguns and then rockets. Two men ran from one of the buildings and were cut down by the miniguns. They sprawled forward and lay still. It was the first time that Cornett had seen gunships kill anyone. They were quite effective.

The flight made a sharp turn, flew to the south and turned again. There was sporadic firing, but it was ineffective and not from the buildings the gunships had attacked. They were too high and moving too fast.

"Flight is turning inbound."

Gunships began working over both sides of the flight path. The rockets walked down the line. Enemy firing tapered off until the flight was on short final, then machine guns opened fire.

"Lead, land just short of the downed aircraft."

"Roger."

They seemed to drop out of the sky in a steep, rapid descent. Cornett felt himself tense. Two rounds came through the windshield. A third hit the instrument panel, destroying a small section of it. Cornett didn't know where any of the bullets had gone after they hit the windshield.

The soldiers dove out of the helicopter, hitting the ground all around them. The flight crew from the downed helicopter jumped out and ran toward the closest one in the flight.

As they scrambled on, Trail said, "You're down with eight. Unloaded."

"On the go."

As they pulled pitch, the soldiers were up and running toward the enemy positions. The gunships were pouring fire into the buildings, and no one was shooting back.

"Lead. You're out with eight."

"Roger, eight."

They turned away from Tan Son Nhut, but didn't climb. Instead, they hugged the terrain until clear of the airfield.

"Flight. Report damage."

Every aircraft reported taking hits. Chalk Four said, "Losing hydraulic power. Several hits in the cockpit. Minor injuries."

That was the worst of it. There were other minor wounds. The air mission commander ordered, "Head for Cu Chi. Shut down on the Three-Quarter Cav pad in front of their hangar. I want a full report on damage."

"Roger that. Four, how you doing?"

"Fighting the controls, but we're good."

There had been other assaults that day into Tan Son Nhut, but that had been the worst. By the time the flight returned, most of the enemy positions had been neutralized. Fires were burning all over the field, the black smoke marking their locations.

Cornett took a deep breath and used the button on the floor to activate the intercom. "That was exciting."

"You ain't seen nothing yet," said Davis. He laughed and added, "That is the first time we ran combat assaults on an active airfield."

That day was the last time that Cornett had been involved with combat assaults in a Huey. After several hours, he returned to his unit because there was a need for resupply and the Chinooks could carry so much more. It was a day that he wouldn't forget.

Because of his flight experience, Cornett had not ended up in an assault helicopter company, but in a detachment that ferried VIPs around Three Corps. Now he had a general in the back, who wanted to survey the area to the west of Tay Ninh. The general didn't want to do that from a fixed-wing aircraft because he thought that he wouldn't be able to see what he wanted to see, and if he wanted to land, a helicopter offered that capability while a fixed-wing aircraft required a runway.

Cornett, and his copilot, First Lieutenant Martin Owens walked up to the Huey. Both were carrying their flight helmets, chicken plates, and wore .38-caliber revolvers in Old West-style holsters. Owens was younger than Cornett, taller, and looked as if he hadn't been in Vietnam very long. He had a sort of dazed look on his face, as everyone who was new to Vietnam did.

The crew chief, Spec Five Hank Masters, said, "Everything is ready, sir. I checked it out." Masters was younger than both pilots, wasn't as tall as either, but had been in Vietnam long enough that he knew the ropes. Keep the aircraft clean, make sure that everything was in its place, and don't say much of anything to anyone. He stayed away from officers who weren't flight crew as much as possible.

Cornett grinned and asked, "You don't mind if I check it out myself?"

"No, sir. But I didn't miss anything."

"I know you didn't." Cornett set his chicken plate and helmet in the aircraft commander's seat. He reached in and got the book. It was a log of every issue found on the helicopter, the flights it had made recently, and other important information. There was nothing significant in it. He put it back, and then began at the aircraft's nose, opening the door over the battery and checking the connections.

"Everything's fine, sir." Masters seemed annoyed that Cornett wanted to do the preflight himself. Cornett was sure that Masters had done a proper job, but it was his responsibility if anything went wrong that should have been caught in the preflight. Cornett would be the one who caught hell for it because he was the aircraft commander.

Spec Four Dick Weaver was working to get the door guns mounted. He was just eighteen and had enlisted before he was caught in the draft. He was skinny, had a bad case of acne, and it looked as if he was losing his hair already. He had dark eyes and a bit of a scar on his chin. He had mounted the M-60 machine gun on his side of the aircraft and was carrying the second M-60 around to mount for the crew chief. He looked up when Cornett arrived but hadn't said anything to him.

Cornett had just finished the preflight when the general, his aide, and his sergeant-major arrived. The general looked at Cornett, saw that he was older than the regular helicopter pilots, and then looked at the copilot, who was a first lieutenant.

The general unfolded a map, laid it on the cargo compartment floor, and pointed to an area near the Cambodian border known as the Angel's Wing. He looked at

Owens. "I need to take a look at a canal system built there and then fly north, toward this jungle area. We think that a Special Forces camp there will interdict the flow of enemy materiel."

The copilot, somewhat embarrassed by the general's mistake, said, "You'll have to tell Chief Warrant Officer Cornett, sir. He's the aircraft commander."

"I don't understand. You have the rank."

Cornett took over. "Yes, sir, but the position of aircraft commander is not based on rank but on experience. This is my second tour, and I have more than twenty-seven hundred hours, of which nearly a thousand in combat in-country. Lieutenant Owens here has been in-country for only a couple of months and has about two hundred hours of combat time."

The general almost said something but thought better of it. He pointed to the map and asked, "Are you familiar with this area?"

"Yes, sir."

"Any problems with heading there?"

"You're close to the border and there are some high-powered defenses there. The triple-A is good to more than eleven thousand feet and I wouldn't be surprised if there were 35-millimeter anti-aircraft in some locations that can reach even higher. They might not engage a single Huey, but the fifty-one cals there can be a real threat."

"How would you avoid them?"

"Real fast and real low, or real fast and real high."

"How high?"

"Five or six thousand feet. Those fifties can reach us, but at that altitude, we're a mile away from the weapon and makes it harder to hit us. We obviously are not pressurized so oxygen can be a problem, but that doesn't kick in until something significantly higher."

The general picked up his map, folded it, and handed it to his aide. "You don't need the map." It was a statement rather than a question.

"I can find the location. Once there, you'll have to direct us to where you want to go. Just remember, we're going to be very close to the border and we don't want to inadvertently cross is."

"I'll keep that in mind, Mr Cornett."

"Then, if you'll get on board, we'll light the fire."

Cornett was surprised that the general had his own headset. It wasn't a helmet, just earphones that would allow him to plug into the intercom system. The problem was, it would take either the crew chief or the door gunner out.

Looking over his shoulder, Cornett said, "Weaver, plug the general into the intercom."

"Yes, sir."

A moment later, the general said, "I'm listening in."

Cornett was tempted to say, "Let's keep the profanity down." Instead, he just reached down and pulled the trigger under the collective, that started the turbine.

The flight to the west was uneventful. They flew south of the Saigon River until Nui Ba Den was in sight. They flew south of the mountain and passed the large base camp near Tay Ninh City, avoiding the traffic pattern, which meant he had no need to contact the tower.

Cornett finally said, "We're getting close to the border, General."

"Parallel the border heading north. Get as close as you can."

"Yes, sir. Altitude?"

"Whatever you think is best."

Cornett lowered the collective and descended until they were no more than fifty feet above the ground, heading toward a finger of jungle that grew to the north. They flew over a cluster of hootches, one that had a mud fence that held a water buffalo. There was a smoking fire on the east side but no sign of human life.

"Can you fly a little higher?"

"Roger," said Cornett and began a gentle climb.

They reached the trees, and the general asked, "Can you circle back over that village?"

Cornett was about to tell him it wasn't a good idea when there was a sudden burst of machine-gun fire.

"Why is the door gunner firing?"

"That's not the door guns," replied Cornett.

He broke to the left, away from the village and the jungle, but moving closer to the border. He dived toward the ground but the firing increased. He felt the rounds hitting the aircraft, but they missed everything that was vital. The door gunner, Weaver, opened fire, but he hadn't seen where the enemy was hiding. He was hoping to suppress the enemy fire until they were out of range.

Cornett realized they had crossed the border and were now, technically, in Cambodia. They were flying over a thicker area of the jungle which hid parts of the expanded Ho Chi Minh Trail. There was more firing. Rounds punched through the rotor blades. That set up a vibration that shook the aircraft.

Cornett keyed the mic. "This is Greensleeves 814, heavy fire near the Angel's Wing."

"Are you going down?"

"Negative. Turning east to avoid it."

A burst of heavy machine-gun fire raked the bottom of the aircraft. It ripped through a bundle of wires, severing the radio communications. A tuning squeal from the Fox Mike filled the earphones. Cornett squeezed the mic button. "Turn it off."

He tried to make another radio call, but he had lost all the radios. No one could hear him. He tried to get away from the heavy machine gun by turning back to the west. Behind him, both Weaver and Masters were laying down suppressive fire. But it was too late. The hydraulics were gone. The controls became stiff and almost unresponsive. He had to fight them to maintain level flight.

"What's happening?" demanded the general.

Cornett ignored the question. He was still attempting to make a Mayday call but didn't believe it was broadcast. He could hear nothing on any of the radios and there was no response to his Mayday call. He was fighting the controls but then the engine quit. He was at three hundred feet and there wasn't much time to react. He looked for a place to set down, but all he saw was the jungle ahead of him.

"We're going into the trees," he said calmly.

He shot the autorotation to the tops of the trees, levelling the skids before they made contact. He had stopped the forward motion, pulled in pitch trying to soften the landing. The helicopter settled into the trees. The weight crushed the upped branches, and they fell toward the ground.

They crashed to the jungle floor nose first. They hit hard. Cornett was momentarily stunned. Someone cried out in pain. He didn't know who it was. The intercom was dead.

Cornett reached out to brace himself against the instrument panel and unbuckled his seat belt. He pushed on the door, but it was jammed shut. He twisted around, kicked at it, but it still didn't open. He felt a hand on his shoulder.

"You okay?"

He nodded at the general. "We have to get out."

"Your door gunner is badly hurt, and I think my aide might be dead."

Without thinking, Cornett pushed himself out of his seat, grabbed at the rear, and hauled himself into the cargo compartment. There was blood splashed around. The aide lay with one arm caught under the troop seat, but he wasn't holding on. Blood was spreading from under him.

The crew chief crawled around and asked Cornett, "You hurt?"

Cornett shook his head. "Just bruised. You?"

"I'm good. I think Weaver broke his arm."

Cornett remembered something that he had learned in survival training. In situations like this, it was imperative to get away from the aircraft as quicky as possible. He also remembered that the survivors didn't take much with them that was not attached to them. The Air Force had survival vests, but the Army had nothing like that.

"Hank. Open the sumps under the aircraft. Get us a pool of fuel under it. We'll use a smoke grenade to set the aircraft on fire."

"No!" The general moved to block him. "It'll give away our position."

"General, this is not a debate. I'm burning the aircraft so that there is nothing left for Charlie."

It took a long time to get everyone out of the helicopter, get the survival equipment, and spread the ammo around. Once they were clear, Cornett pulled the pin on a smoke grenade. As he tossed it into the pool of JP-4 under the wrecked Huey, he said, "Goodbye, old friend. You did a fine job."

As they pushed into the jungle, the flames began to spread. Minutes later they heard some of the M-60 ammo cooking off and then a larger boom as the helicopter began to destroy itself.

CHAPTER 4

The MACV Headquarters in Saigon had been built on a soccer field near Tan Son Nhut airport and covered several acres. It was a modern, two-story building that was air-conditioned because no one liked to see generals and senior NCOs sweat. At least that was the perception of the common soldier in Vietnam who found himself on a fire support base, living in a sandbagged bunker that not only didn't have air conditioning or electricity, but also housed all sorts of vermin, some of them deadly.

James Cooper was a newly promoted captain who had not been in the field in Vietnam and there were no real prospects of him finding himself in the field any time soon. His quarters, on another section of the MACV compound, was air-conditioned and had a small black and white TV that easily picked up the television broadcasts from AFVN. He didn't see many of the shows, given his schedule, but that didn't matter to him. He was serving in Vietnam as an intelligence officer, which would look good on his record when it was time to think about being promoted to major.

Cooper was a stocky man with jet-black hair and a premature balding spot on the back of his head. He could hide it by keeping his hair a little longer on top and combing it carefully to conceal the baldness. He had dark eyes, a strong chin, large ears and hands that looked as if they belonged to someone older and larger than he was. There were those who believed he had been assembled from leftover parts late on a Friday afternoon by someone interested in starting the weekend early.

There was a tap on his open office door. He glanced up and saw his Air Force counterpart standing there. The man said, "You have a minute?"

Cooper closed the folder on his desk and waved Davis in. Ralph Davis was also a captain, but his date of rank was nearly a year earlier than Cooper's. That meant that technically, Davis outranked him. Cooper didn't care about that, and Davis seemed to be unaware of it. Besides, they were both captains and that was all that really counted.

Unlike Cooper, Davis was a tall, thin officer with a full head of brown hair. Unlike Cooper, Davis had his jungle fatigues starched and pressed so that it looked as if he was ready for the parade ground or to meet with a general. He was a graduate of the Air Force Academy, and unlike some, he usually managed to get that fact entered into the conversation at some point.

As Davis entered the office, Cooper pointed to one of the chairs in front of him. "Have a seat? What's on your mind?"

"First, why do you keep it so cold in here? This must be the coldest room in the building."

Smiling, Cooper said, "I figured I'd keep better in the colder climate. Don't want to spoil in all that heat outside."

"I'm not sure how solid that theory is."

"Ralph, I'm sure you didn't come down here to comment on the weather in my office. Or my theories on aging in a tropical environment."

"No. And I'm not sure if I have a problem but at the Academy, they taught us to plan for all contingencies. I was talking to our Ops guys. They say they're missing an aircraft. It's overdue by about two hours and they think it's down somewhere just east of the Cambodian border in Three Corps. Up around the area of Tay Ninh."

Cooper rocked back in his chair. "Two hours isn't much. They could have landed at any number of bases or camps with an airstrip. You get a Mayday call?"

"We've heard nothing from them and even if they had lost their radios, they would have communicated before now."

"I don't know, Ralph. I think you're overreacting here."

"There was a general on that helicopter. There were extra radios, and they had been in contact with MACV-SOG here in Saigon. There is no way that they should have been out of radio contact for two hours and if they had been forced down at one of our bases out there, they would have had landline contact. Some of the brass are quite worried about this."

"Okay. Just what would you have me do? Search and rescue are not in my wheelhouse."

"Contact some of your Army people in the area. Ask them if they have seen or heard anything."

"You have a flight plan?"

Davis shook his head. "Just that they were going to an area known as the Parrot's Beak. Well, they were going to fly north from there. They were going to play it by ear. See what they could see and then turn around and head back here."

"It would seem to me that your aviation assets would be of more value in any search than the ground forces that I could deploy."

Davis shook his head. "No. You Army guys have all those helicopters flying all over the place. They're better for searching than a fighter flying at five hundred knots or a B-52 flying above thirty-three thousand feet."

"You have Sidewinder Control. They've got some slow propeller jobs and high wings that allow a good view of the ground."

"They're based here and not set up for search and rescue. They don't have the assets for a search and are not set up for any type of rescue operation. We have to move fast on this. General Dekker has his panties in a bunch and he's going to be all over this."

When Davis left, Cooper sat at his desk, staring at the folder. The ink on one of the top-secret stamps was slightly smeared, which he found strange. But it was all just a way to avoid having to think about the problem Davis had brought. Was the helicopter really missing or had it landed at one of the forward bases?

Cooper knew that one of the benefits of being in Saigon was that it was the hub for tons of supplies brought in by ship. Because the top brass was there, they managed to gather most of the good stuff. You might not be able to find a Coke at Tay Ninh, but there were pallets of it available in Saigon. They never ran out of the comfort supplies.

What that meant was that the communications for the military organizations around Saigon was much better than it was for those bases and camps to the west, especially those near the Cambodian border. He left his office and found the signal officer, another captain whose jungle fatigues were so faded they were almost gray. It meant that he had been in Vietnam for a long time and was probably a short-timer.

Cooper approached him and asked, "You have working communications with the bases out near the Cambodian border?"

"Define working and define bases."

Cooper looked puzzled. "Working means that you can hold a conversation with them and bases would mean fire support bases and Special Forces camps."

"Then yes, sort of, and yes, to some."

"You're not being very helpful, Captain."

"I'm telling you that our communications are sometimes spotty. Land lines are severed by tracked vehicles, or the Vietnamese steal the wire and sometimes it just breaks. We have radio communications with some of the fire support bases, again based on various things including the weather and the atmosphere."

"Let me try this again," said Cooper. "Have there been any calls for assistance? Aircraft in distress, for example?"

"We monitor the guard frequencies, both Fox Mike and Uniform. There has been nothing like that, and we can pick up some distress calls from a hundred, hundred fifty miles away depending on the atmospherics and the altitude of the aircraft."

"I take it from your answer that you've heard no Mayday calls in the last two or three hours?"

"Nope. You can look at the logs and since you're an intelligence officer, I will assume you have a top-secret clearance."

That surprised Cooper for a moment. He wondered how the man had known he was an intelligence officer and then remember the branch insignia on his collar would have given him the information. His assumption about the clearance was related to his position, but Cooper knew the man should have asked for proof.

"I don't suppose that will be necessary. I don't need access to anything classified. Could you send out a message to those locations that have a landing strip or helipad associated with their base?"

"Most of the fire support bases and small camps have helipads but no airstrip. Special Forces camps usually have a landing strip, but they aren't very long and are not paved."

Cooper didn't like the way the man was sharing information. True, he didn't look like a VC spy, but Davis didn't know that. He should be cautioned about sharing too much information with someone who hadn't presented credentials to prove he had the proper access. Then again, they were both inside a building that required identification before they were allowed to enter.

"If you hear anything, can you let me know?"

"Sure. Who are you and where do you work?"

Cooper told him and then left, figuring that it was a wasted effort. A helicopter could be down at one of those camps without a landing strip and there were many of those sorts of installations.

United States Army Special Forces Colonel Alan Bates knocked on the door to Gerber's office. He didn't wait to be invited to enter because he outranked Gerber, and they were friends. "We might have a problem," he said without preamble.

Fetterman looked up from the official report he was reading and asked, "Why does he never visit unless he has a problem?"

"Because he knows that you know everything, Sergeant Major, and wishes to tap into that massive brain."

Bates was not going to let them get away with that. "You mean that massive ego," he said.

"Ego? Brain? What's the difference?"

Bates decided to ignore the question. "You have anything to drink around here?"

Gerber looked at his watch. "You looking for something cold, or something with a bit of a bite to it?"

"Just something cold. I have real work to do, but that's not why I've dropped by. You heard there might be an aircraft down near the border, somewhere around Tay Ninh?"

"No, sir."

"I got the heads-up from Saigon a few minutes ago, wondering if we'd heard anything."

"What do they think we might have heard?"

"Mayday call. Anything like that."

"Nope."

"Who do we have in that area?"

Gerber realized that Bates was serious. "What's going on?"

"An aircraft seems to be missing with a Saigon general, one of ours, on board. There was no Mayday call and it's overdue."

"Well, depending on where you think it might be, I've got a guy north of Tay Ninh and he's set up ten, twelve klicks from the border. Bromhead is in that area, but south of Tay Ninh. Bromhead's strikers are better trained."

"Why do you say that?"

"He had a patrol ambushed. The VC triggered it early and the strikers attacked it. They had no casualties, but killed a couple VC and captured some of their weapons."

Fetterman handed Bates a Pepsi. "It's not real cold. Best we can do on such short notice, since you aren't interested in anything stronger."

"Thanks. I haven't had an after-action report on that."

Gerber tapped the folder on his desk. "I've got it right here. I was just reviewing it before sending it up to you."

Bates set his Pepsi on the floor near his chair. "Want to let me see it now?"

"It's really nothing special. The VC ambush was not well organized. I'm just wondering if it suggests a large force in that area. We've heard some intel, well, rumors actually, that the

NVA has infiltrated about two regiments into that area. Might be some sort of recruiting mission but I don't think they'd use two regiments for that. A platoon, maybe. A couple of regiments suggest something a little more important is going on."

"You're thinking they're going to try to overrun one of our camps?"

Fetterman nodded. "Be good propaganda for them if they can pull it off."

"Can they?"

"No, sir," said Fetterman. "All our camps are under the umbrella of fire support base artillery, and we can get gunships there within minutes. If we need fast movers, it'll take a little longer, but we can get them too. Camps are designed with interlocking fields of fire, and the strikers are better trained than they were a couple of years ago."

"There is one other thing that we should note," Gerber said. "I believe the NVA might have spread those forces out over a large area to keep us from finding them. We might find a platoon or company, but not the entire regiment."

"Why would they do that?"

"Keep us asleep. If we run into anything, it's not a large force. We don't see anything that hints at something more substantial."

"Are you doing anything about that?

"There will be an after-action report to you in a day or two. We did use a LRRP team, and they found evidence of NVA units on our side for the border. We did take some fire…" said Fetterman.

Gerber shrugged. "We made a reconnaissance flight over the area earlier. The aircraft didn't take any hits, and the aircraft commander called in artillery. We put the LRRPs in to take a quick look. They found some evidence of enemy activity, but pulled out. Their job had been to see if the artillery had been on target, not to engage or be seen. I didn't want any VC in the area to know that we had an interest in it."

"And when did you plan to share that information with me?" asked Bates.

Gerber grinned. "Why, now, sir. Of course."

Bates waved a hand as if trying to wipe the slate clean. "We're drifting off the original problem. We've lost a helicopter with a general on it." Bates looked at his watch. "Unless something has turned up in the last twenty minutes, it's been almost four hours."

"Are you going to tell me that these two events are related?" Gerber glanced at Fetterman, who nodded his agreement.

Bates hesitated before speaking. "I think we have detected an increase in activity in that area that we need to exterminate. You've just added to that pool of information."

"Exterminate?" asked Fetterman.

Bates was surprised by the comment. "Yes, Sergeant Major, exterminate. We don't need them gaining a foothold in an area that is considered to be pacified. The Vietnamese there are more or less on the side of the government."

"Captain Bromhead is capable of handling the situation," said Gerber.

"Are you sure?"

"I trained him —"

Fetterman interrupted. "We trained him, and we've kept an eye on him. Yes, he can handle it."

Bates reached down and picked up his Pepsi. He took a drink and said, "This isn't very cold."

"I warned you about that and you put it on the floor for the last twenty minutes. What did you expect?"

Bates chose to ignore the comment. "I ask again. Can he handle it?"

"It'd take more than a couple of regiments to overrun his camp, if that's what you mean. If you want him to set up a search for the missing general, I would say that is in the bailiwick of the Air Force, and not us. They have the aviation assets to conduct the search."

"Army Aviation can do it, too," added Fetterman. "They could also supply the ground forces, if necessary, for the rescue without bothering us."

Bates looked directly at Gerber. "I'd be happier if you'd head out to Bromhead's camp and take a look around. Maybe add some guidance, if he needs it, and be sure that his strikers are up to the task."

"I'm sure that he can handle anything that is thrown at him," said Gerber.

"Did I mention that I'm on the brigadier general list?"

"Is that relevant?" asked Gerber, grinning.

"I thought you might be inclined to take my suggestion for what it was if you knew that."

"Let me say congratulations to he who is about to enter the big time, and I take it your suggestion is more in the form of an order than a suggestion."

"You have an acute understanding of military protocol, Major."

"When would you like us to fly out there?"

"This afternoon too soon?"

"Getting late in the day. A late flight would draw undue attention," said Fetterman.

"Humor me, Sergeant Major."

"Yes, sir."

After Bates had left, Fetterman looked at Gerber. "Are we going today?"

"You have something going on that I don't know about?"

"Nope. It just seems that this hasn't been thought all the way through."

Gerber closed the folder on his desk. "All I have to do is put this back in the safe and grab my weapon and I'm ready to go."

"It just seems that there is no planning behind this."

"What is your reluctance, Sergeant Major?"

Fetterman rubbed his chin and glanced upward, as if asking for divine intervention. "There is no reason for an immediate response. There is no hard intelligence suggesting that Bromhead's camp is in any imminent danger. We have some intelligence that there might be a large force gathering, but we don't have any hard intelligence about the location and size of that force. I'd prefer to take a step back to gather more information."

"Well, I would say that your words move me, but we have our orders. Besides, we'll have a chance to visit with John and we'll be on hand if something does happen, not to mention we can say that we are looking for that missing general for the brass hats in Saigon."

"Don't misunderstand, Major. I'm just saying I don't understand the rush here."

"Why don't you grab your weapon, and I'll go over to Operations to see about getting us a ride out there in the next hour or so."

Fetterman grinned. "Just my weapon?"

"I don't see us being gone all that long. If there is something else that you think you'll need, grab that too. But I can't see us being there more than a day or two. They'll have everything we need, and I don't plan to leave the camp."

"I'll meet you in Operations."

"No, meet me at the hootch. There are a couple of things I want to grab."

"Yes, sir," said Fetterman, grinning broadly. "You're beginning to sound like a real live field grade officer."

"I figure if Bates can make brigadier general, then there is hope for me yet."

CHAPTER 5

They arrived about twilight in a cloud of swirling red dust. As soon as they were off the helicopter, it lifted off, climbing rapidly to the southeast, away from the dense jungle that could hide hundreds of enemy soldiers. Gerber had knelt on the rough gravel of the runway so that he wouldn't be hit by the rotor blades. Fetterman, bending low, scrambled to the edge of the runway, his eyes closed against the dust.

A jeep raced out of the Special Forces camp. As the helicopter disappeared into the distance, the jeep slid to a halt. The man in the passenger's seat leaped out and asked, "Need a ride, soldier?" He then noticed the gold oak leaf of a major and added, "Sir."

"Be delighted, Lieutenant."

He glanced over at Fetterman, who was standing erect and brushing the dirt off his uniform. "Captain Bromhead is waiting in the team house."

"Let's go, Sergeant Major," said Gerber.

They climbed into the jeep for the ride that was only about a hundred yards long. They sped through the gate and stopped near a long and narrow building. There were sandbags halfway up the wall, and more scattered across the corrugated tin roof that had rusted to a dull orange-brown.

Gerber got out of the passenger's seat as the door to the team house opened. "Welcome to our camp," said Bromhead. "What brings you here?" He didn't bother to salute, and Gerber didn't care that he didn't.

"Soon-to-be General Bates thought it would be a good idea," said Gerber.

Fetterman, who had joined them, added, "But we really got tired of all the comforts at the base camp and thought we'd come out to see how you peasants lived."

Now Bromhead grinned. "Better than we did back at the old Triple Nickel. The generator rarely fails, we have air conditioning in some of the hootches, and cold beer and soft drinks. We even have ice cream once in a while."

"Even way out here in the boondocks?"

"You'd be surprised." Changing the subject, Bromhead said, "Let's get out of the open. One grenade could get us all."

Gerber laughed. "Haven't heard that in a while."

Once inside the team house, Bromhead asked, "What's your pleasure, gentlemen?"

"A cold Pepsi would be fine," said Gerber.

"Nothing stronger?"

"Not till we get the lay of the land. We're looking for any intelligence you might have on a large force of NVA in your AO."

Before Bromhead could answer, there was a flat bang. "Rocket," said Gerber.

Bromhead, grabbing his weapon, said, "That's new. We get mortars, but not rockets. I'm going to the fire control tower."

"I'll go with you." Gerber turned to Fetterman. "You want to go to operations?"

"Sure."

There was another detonation, this one closer. Bromhead and Gerber sprinted across the camp to the fire control tower. Bromhead started up the ladder first. There was a third rocket, closer. Bromhead leaned forward, grasping the ladder, but the shrapnel didn't reach that far. The rocket had landed in the wire more than a hundred yards away.

As he scrambled over the sandbags protecting those in the tower, he asked the strikers there, "You see where they came from?"

Just as Gerber arrived, one of the men said, "We see one place. One came from there."

Bromhead took the binoculars from the striker, who pointed toward the jungle.

There was another detonation, but this one was on the other side of the camp, out in the wire. "Nothing hit us," said the striker.

"They can't aim the rockets," said Gerber. "They just point in the general direction and hope to hit something important."

"Yes, sir."

Bromhead scanned the jungle around the camp, but there was nothing to see. It was too dark now and no more rockets were fired. "That was strange," he said. "They usually use mortars. At least they can aim those."

"No use in calling in counter-battery," said Gerber. "Even if you knew the exact spot, the crews would all be gone by now. That's if the rockets weren't delayed fired."

You going to send out a patrol?"

Bromhead lowered the binoculars and handed them back to the striker. "No. Best case scenario is that they don't find anything. Could be an ambush set up to catch anyone we send out. Besides, we don't know exactly where the rockets were. Best to keep a good watch and wait for the next move, which will probably be sometime after midnight and probably be mortars."

"You know best," said Gerber. "There going to be another attack tonight?"

"I doubt it, sir. As I said, they usually just hit us once, though they might try to drop in a mortar round or two about three."

"What's your alert status?"

"Skeleton crew. Tower manned, and strikers in points around the perimeter. You're not expecting a ground attack?"

"Not really," said Gerber. "Our mission here is to determine if there is a buildup in enemy forces that might lead to a ground attack." He glanced at the strikers and added, "There might be another mission, but that can wait until tomorrow."

"Then let's get out of this tower and see about getting something to eat."

When they stopped for a brief rest, General Patterson moved closer to Cornett. Keeping his voice low, he asked, "Are we getting close to Vietnam?"

Cornett hesitated. "We're moving away from South Vietnam."

"Why in the hell would you do that?"

"Because we're in Cambodia and Charlie would expect us to take the shortest route to get us back to Vietnam. I'm putting distance between them and us. We'll change course tomorrow and head back, toward Vietnam."

"Don't you think you should have discussed that with me first?"

"Well, General, we're in a strange situation here. I'm the aircraft commander, which puts me in charge of the flight crew and the passengers. The chain of command becomes murky when we are down and escaping. You are the senior officer present, but my responsibility didn't end when we hit the ground. Given that I am the aircraft commander, I believe I have the ultimate authority here."

"Mr Cornett, I am a general."

"Yes, sir. But are you versed in escape and evasion in a combat arena? I have been through survival training while here. Part of it was to provide guidance for escape."

Patterson thought about that. He knew that he was out of his depth here. His training was two decades old, and he had been in what was thought of as combat support, rather than direct combat. He shouldn't be in the position he found himself in. He knew, from his years working his way up to general, that there were people at low ranks who knew more than he did about their field of expertise. He couldn't fly a helicopter, but Cornett could. He hadn't been through the survival training or the escape and evasion training that Cornett had. He decided his best course of action was to listen to Cornett until they came to a point where Cornett's expertise was no longer relevant, or they reached a point where he believed he needed to assert his authority.

Patterson said, "I seem to remember that we're supposed to hide during the day and move at night."

"That is good advice if you're in North Vietnam trying to evade a search party. Here, we're close to the terminus of the Ho Chi Minh Trail. The NVA are very active at night and they're hiding during the day to avoid detection by our Air Force. We have less chance of encountering them during daylight hours."

Patterson nodded. "That makes some sense. When do we turn toward Vietnam?"

"When we are far enough away from the helicopter. I don't know how thorough their search is going to be. They'll find the body of your aide, but I don't think they'll stop searching then. They'll be looking for more, but I don't know how far they'll carry that out."

Cornett fell silent. He listened to the noise of the jungle around him. It sounded natural. The monkeys were chattering at one another. There were birds calling and he heard a couple of large animals moving around somewhere. To him, it suggested that there were no humans in the area other than his small band.

"We should eat something now, drink some water and wait for nightfall. We can't have any fires because the smoke would give us away. We need to bury any trash that might provide clues that we have been here. And we need someone to remain alert as we do this all this."

Patterson shrugged. He had learned long before that it was a good idea to lead by example. He knew soldiers resented the idea of rank having privilege. But he also knew that he had earned the privilege by going through what the other soldiers were going through now. They didn't consider what he had done to get to his position, only that he now could do things they couldn't because he was a general.

"Why don't I take the first watch while your aircrew eats?" asked Patterson.

"I need to take a look at Weaver's arm. He's in pain and he could slow us down."

"Isn't there anything you can do for him?"

"Our first aid kits are basic. I have some aspirin, but I don't think it will relieve the pain. We'll have to get his arm immobilized and we'll have to keep an eye on him."

Owens, who had crawled up and overheard the last remark, said, "That aspirin couldn't hurt."

Cornett looked at him and then back to the general. "We need to hold down all this discussion. Talking can alert the enemy if they're in the area."

Owens shook his head. "Not with all the noise the monkeys are making. They'll drown out the sound of our voices."

"I'm not here to debate you," said Cornett.

Patterson almost laughed. "You realize that he outranks you?"

"Yes, sir, but I'm in charge. Remember?"

"So you are," said Patterson.

Cornett stood up. "We'll get moving in about an hour, when it gets really dark."

Captain James Cooper had tried to find out where General Patterson was. He had used every resource available to him and called in several favors. In the end he had concluded, based on the information he gathered, that Patterson's helicopter was down, probably somewhere near Tay Ninh and the Cambodian border. There had been no distress call, which suggested that whatever had happened was instantly catastrophic. There had been no time for a distress call. He didn't know that his thinking on that point was inaccurate.

That was the problem. There was no requirement to file flight plans and there was no flight following available. Thousands of helicopters filled the sky, and it was surprising that more of them didn't run into one another. Cooper knew of one case where an American artillery round had detonated near a high-flying command and control helicopter. No one was hurt, but the aircraft had been riddled with shrapnel. They were able to return to their home base, but the helicopter had taken hits to some hard-to-repair areas. It would be weeks before it would fly again.

Cooper was trying to figure out what do to next and wondering why the Air Force, which had units dedicated to search and rescue, weren't out searching for the general. He glanced up, saw an Air Force officer standing in his doorway and then noticed the black eagles on his collar.

Cooper stood and asked, "May I help you, Colonel?"

"You running the search for General Patterson?"

Still standing, Cooper said, "I'm not sure that I'm running the search, sir. I have contacted several of our bases out near the Cambodia border. I haven't learned much of anything. I have provided the little information I found to General Dekker, but I don't think of that as running the search."

The colonel, whose nametag said "Evans," entered and dropped into one of the visitor's chairs without invitation. He waved a hand, motioning Cooper to sit down. Evans said, "You know the importance of this?"

"Sir, you're outside of my chain of command."

"Meaning what, Captain?" He said it as if captain was a dirty word. His face was hard, looking angry. He stared at Cooper, waiting for an answer.

"I was asked by Captain Davis to ask a few questions. I have done what I could and as I said, I haven't learned anything."

"That didn't answer the question."

"No, sir, it didn't. But you are an Air Force officer and I'm in the Army. While I'm all for interservice cooperation, it means that I have my work to do and if you need my assistance, then you should speak to my immediate superior."

"It is getting late, Captain, and I don't have time to play those political games. We, and by we, I mean you, need to expand your activities. This is becoming a priority mission given the rank of the missing officer and the importance of the mission he was on."

"You're still outside of my chain of command," Cooper repeated.

"I'm sure that you know General Dekker? You mentioned him yourself. He in your chain of command?"

"Yes, sir, I know the general, or rather I know who he is. Yes, he's in my chain of command."

"Do I have to get him on the phone so that he might tell you that more is necessary in this search?"

"No, sir." Cooper felt a tightness in his belly. He didn't like the direction this conversation was taking and feared that he was about to find himself in the field.

"As I said, General Patterson was on an important mission. Even if he was sightseeing, we can't lose a general officer or, rather, have a general officer disappear. Your mission is to find out what happened to him. This is a priority mission."

"Yes, sir. May I ask a question?"

"Of course."

"Why me?"

"Because you are already aware of the problem and quite frankly, because you're here. I don't want this information and our concern for General Patterson to become public knowledge." He glanced around, almost as if looking for spies. He lowered his voice and said, "It is imperative that we find out his fate."

Cooper said, "Yes, sir." It was the only thing that he could think of at the moment. It was always a safe reply when talking with a higher-ranking officer who was already annoyed about something.

Evans stood up. "I'll expect a report in the morning. I want something more than you checked with various airfields and base camps but have nothing." Evans glanced at his watch. "You have a little over twelve hours to come up with something better than that."

Cooper stood too and said, "Yes, sir." As he sat down, he didn't know what he was going to do. He didn't have any idea where to start. And he didn't know why this had fallen into his lap.

When it had been completely dark for a while, and Cornett had never been anywhere that was so completely dark, he said that it was time to move. There was no moon, and the stars, the few that were visible through the jungle canopy, didn't do much to light the landscape. He couldn't see any of the soldiers with him except Patterson, who was a dark gray lump about two feet away, sitting on the ground holding a pistol in his hand.

Cornett stood up and quietly gathered the men together. "We need to get going," he whispered. "We need to stay in physical contact with one another, otherwise we're liable to get separated. Weaver? How are you doing?"

"I'm fine, sir." His voice was tinged with pain that he was attempting to conceal.

"You don't sound fine."

"There is pain in the arm and it's making me slightly sick and dizzy."

"We'll be moving very slow. We don't want to make any unnecessary noise. Can you keep up?"

"You can't leave him," said Masters.

"Nobody said anything about leaving him. We're going to be moving slow. I just want to make sure that he's going to be able to keep up with us."

"Don't worry about me, sir. I'll keep up."

"I'll help him," said Masters.

"We'll help each other." Cornett paused and then said, "General, you are right behind me, your sergeant-major behind you. Weaver, you're behind him with Masters, and Owens you bring up the rear. We can't afford to lose contact with one another. Any questions?"

There were none. Cornett turned and picked up his gear, waited until he felt Patterson's hand on his soldier. He said, a little louder than he meant to, "Everybody set?"

When everyone had answered, Cornett stepped out and then realized he would need to feel his way along. He stopped and said, "Everyone remain in place."

He bent down and felt the ground in front of him. He felt nothing but the soft jungle floor that was slightly wet. As he touched something that moved, he realized that this was a bad idea. He wanted a walking stick but after the encounter with the unknown creature, he decided that he would have to take his chances and move more carefully.

He stood up and touched Patterson and said, "Hang on. Here we go."

He reached out with his left foot, carefully felt the ground and moved forward, doing the same with his right foot. Patterson tugged on his shoulder but didn't remove his hand. It was going to take a long time to move a hundred yards and Cornett wished that there was a partial moon.

They moved steadily for thirty minutes. Cornett figured they might have walked half a klick. They were getting farther away from the crash site and if the enemy found the wrecked helicopter, they wouldn't know where the crew had gone. In daylight, they might be able to follow their trail, but Cornett didn't think they had left much in the way of a sign.

There was a crash behind him and a loud moan. Masters said, just loud enough to be heard, "Weaver's down."

Cornett worked his way back to Weaver, feeling his way by touching the men behind him. They were crouched down.

Cornett couldn't see much. Weaver was nearly unconscious, his breathing erratic and shallow. His uniform was soaked. Cornett felt for his pulse. It was weak.

Patterson was suddenly kneeling near him. "How is he?"

"I don't think he's going to be able to walk anymore tonight."

"We can't stay here."

"Why not?"

"You said it yourself. We must put distance between us and the crash site."

Cornett thought for a moment. "We don't know that anyone has found it. If they have, we don't know if they are inclined to follow us, which might be determined by any sign we might have left as we moved out. We don't know that they'd have anyone with them that can read those sorts of sign. With us gone, they might just believe that we got away."

Patterson whispered, "I can't be captured."

Cornett's immediate thought was that of course he could be, and then he realized that there was more to that comment. "Just what were you looking at as we flew around the border."

"That's the problem," whispered Patterson. "I am privy to some highly classified information that…" His voice trailed off.

Cornett said, "We'll rest here. Set up a perimeter."

"I'm afraid that I'm going to have to override that decision," said Patterson.

"General," said Cornett carefully, "we cannot leave Weaver. We are safe here for several hours at least. We'll stay put through the day. That gives Weaver time to recover slightly. The break isn't too bad, and some rest will do him good. We'll know more tomorrow and we're not making much progress tonight."

Patterson was quiet for almost a minute. Finally, he said, "We are putting a lot of lives at risk for the sake of one man."

Cornett grinned, knowing that Patterson wouldn't be able to see it in the dark. "Specialist Weaver is my responsibility. As the aircraft commander, I am responsible for the lives of my crew and any passengers that I am carrying. I will not leave him here. We simply don't leave our soldiers in the field."

"Stay with him then. Sergeant-Major Stein and I will go on."

Cornett chuckled. "Which way are you going to go?"

Patterson looked up at the jungle canopy, but couldn't see any constellations that would help him navigate. There was no moon. He didn't know exactly where they were, and he didn't know how close they were to the border or to any friendly installations. He didn't know where the Ho Chi Minh Trail might be, where they stood a good chance of running into the enemy.

"I could order you to leave him."

"You certainly could, but I seem to remember one of the laws of command is to never issue an order that you know won't be obeyed."

"You'll be court-martialed when we return."

"No, I won't," said Cornett. "You're not going to court-martial me for staying with my injured soldier."

Patterson realized that they had reached an impasse. "So, what do we do now?"

CHAPTER 6

Captain James Cooper had tried to figure out how to gather more information now that the sun had set, and part of the telephone system was down again. He suspected that someone had cut a critical wire, taking out a large part of the system. That was something that made the landlines problematic. So, he walked over to the Intelligence Center, knocked on the door, and when it opened, he entered.

Because the soldiers inside dealt with highly classified material, the door had been locked. Inside, where the air conditioning was on at such a low level that it was nearly freezing, was a large, brightly lit room. There was a half dozen or more old military desks, that all looked as if they had been salvaged from the dump. There were teletype machines lining one wall and two of them were spitting out yellow paper. And the walls were of plywood that had been scorched by blowtorches to bring out the grain as a sort of decoration.

Cooper felt the chill the instant he entered and noticed that some of the soldiers were wearing gloves to keep their hands warm. Someone had said that those soldiers were attempting to drop the temperature below freezing, just to see if they could do it. Their excuse was the radio gear and other electronics worked much better in the colder environment.

Once inside, he asked to see the intelligence officer, a lieutenant colonel named Washington. He was a large, Black man with little hair and a neatly trimmed mustache. He wore a weapon as if he expected an attack at any moment or maybe feared someone would try to steal classified information. When the door to the Center opened, he had come out of his office to see who had arrived.

"What can I do for you, Captain?" he asked as he approached Cooper.

Cooper looked around. Everyone in the Center had a top-secret clearance, but not everyone had a need to know. Cooper thought that the information about Patterson was restricted, and he didn't want to mention it where others could overhear, though the roaring fans made conversation difficult. He lowered his voice anyway and asked, "Can we talk in private?"

Washington stared at him for a moment. Then he grinned and said, "Sure. Follow me."

Washington opened the door to his private office at the far end of the outer room and waved Cooper through. Washington sat down behind his desk, which was a slight improvement over those in the outer room. He indicated the chair opposite. The office itself wasn't large. It contained a desk, two mismatched visitor's chairs and a small bookcase that held three-ring binders, each labeled. The only additional piece of furniture was a safe that had some sort of wilted plant on top of it.

"Is it always this cold in here?" Cooper asked.

"You noticed?"

"Is it true about wanting to see how cold it can get?"

"You didn't come here to learn about our private indulgencies, did you, Captain?"

"No, sir. Colonel Evans…"

Washington nodded, indicating that he knew who Evans was.

"Which is to say, General Dekker, is concerned that General Patterson has disappeared."

"I heard his helicopter was down."

"Yes, sir. I have been tasked with finding him and all I really know is that his flight was somewhere along the Cambodian border, north of something called the Angel's Wing or Parrot's Beak and near Tay Ninh."

"I have heard about that."

Now Cooper shrugged. "I have no other information, other than I contacted about a dozen fire support bases and Green Beret camps in that area but none knew anything useful. They hadn't seen Patterson or his helicopter, and they knew nothing about him."

"And you want what from me?"

"Anything that you can tell me that might help locate the general."

"You know as much about it as I do."

"What was he doing flying around in that area? Most of the Army stays as far from the border as they can get. There's not much there, except for the triple-A threat that reaches eleven thousand feet. There is a lot of open ground and some NVA infiltration routes."

"Out of school, Captain?"

"Anything I hear in here goes no further. My mission is to locate the general."

"There are rumors of some sort of cross-border operation being planned and Patterson is one of the senior officers planning it." Washington held up his hand to stop the obvious question. "I mention this only because it is imperative to learn Patterson's fate as quickly as we can."

"In the spirit of that," said Cooper, "what can you tell me about his flight?"

"That he was doing a reconnaissance of the area, surveying the terrain, obstacles, villages and about anything else he could see that might present a future problem. I'm not sure if he has been read into the plan at this point, but he surely has some inkling that a cross-border op is in the works."

"Wouldn't you be able to supply that information?" Cooper waved a hand at the office door, indicating the intel center beyond.

"Why, thank you, Captain. I appreciate the compliment. We did work up a complete analysis using recon photos taken in the last week by the Air Force. But there is nothing like seeing the area firsthand. There was little danger of flying over that area as long as they didn't get too near the anti-aircraft guns that have you worried, or blunder into some unidentified enemy force."

"I don't think that helps much."

Washington tented his fingers under his chin. "If General Dekker sent you here, then you probably have the need to know. I'll take a chance here. We used the DoD Evasion Chart, that is EVC five hundred dash three. Covers all of Four Corps and a lot of Three Corps up beyond Tay Ninh to the north."

Cooper was thrilled with the information and was about to get up to search for the chart and then thought it through. "Do you have a copy of the chart and the route they took?"

"Yes, I have one of those charts." Washington stood up and opened his safe. He took out a large, folded piece of vinyl and began laying it out on his desk. Cooper saw that it was EVC five hundred dash two, but Washinton turned it over as he folded it to a more manageable size. It had EVC dash three on the back. He wondered how widespread the charts might be. There were no classification markings on it. He suspected that it would become classified once tactical data were added to it, but the chart itself was just a detailed map of the area that was probably available from a variety of sources, including shops on Tu Do Street.

Washington picked up a pencil to use as a pointer. "As you can see, the Angel's Wing is nearly due south of Tay Ninh."

"I see why they call it the Angel's Wing. And there is the Parrot's Beak just south of it."

"Right. Patterson's flight was to head for the Angel's Wing, which is flat and open to an extent, flying north, along the border, past Tay Ninh and into this area that is heavily jungled. It's not all triple canopy, but it provides good cover from aerial surveillance. That's why the NVA like it and why there is a suspected NVA new terminus to the Ho Chi Minh Trail."

"Where's the Ho Chi Minh Trail from there?"

"On the other side of the border, but in places it nears the border until they reach a crossing point. Those shift around as we interdict them. Patterson was checking all that out in person. He was tasked with identifying areas where armor can operate. It's not much good in thick jungle."

"Still sounds like aerial surveillance would be a better way to do it."

"Looking at a chart tells you what is there, but it doesn't show you what it looks like. Nothing beats eyes on. This open area here, is jungle, but you don't know that by looking at the chart, or how thick that jungle is."

Cooper was going to ask for the chart but then realized he could get his own by asking Dekker's aide for one. Wouldn't be much of a hassle to do that, and he'd probably have it inside an hour. People responded quickly to a general's aide's request, always assuming that it was for the general.

"Do you know where they were going to land to refuel?"

Washington shook his head. "I would suspect either Tay Ninh or Dau Tieng. Both have refueling facilities and you don't need any sort of special permission to use them as long as you're in a military aircraft. Dau Tieng isn't all that close to the border, though. Just check in with the tower and you'll be good to go."

Bromhead knew better than to abruptly awaken Gerber or Fetterman. Both were old combat veterans who slept lightly when in the field. It was a learned talent that Bromhead understood, having recently developed it himself. The slightest change in the environment could cause him to grab for a weapon almost before his eyes were open. Instead of entering the hootch, he stood to one side and said, in a nearly normal voice, "Major Gerber."

There was scrambling in the hootch and Gerber appeared at the door. "What is it, Johnny?"

Bromhead ignored the use of his childhood nickname. "Got a special message, sir." He emphasized the "sir."

Fetterman said, from the dark. "What is it?"

Gerber stepped out. To Bromhead's surprise, Gerber was fully dressed, though his boots were not tied. Gerber didn't like the zippers that some soldiers used so they could slip into their boots faster. He held his pistol in his right hand, down by his leg, so that it wasn't easily visible to an outside observer. He raised it, his thumb on the hammer, and carefully uncocked it.

Bromhead said, "I have been told that a flight of Hueys will land here at first light. I'm to have a striker company ready to board them, but not what the mission is or where they are going. There is no timetable other than the flight will arrive about dawn."

Gerber glanced back over his shoulder at Fetterman. "Tony, let's go get something cold to drink."

"In the team house?" asked Bromhead.

"Yes."

"Do you know what this is about?" Bromhead asked.

"I have a suspicion, but I don't really want to talk about it out here." Gerber sat down on the steps and tied his boots. He picked up his weapon and holstered it.

When they reached the team house, had turned on the light and were seated, Gerber said, "I was going to mention this later in the morning, but I didn't know what role you would play, if any."

Fetterman opened the refrigerator, took out two Pepsis and a Coke. He set them on the table but didn't say anything. He looked annoyed. He didn't like to be awakened at three in the morning when, in three or four hours, he would have awakened normally. He didn't like the duty day beginning so early because it threw off his normal routine. By noon, he would be tired.

"There is an aircraft down somewhere around here with a general on board. Search operations start at dawn. I guess they are prepositioning assets for a quick response in case they're needed."

Bromhead, holding the Coke, asked, "Why don't they know where they went down?"

"Flight plan was rather vague and there wasn't any distress call."

"The aircraft blew up. Hit by an RPG or artillery or even small arms fire. The general is dead, along with the flight crew."

"That's probably true," agreed Gerber. "But with a general on board, they're mounting a massive search."

"And what about the two or three regiments that have been infiltrating into the AO?" asked Bromhead.

Fetterman set his Pepsi down on the table. "I suspect that the missing general is more important than what Saigon probably thinks of as a phantom force invading territory that we already control. A regiment or two running around out here is no real concern to them. It is no threat to them, but the wrath of a missing general could end careers."

"Very cynical of you, Sergeant Major," said Gerber. "Unfortunately, that's probably an accurate assessment of the current situation."

"Well, that doesn't actually change much. I was going to send out a couple of patrols about dawn to search for those rocket-launching sites. We'll just keep them here and wait to see what happens."

Gerber drained his Pepsi. He looked around and then said, "I'm wide awake now. I think I'll go up into the fire control tower to see what I can see."

"If they were going to hit us with any sort of a ground attack, they would have done it by now," said Fetterman.

"I know that, but I'm too keyed up to sleep," said Gerber.

"Well, tomorrow could be fun," said Fetterman. "I'll be sleeping if you need me."

Cornett had just fallen asleep when Owens shook him awake. "Weaver's not having a good night."

Sitting up, Cornett asked, "What's the problem?"

"His broken arm. It's causing him great pain and there isn't much we can do about it. He's going to slow us down when we begin moving again."

"You're not back to thinking we should leave him here, are you?"

"We could find him a good place to hide, give him most of our rations and water and all the smoke grenades. When we get back to Vietnam, we can tell them where to find him."

"There is no reason for us to travel during the day. I told you that. We lay up here and keep quiet. Give Weaver a chance to get some strength up. I'm not going to leave him. We do not leave our wounded or injured in the field. Our best chance is to remain calm and stay together."

"Look, Cornett, I'm a lieutenant and on the ground, I outrank you, as does General Patterson. I say that we leave him here and come back to get him later."

"Here's your problem, Owens, I'm still the aircraft commander —"

"We have no aircraft."

"Shut up and listen. Neither I nor Masters will agree to that. You're outvoted, and General Patterson already tried to pull that shit. When we get back, I'm going to let our CO know about your attitude."

"Are you threatening me?"

"No, sir. I'm giving you the facts of life and I'll add one more. If you force this issue, I'll guarantee that no one in our company would help you if you happened to be shot down again, or if you had an engine failure. You'd be on your own because they would know what you did here."

Masters crawled up and whispered, "I think I saw some movement out there."

Ignoring Owens, Cornett asked, "Where?"

"Maybe about a hundred yards off in that direction." He pointed to the south but in the dark, Cornett couldn't see the gesture.

"Show me."

Masters crawled past Cornett, who followed. When Masters stopped, he said, "Out there. Maybe a hundred meters or so."

Cornett still couldn't see anything and wondered if Masters was seeing things. Everything looked strange when there was little light, and they were in unfamiliar territory. Bushes appeared to be hunched over enemy soldiers. He knew that one night, on the bunker line, one of the soldiers on guard duty shot at an enemy just outside the wire. Turned out to be a Vietnamese headstone that had been there for years. The soldier hadn't recognized it for what it was and opened fire.

Cornett was about to tell Masters to relax when he caught movement out of the corner of his eye. He turned and watched as the man-shaped shadow made it's way toward him. Cornett didn't think the man had spotted them. He was just walking along. He didn't seem to have a weapon, but Cornett slowly turned his M-16 around and felt for the selector switch. He moved it to single shot, just in case.

A second man appeared, walking behind the first. Cornett now knew that both had weapons. He leaned close to Masters and whispered, "Go to full auto." With that, Cornett moved the selector switch.

When it was clear that the enemy was walking straight for them, Cornett knew there was nothing he could do. The enemy would find them. It was just bad luck. He let them get closer. At twenty yards, he pulled the trigger.

The muzzle flash nearly blinded him. It reached out three feet from the weapon. It destroyed his night vision, but he saw the first man fall. The other man turned as if to flee and was cut down by Masters. He dropped his weapon without firing.

Patterson rushed to them. "What in the hell?" His voice was loud and unnaturally high.

"We've got to get out of here."

"What happened?"

"Enemy soldiers. I don't think it was a patrol. They weren't searching for us, but someone had to hear the shooting. They wouldn't be walking around out here if they were alone. There will be follow-up."

"Were they armed?"

"Of course they were armed," snapped Cornett. "Why do you think we killed them?"

"Are you going to pick up the weapons?"

"No. We don't need the extra weight. We don't need any souvenirs. We've got to get out of here, before someone investigates the shooting."

Patterson turned to Stein. "Sergeant Major, you're with me."

"What are you doing?" Cornett asked.

"I'm going to find and disassemble the weapons. Just take the bolts. It will deny the enemy the use of the weapons."

Cornett said, "Owens, get Weaver ready to move. Load him up on the aspirin. Might make his life a little easier. Stay close to him and help him as much as you can. General, we don't have much time. There might be more enemy around and if there are, they heard the firing and they're going to be looking for the source of it."

"But they'll think it's their own men," said Patterson. "They won't expect us around here."

"General, I can tell the difference between an AK-47 and an M-16. I will assume that there are enemy soldiers who can also do that. If they heard the shooting, they're going to come looking. They'll know that there were no Aks shooting. It'll take them a little time to get organized, but they will come looking. We have to move."

Without a word, Patterson pushed past Cornett. He jogged out, looking right and left, but didn't see anything. He nearly tripped over the first body. As he bent down to grab the weapon, the man moved slightly and groaned. It surprised Patterson and he fell back into a sitting position. He grabbed at his holster, drawing his .45-caliber pistol. He thumbed back the hammer and pulled the trigger. The weapon fired but the man didn't move. He waited, not sure if he had hit him or not.

Stein knelt near Patterson and whispered. "You all right, General?"

"I'm fine. Get the weapon and break it down. Keep the bolt."

"Yes, sir."

Patterson got up and found the other dead man's weapon. He wanted to keep it as a souvenir. It would look good, mounted like a game fish and hanging in his office. He wasn't going to let a warrant officer tell him what he could or couldn't do. If he wanted a souvenir, it was no one's business but his. If he wanted to carry the extra weight, there wasn't a warrant officer in the world who was going to tell him different. He slung the weapon and watched as Stein crouched down and picked up the first man's AK. He heard him disassemble it to get at the bolt. He tossed the pieces into the jungle and slipped the bolt into a pocket.

Cornett caught up with them and asked, "You have everything you need?"

"Yes. We've destroyed the weapons."

There was a groan and Weaver asked, "Can I sit down for a moment?"

Cornett looked back and could see a charcoal shape. Sunrise wasn't far off. "We have to move, Dick."

"I'll keep up, sir."

Cornett noticed that Patterson had one of the AK-47s. He stared at it, then shrugged. He wasn't going to tell the general to leave it. He suspected that Patterson wouldn't listen anyway. This was not the time or place for an argument over what could become trivia. Cornett had pushed the general about as far as he could.

Cornett turned his attention to Weaver. "If you need some help, let us know, but we have to get out of here."

"Yes, sir."

CHAPTER 7

Captain James Cooper had spent most of the night looking for the gear that he would need to go into the field. Because he was assigned to MACV in Saigon, he had no need for the equipment that was issued to the soldiers in the field. He had a .38-caliber Smith and Wesson revolver that held the standard six rounds. He laughed when given the standard issue of ammo for the pistol. It was twenty-one rounds. He could reload three and a half times. Someone told him that the standard issue was based on the .45-caliber ACP, which held seven rounds.

He had a steel pot, but he hadn't worn it since it had been issued. What he really wanted was a flak jacket. It wasn't much good for stopping a rifle round, but shrapnel normally wouldn't penetrate it. It provided protection from artillery and mortars.

His web gear included a pistol belt that held a canteen, first aid kit, and pouch for spare ammo The ammo pouch was for the spare magazines for the .45 and not much good for the .38 ammo. It followed the tradition of basing everything on the .45. Cooper had seen soldiers, mostly pilots, who had Old West-style holsters that had loops to carry the spare rounds. He now understood why they had those holsters and wondered where they found them.

Satisfied that he had the equipment he would need to survive in the field, he left his quarters and walked over to Operations. It was situated in a building that was guarded by two soldiers armed with M-16s. As he approached, they saluted but didn't move to open the door for him. He ignored the slight, figuring that their job was to keep unauthorized personnel and the enemy from entering, and were not a decoration.

The interior was dimly lit, given that it was so early in the morning. There was no one in the lobby area but as he opened the door leading deeper into the interior, he found a desk manned by an old sergeant who was armed with a pistol.

The sergeant, who seemed to be half asleep, looked up and asked, "How may I help you, sir?" His words were slightly slurred, and Cooper wondered if he had been drinking.

"I need to see the senior officer on duty in Operations."

"Yes, sir. Who might that be?"

Cooper stared at the man. He had no clue who would be on the night shift. Invoking the protocol that he knew would work, he said, "I'm here on orders from General Dekker." It wasn't quite the truth, but then again, it wasn't completely inaccurate. Colonel Evans had made it clear that he was under orders from Dekker.

"Yes, sir," said the sergeant. "That would be Lieutenant Colonel Cobine. He's in the last office on the right."

"Thanks."

"Sir? I need to see an ID."

Cooper stopped. "Are you serious? I'm here, in uniform, I have told you who sent me and I am clearly authorized to be here."

"Yes, sir. ID?"

As he pulled his wallet from the right-hand pocket of his jungle jacket, he realized that he shouldn't be carrying his ID into the field. He showed both his regular Army ID card and his access badge for the building and most of the offices inside. Although he thought the enemy knew what the standard ID card looked like, he didn't think the VC knew what the local assess badges looked like.

The sergeant scanned it carefully. "Thank you, sir. Please sign in." He pushed a clipboard around for Cooper's signature.

Cooper signed in and then walked down the corridor. Rather than the linoleum tile in many buildings, this one was carpeted. It looked as if it had just been vacuumed. That was the advantage of working in a building that housed so many senior officers.

He came to the office and knocked on the door. It was opened a moment later. "Colonel Cobine?"

The man pointed over his shoulder at a soldier standing near a situation board that was attached to the wall. He was using a rag to wipe grease pencil marks off it and then adding others. He was a tall, thin man, nearly skinny. He had dark hair but very light skin, as if he didn't get out in the daylight often and certainly not out in the field.

"Colonel Cobine?"

"Yes?"

"I need to get out to one of the Special Forces camps near the Cambodian border and south of Tay Ninh."

"Good for you. That's my problem, how?"

"I'm working with Colonel Evans on orders from General Dekker." Cooper hesitated and then decided that Cobine had to know about the search for General Patterson.

Cobine answered the question for him. "You part of the search?"

"Yes, sir."

"Okay. We can get you a ride out to one of the Special Forces camps. Be right in the middle of the search area." Cobine looked at his watch. "Be at the main helipad in about thirty minutes. That going to be a problem?"

"No, sir. I'm ready now."

*

Although Kendall Stacy was a civilian and had no role at MACV, he was an accredited reporter from a small-town newspaper who had wormed his way into the upper echelon of the local power structure. He had done it with flattering stories about the generals and senior colonels who had appreciated his kind words published about them. They didn't care that the stories were not picked up by a major newspaper or the wire services. That those stories were published was enough. They then looked out for Stacy in ways that annoyed the other reporters who didn't write the puff pieces.

Stacy was in his mid-forties and had a career that was less than sterling. He had worked for several newspapers, was an adequate writer, but had no real understanding of what made a good story. He chased the wrong angles, talked to the wrong witnesses and had no sense of rhythm when putting together a paragraph. But he accepted all assignments with enthusiasm, and if he was annoyed, his editor never knew it. That was a major reason that he stayed employed.

But now he was in Vietnam, working on a more or less freelance beat, still trying to find that one story that would catapult him to the top. A master sergeant he knew, who he often bribed with alcohol, told him about the current major rumor. The sergeant had leaned in close while sucking down another bourbon and coke, and whispered that he wasn't sure, but he heard that a general had been captured by the VC. The enemy had him in Cambodia and were trying to get him north for proper interrogation by the experts.

"There's a big search to be launched at dawn. Lots of assets being moved around for the search."

"How sure are you?"

"Well, I'm not supposed to know anything about it, but I was there when the OPORD came down. Missions cancelled and whole helicopter companies being ordered south of Tay Ninh. They're stationed at several of the fire support bases and Special Forces camps in the area. A thousand or more men are involved in some capacity."

Stacy asked again, "How sure are you?"

"All I can say is that the orders have gone out and the assets are being moved, and I saw them. The orders, I mean."

Stacy ordered another round and leaned back, looking at himself in the mirror on the other side of the bar. Even if it wasn't a search for a lost or captured general, something big was being organized. He realized that this might finally be his chance. He dropped a wad of MPC on the bar to pay for the drinks and said, "I've got to run."

The master sergeant realized that there was enough money in the wad to keep him in booze for a couple of days. He didn't say anything as Stacy disappeared through the door.

As Stacy walked out into the late-night humidity, he wondered what to do next. He needed to get into the field but had spent the last seven months in Saigon, listening to the canned briefings and interviewing the colonels because most generals had no real time for him, except when they wanted a story about themselves sent out. They knew that he didn't have a high-profile news affiliation that would make the story national. That was the trouble with being freelance.

He didn't know where to go. He thought about Hotel Three, the heliport at Tan Son Nhut airport. There was a small terminal there where soldiers caught rides back out into the field. He could find a ride that would get him to Tay Ninh, but not necessarily to where the search was happening.

He thought about trying to convince one of the helicopter units here to give him a ride. If he found the right one, they might just drop him into the middle of the search. During his time in Saigon, he had discovered that several units were based at Long Binh.

The first trick was to find a ride to Long Binh. That wasn't difficult. He knew of a transportation company that often sent vehicles there, or sent out crews to recover damaged vehicles. They operated around the clock. He looked at his watch and figured that someone would be going to Long Binh even at that late hour.

He walked across the compound, found the operations bunker for the company, and walked in. A chubby, older sergeant first class was sitting behind the counter. He was pretending to read a magazine, but looked as if he was about to fall asleep.

"Hello, Sergeant First Class Torrence. How are you this fine evening?"

Torrence sat up quickly, as if horrified that he had been caught napping. He then recognized Stacy as no threat. "What can I do for you at this ungodly hour?"

"I need to get to Long Binh as quickly as possible."

Torrence sat up straighter. "What in the hell is going on over there that would interest you?"

"Don't know exactly, but I want to find out. I need a ride over there."

Torrence grabbed a clipboard, flipping over a couple of sheets. "Got a three-vehicle convoy loading with a departure time in —" he looked at his watch — "about fifteen minutes. That do you?"

"That would be perfect."

"They're out by the motor pool. Anybody gives you any grief, you let them know that I said it was okay."

"Thanks, Torrence. Take a commendation medal out of petty cash."

"Ten bucks would be more useful."

"Isn't that bribing an NCO in the completion of his duties, or some such nonsense? I mean, we're talking court-martial here."

"Probably is against regulations. Guess you can keep your ten bucks, though if I saw you in the NCO club, no one would think of it as a bribe if you bought me a drink or two."

"Fine. Find me later and I'll buy you that drink or two."

"You've got a deal."

Stacy had no trouble finding the convoy and the sergeant in charge didn't care that Stacy needed a ride. He just pointed to one of the trucks and said, "Go sit in the cab and don't get in our way. Don't talk to the driver."

Once at Long Binh, he went to the office of one of the aviation companies. The operations officer was less than delighted to see him and tried to ignore him. Stacy found the senior NCO, told him what he needed, and let that man talk to the officer.

Stacy watched the conversation and saw the operations officer shrug and then glance his way. He raised his voice and called, "Stacy, you pain in the ass. We'll get you out there, but I will not guarantee a ride back. Once you're out there, you're on your own."

"Thank you, sir. I understand."

Stacy was surprised that it had been that easy. He hadn't had to bring up the First Amendment or the peoples' right to know or any of the other arguments that only worked sometimes. He figured the man must be tired or too busy to worry about a reporter flying out into the middle of a classified mission, if that is what it was. He got out of the office as quickly as he could and found the helicopters were manned, but the rotors were not turning. They'd take off when the order came through.

He found the flight lead. "Ops guy said that I could hitch a ride with you?"

The man, a young warrant officer who looked as if he was trying to grow a mustache and failing, said, "We're just flying out to some Special Forces camp, and we'll be there on standby until called." It sounded more like a warning than a statement of fact.

"That's fine with me."

"Hop aboard trail." He glanced at his watch. "I check in with Ops in ten minutes. They're supposed to give me a take-off time."

"Thanks." Stacy turned and walked back to the last aircraft in the line. He was again surprised how easy it had been to find a ride into the field. As he climbed into the helicopter, he realized that he'd left his camera in his quarters. He had no way to recover it now. That had been a huge mistake.

As the sky began to lighten, Gerber climbed down from the fire control tower. There had been nothing suspicious in the jungle to the north of the camp, and the open ground to the south was not a good approach for an attacking force. Gerber figured they would have nothing to worry about during the day. It was too late for any sort of enemy attack on the camp. There might be ambushes along the trails in the jungle, but the strikers who would be patrolling knew to stay away from the trails and how to respond to an ambush.

Bromhead met him at the bottom of the tower. "Anything interesting out there?"

"Nope. You get word on the incoming flight?"

"Not yet. I don't know if they would take off in the dark or wait for dawn."

"My understanding," said Gerber, as he started toward the team house, "is that they'll be arriving anytime now."

Fetterman joined them. "We all set?"

"We have time," said Bromhead. "We'll make sure the first strike company is ready when the helicopters arrive. Others can filter out later."

"We going out with the strikers on patrol?" asked Fetterman.

"I hadn't planned on it," said Gerber. "I thought I would coordinate with the lead pilot. See what specific orders he has. Other than that, I think of myself as an observer. John is in charge here. I'm just making a nuisance of myself because, well, I can."

"I'd like to accompany one of the patrols." Fetterman looked at Bromhead for permission.

"I have no objections, Sergeant Major. I'm not sure that I'd want to voluntarily wander around in the jungle today. Especially as it's going to be hot later."

They entered the team house and sat down at the main table. Gerber looked at the refrigerator but didn't move. "Do we have any coffee ready?"

"No, sir. I can get some started."

"Don't bother. Besides, I think I would rather have something cold."

Bromhead pushed back his chair but as he did so, Staff Sergeant Travis Peterson entered and headed toward him. He leaned close to the captain's ear and said, "We have a flight coming in on long final."

Gerber overheard the comment. "I guess that means things are beginning."

"Get the First Striker Company ready," ordered Bromhead. "They'll stand by at the helicopters. I'll want two platoons from the Second ready to begin patrolling after they have breakfast."

"Yes, sir," said Peterson. "I'll alert Lieutenant Nguyen."

"No, tell Captain Trang. Have him select the platoons and issue the specific orders. That keeps the striker chain of command intact."

"Yes, sir."

When Peterson was gone, Bromhead said, "I guess it starts."

"I'm not sure how," said Gerber. "We don't know where that general went down, or if he is even alive or a prisoner. Could be closer to one of the other camps. We might just spend the day waiting for something to happen."

"We still have those new regiments to worry about," Fetterman reminded him.

"True."

"I'm sending an awful lot of my strikers out," said Bromhead. "We're going to be shorthanded if those regiments attack us while the strikers are riding around in helicopters."

"It's only two platoons in the field," said Gerber. "Your first company is here. They're just on call and if anything happens where they are needed, it will mean that the enemy isn't close to us."

"I'm not thrilled with that assessment, Major. I'm being stretched too thin for my taste."

"The orders have come down from on high. They're not my orders, but someone whose pay grade is far above mine. Besides, the odds are that nothing is going to happen here while your strike company is gone. All will be well."

"Yes, sir."

"You remember what Georgie Patton used to say. That's the real one and not the kid here in Vietnam. He used to say that you shouldn't take counsel of your fears. It means —"

"I know what it means. But I thought good planning was anticipating the enemy intensions, which is not the same thing."

Fetterman laughed out loud. "Are you two really going to argue about the meaning of Patton's sayings. Are you even sure that he said it, and it's not some quote attributed to him?"

"Doesn't matter, Sergeant Major. It just means to not overreact until all the facts are in."

They heard the approaching helicopters as they descended toward the end of the runway and then hovered forward until they were close to the entrance to the camp. Gerber, Fetterman and Bromhead left the team house so that they could greet the pilots. As they walked toward the runway, Bromhead said, "I'll go and alert the strikers."

As Gerber and Fetterman left the camp, they saw the helicopters shutting down. A man wearing a flak jacket and steel pot jumped from the trail aircraft. He held one hand on the top of his helmet as if the rotor wash would be able to blow it off.

"He doesn't have a weapon," said Fetterman.

"No, he doesn't," said Gerber. "I think he might be a reporter, but I don't see a camera. I don't think he's CIA."

"Why not?"

"Because he doesn't have a weapon and he jumped out of the helicopter without waiting for the rotors to stop." Gerber grinned. "And he was holding onto his helmet."

The man approached, looked at them, and asked, "Who's in charge here?"

"And who might you be?" asked Gerber.

"Stacy. I'm with the press."

"Press? What press?"

Stacy looked uncomfortable. "I'm working freelance."

"Just who authorized your flight here, Mr Stacy?"

"I have permission from Colonel Evans." It was the first name that popped into his head.

"We don't have a Colonel Evans in our chain of command," said Gerber. "I'm going to verify your claims with MACV."

Stacy was saved from having to come up with another explanation as Bromhead caught up with Gerber and Fetterman. He had alerted the strikers. He then looked at Stacy. "Just how in the hell did you get on that helicopter to come here?" he demanded.

"I talked to the officer in Operations. He said it would be okay."

"I meant, what is your authority? Not who you talked to who doesn't seem to know his ass from a hot rock?"

Stacy held up his hands as if to surrender. "Hey, I'm on your side."

Bromhead started to speak but Gerber cut him off. "It has been my experience that the press is not on our side."

"Just who are you?" asked Stacy.

Gerber ignored the question. "I think the real question is how soon we can get your ass out of here."

"Maybe we should take this discussion into the team house," suggested Fetterman.

There was an awkward silence. Stacy, becoming nervous, finally broke it. "I just want a story. I want to know what is going on. There is a big flap at MACV. Something about a general disappearing. Maybe captured by the VC."

"We have nothing to do with that," said Gerber.

Stacy glared at him. "I know the truth. I know about the general, and there is a big search that is going to start in a few minutes."

"Not from here."

"Then why are all these helicopters here?"

"That is none of your business. We have search-and-destroy operations to run." Gerber turned to Bromhead. "You have facilities for the prisoner."

The color drained from Stacy's face. "Prisoner? I'm a prisoner?"

"You are not authorized to be on this facility. You have stumbled onto a classified operation, and we can't afford compromise."

"What do you mean compromise?"

"There is nothing that I can tell you other than you don't belong here."

"Major," said Fetterman. "He doesn't have a way to communicate with anyone without using the radios here. He can't leave unless we allow it, other than to let him walk off the runway. But where could he go? If he agrees not to publish anything until we clear it, and he remains here quietly, then no harm, no foul."

"You might be right," said Gerber.

"We could put him in the team house. We can put a guard on him if that would make you more comfortable?" said Bromhead. He had picked up on what Gerber and Fetterman were doing.

Quickly, Stacy said, "I won't file anything until you tell me that it won't harm your mission."

Bromhead said, "Let's get out of here. The sun is beginning to bother me."

"You have all your gear?" Fetterman asked Stacy. "Your ride out of here might not be with the same unit."

"I have everything I need right here." Stacy patted his canteen.

Gerber turned and walked off. He heard Stacy ask, "Is this really a Green Beret camp?"

"You noticed the headgear, did you?"

"Yeah. I've never seen a Green Beret camp. I've been in Saigon."

"Well, we don't have the comforts that you had there. We are a little... I think spartan is the word."

As they entered the camp proper, Stacy grinned. He felt relieved. At least they hadn't shot him or ordered him back on the helicopters. That would have ruined everything. Stacy believed he had found his ticket to a major newspaper and a choice assignment ... if he wasn't killed first, but he didn't think that would happen. The real danger was with the helicopters, if they were called out.

CHAPTER 8

Although they were moving through thick jungle, the sun broke through, creating shafts of green light. Now Cornett could follow a straight line, leading off to the southwest in his attempt to avoid any enemy search parties. He was trying to figure out when they should turn back east. It was a tricky question. Cornett wished that there was an infantry officer with them. Patterson's aide had been wearing the crossed rifles of an infantry officer, but he was dead, his body burned in the helicopter.

They came to a dark area, in what looked like triple-canopy jungle. The vegetation was as thick as it was in other areas, but there was a rocky outcropping that looked almost like part of an ancient wall. There were tool marks on them. The wall offered a bit of protection and was a defensible position. Cornett called a halt.

Weaver's face was covered in sweat, his uniform nearly black. He was pale. He hadn't complained but had slowed them down slightly. He was breathing heavily and when Cornett held up the balled fist signaling a halt, he dropped to one knee, his head bowed.

Patterson moved around Weaver and leaned close to Cornett. He spoke quietly, though he didn't believe there was anyone around them. "Mr Cornett, I don't question your decisions, but we do have to get out of Cambodia. The Army won't be searching for us here. They'll be looking for us in Vietnam."

"I know that, General, but I'm trying to keep us out of the hands of the NVA. I'm trying to anticipate their search patterns so that we might avoid them."

"This is an interesting position. It would offer your injured man protection and allow us to move faster toward Vietnam. It's a landmark that could be seen from the air."

"General, I was taught from the very beginning of my military career that we don't leave our wounded in the field. We have an obligation to them."

"Sometimes the needs of the many outweigh the needs of the one."

"And we induce men into dangerous positions with the promise that they won't be left alone. They believe that they won't be left behind."

Patterson wiped his sleeve across his forehead. "I understand your position, but I insist that we get out of here."

"You can insist all you like, sir, but as the aircraft commander it is my responsibility to protect all my crew and passengers. I will not leave Weaver behind."

"I didn't want to say this, but your aircraft is a burned wreck several klicks away. As the senior officer present, I will now assume command and responsibility."

"This is not the place for a power struggle," said Cornett.

"There is no power struggle. I have assumed command. Sergeant Major Stein will back me on this, and any more discussion will be seen as a refusal to obey lawful orders in the field. It could be considered making a mutiny."

"Really? You're going to pull that chestnut on me when you have no idea where we are or how to get back to Vietnam?"

"I know which way is east and that's all I need to know."

Stein, who had approached them quietly, said, "General, I think we need to table that discussion. Someone is coming."

"Where are they?" asked both Cornett and Patterson.

"There, I believe," said Stein, pointing. "They aren't following noise discipline. If we were in Vietnam, they would be moving cautiously, but here?" He shrugged.

"Okay," said Cornett. "We stay here. Use the wall for protection. Get Weaver situated in the corner and then we spread out. We lay chilly and hope they just pass us by."

"And if they don't?"

"Then we'll just have to use the element of surprise to overcome them."

When the door to his office opened without the courtesy of a knock, Colonel Evans didn't bother to look up. He wanted to make whoever it was wait as he finished what he was doing. It was just a minor way of maintaining control.

"A moment of your time, Colonel."

Evans recognized the voice. In one smooth move, he pushed his chair back and stood up. "I would have come to your office, General."

Dekker waved his hand, dismissing the remark. He dropped into the nearest chair without invitation. "I want to know what is going on with the search for General Patterson."

"I'm waiting for additional information from Captain Cooper. I gave him the task of gathering as much information as he could and report to me. I should have heard from him by now."

"Given the importance of this mission, do you think assigning this to a rather junior officer was the appropriate course of action, especially since you apparently have heard nothing from him?"

"I am keeping control of this, sir. Cooper is on his way out into the search area."

'It seems to me that you're sitting here, waiting for this captain to do what I had hoped you'd be doing."

Evans took a deep breath and let it out slowly, trying to control his anger. He knew that Dekker could wreck his career with a careful word spoken to his rating officers. "At the moment, sir, there isn't much we can do. The sun hasn't been up long, but several companies have been deployed into the forward AO. Aerial searches should be launching about now. There are quite a few assets being employed."

"Should be launching, Colonel? Are you guessing or do you have specific knowledge?" Dekker's voice was calm, almost to the point of real annoyance.

Evans caught the drift. "General, while you wait here, why don't I ensure that the proper orders have been issued. I'll check with Ops."

Before Dekker could respond, a master sergeant opened the door with his shoulder. He was pushing fifty, balding, and what little hair he had left was gray. His uniform looked as if had just been pressed. There was not a stain on it, but it was faded from many washings in the laundry's harsh detergents. He was carrying a tray that held three glasses of juice and a variety of pastries.

"I thought the general might like a pastry and some freshly-squeezed orange juice."

"I do not like being interrupted, Sergeant, but I do wonder where you could find freshly-squeezed orange juice at this hour?"

"In the world of the Air Force, sir, I find it helpful to provide colleagues with assistance when they need it, some advice periodically that might be helpful, and warn them of impending problems so that they might be able to correct them before they are found by the brass…" He trailed off, realizing that he had been too candid.

Dekker couldn't help but smile. "And you have contacts at the mess halls?"

"We call them dining facilities, sir, but yes. The senior master sergeant owed me a favor or two and I thought you would appreciate the pastry and juice, given the circumstances."

Evans hadn't moved. He stood there, looking at the master sergeant. He was a good man, but it wasn't until that moment that he realized just how good. He said, "If you will excuse me for a few minutes, General, I'll gather some information for you."

He left his office and went in search of Cooper. When he couldn't find him in his office, he asked one of the NCOs. "Do you know where Captain Cooper is?"

"No, sir. I understand he was here until two or three in the morning. Maybe he's in his hootch."

"And where might that be?"

"Out the main door and turn left. It's one of those hootches there, but I'm not sure which one."

"If you don't know which one, what do you do if you need him quickly?"

"Tell Sergeant Steward that we need Captain Cooper."

"And where might I find Sergeant Steward?"

"He's probably in his hootch. Out the door, turn left, and I think it's the third one on the right."

"Thank you, Sergeant."

Evans left the building but couldn't find Cooper or Steward. In desperation, he hurried to Operations. He asked around but no one there knew if Cooper had been there and if he had, where he had gone from there. He returned to his office, trying to figure out what to say to Dekker.

He found the master sergeant still in his office, but now sitting in the other visitor's chair, chatting with the general as if they were old friends. It made sense. A senior master sergeant was nearly at the top of the NCO ranks and a general was nearly at the top of the officer ranks. Both had been in the service for twenty or more years and had advanced nearly as far as they could on their particular career paths. The smart officers listened to what the top NCOs had to say.

"Colonel Evans," said Dekker. "What'd you find?"

Evans hesitated. "Captain Cooper is in the field gathering as much information as he can."

"He couldn't do that here?"

"He could, but he'd gather better information in the field. He'd be able to get it faster that way. You can talk to one or two guys on the field phone or radio, but if you're on the scene, you have the opportunity to talk to more people and they tend to say more in those circumstances. With a helicopter, he can get around quickly."

Dekker set his glass on Evans' desk. "Keep me in the loop."

"Yes, sir."

"Sergeant. Good to meet you. If there is anything that I can do for you, let me know."

"Thank you, General."

When Dekker was gone, Evans asked, "What did you and the general talk about?"

"Just compared stories. We knew some of the same people. I told him that I'd ask around to see if any of the lower-ranking NCOs knew anything about Captain Cooper. Those at the lower end of the spectrum sometimes don't want to talk to the brass."

"Well, that was a nice play with the pastries."

"Thank you, sir. I'll take the glasses and the tray back to the mess sergeant."

Major Edward Gore, a tall, heavy-set man with a hairline in full retreat and skin that was perpetually red even when he avoided the sun, walked to the center of the room. "Gentlemen, we have been tasked with a mission that has nothing to do with forward air control. Because we have slow, high-wing aircraft, which, I'm told are best for search operations, we will be withdrawn from our normal role as FACs. We are now going to search for a missing helicopter."

"What in the hell is so important about this missing helicopter?" asked one of the assembled pilots.

"Other than it carried a crew of American soldiers and we have an obligation to find them?"

"Yeah."

"One of the passengers was a general officer."

"Well, that explains it." The sarcasm was not lost on Gore or the others in the briefing room.

Gore walked to the front of the room where there was a large map of Three Corps. There was nothing special about the map, which meant that it wasn't classified. He pointed to a large area south of Tay Ninh. "This is the search area. We'll be operating close to the border where there is a heavy presence of anti-aircraft defenses, which I'm sure you already know about."

"How is this affecting other operations?" One of the pilots was waving his hand to draw attention to him but hadn't waited for Gore to acknowledge him.

"Not that it's any of your business, Lieutenant, but several aviation companies are on standby around the area in case they're needed. We have not been tasked with any specific missions today, other than provide aircraft and teams for the search."

"If they were operating that close to the border, what's to make you, or anyone else, think that they didn't crash into Cambodia?"

Gore looked at the man as if angry that the question had been posed, but said, "Assigned areas of search will be provided in Operations. You have about two hours to search and then return here. Aircraft commanders will be handed a special code to report findings, if any."

"This doesn't seem to be well thought out," said someone in the back.

Gore held his hand to his eyes and stared. "That you, Becker?"

Becker stood up. "No, sir. I would never question the orders of my superiors in such a cavalier fashion."

"Thank you, Mr Becker. I'll see to it that you get the worst search area."

"I figured I had already been assigned that."

There was laughter. Gore said, "If there are no further questions, Peter Pilots, your assignments remain the same as they were last night, in case you were unsure. Let's get out there."

As the rotors of the Huey stopped turning and the two pilots removed their flight helmets, Captain Cooper knelt between them and asked, "Your orders are to remain here?"

"Unless something is found. Then we load the troops and take off. Once we've made the insertion, we'll either return to our home base or return here in case we need to extract the troops. The situation is very fluid, and I can't say that I'm thrilled with our instructions."

"Why would you need to extract them?"

"Heavy contact. No contact. Move them to another location. Hell, Captain, I don't know. We just sit here with the Prick-25 and wait for C and C to contact us and tell us where we're needed."

Cooper patted the pilot on his shoulder. "Thanks."

He jumped out of the cargo compartment. He saw that the officers who had been standing at the edge of the runway as the flight landed were now moving into the camp. The reporter was with them. Cooper was surprised they hadn't ordered him to stay with the flight.

He hurried after them. He didn't know who they were or what ranks they held. He shouted, "Sergeant?" Surely one of them was a sergeant.

That stopped them all. They turned and when they did, Cooper slowed to a walk. He caught up with them and saw that one of them was a major. He saluted.

"We don't do that in the field," said Gerber. "Tells the enemy who to shoot first. That would be me and then probably you."

"Sorry, sir. I forgot."

"Well, now that you've identified that two of us are officers, let's get out of the line of fire."

They reached the team house and went inside. Gerber ignored the reporter, but Bromhead took him aside to talk to him privately. Gerber said, "And just who are you?"

"Captain Cooper, sir. I've come from MACV."

Fetterman laughed out loud. "Is that supposed to mean something?" He didn't mention that it seemed that everyone who was showing up suddenly said they were from MACV.

Cooper turned his attention to Fetterman. He was about to say something snide but saw that he was a sergeant major.

There was something about the man's eyes that almost frightened Cooper. He said, "No, Sergeant."

"Sergeant Major," Gerber corrected.

"Yes, sir. I just meant that I came from MACV with an important mission."

"I didn't think you were out here on a sightseeing tour," said Fetterman.

Cooper glanced over his shoulder at Bromhead and the reporter. They seemed to be deep in a private conversation. They weren't paying any attention to him. He lowered his voice. "There is a general's aircraft missing in this area and I'm here to assist where I can and provide an update to General Dekker."

"We know," said Gerber.

That surprised Cooper. "Then you know where he is?"

"We know that he's missing. But we're not involved in the search operations right now. We have a striker company standing by in case there is the need for a strike force for extraction of the general and the aircrew, but we are not actively looking for him."

"You could send up some of those aircraft to search."

Gerber shook his head. "Do they just send the dumbest officers to MACV? We don't know where to look, we are not involved in the search operations. We are standing by in case a larger force is needed. I doubt they'll be called out. More than likely, they'll use a Medevac helicopter to retrieve the dead."

"Dead? You think they're dead?"

"Or captured. There wouldn't be a large search operation beginning if there had been contact with the aircrew and as far as I know, there has been no contact with them for the last twelve to fifteen hours Maybe more."

Cooper fell back in the chair. That answer sounded right to him. Since they hadn't heard anything, it was clear that they'd find the wrecked helicopter with the bodies inside.

"I need to go back to Saigon."

"Good luck with that," said Fetterman. "Those helicopters are not going anywhere until released by a higher authority."

"On the bright side," said Gerber, "you can get breakfast here if you ask nice and say please."

CHAPTER 9

Fetterman left the team house, returned to his temporary quarters and grabbed his web gear and M-16 rifle. He also had a pistol hidden in his gear. Concealed weapons were a court martial-offense, but in all his years, he had never heard of a soldier who had been court-martialed for having such a weapon. The attitude seemed to be that it was better to have it and not need it than to need it and not have it.

He found Gerber and Bromhead talking with Lieutenant Nguyen. The striker platoon was assembled in the limited shade provided by the buildings. As Fetterman approached, Gerber asked, "Is this a good idea, Tony?"

"Just recon. Might find a clue to the missing general."

"Fat chance," said Bromhead.

"I'll be looking for clues about those regiments intel has reported and keeping my eyes open for anything that would lead us to the general."

"Don't do anything stupid, Tony."

"Never happen, Major."

Nguyen said, "We go now?"

"Yes. We go now." Fetterman turned to Gerber. "We'll be back no later than noon tomorrow, if not by sunset tonight. Depends on what we find and how far we range."

"I've plenty to do here, Tony, and don't feel the need to head back to the office today. Stay in radio contact, and we do have access to a flight of helicopters to move the strikers for assistance if you find something interesting. I might have to bend some rules, but we'll get you help if you need it."

"Yes, sir." He turned to the striker. "Let's go, Lieutenant."

They walked toward the striker platoon. Nguyen waved at the senior NCO who turned, waved his arm and the strikers spread out, walking in a trail formation. They worked their way through the wire and then across the killing field. They disappeared into the tree line.

After they were gone, Gerber said, "Let's go to the communications bunker."

"Any reason?" asked Bromhead.

"To get out of the sun, but mostly to stay away from the rear-area wienies. Besides, it's air-conditioned."

"Shouldn't we keep an eye on them?"

"Tell Sully to entertain Cooper, answer his questions and to keep him away from us. There is something about that guy I don't like."

Bromhead laughed. "I know what you mean. I don't know why, but I just didn't like him."

"I think it might be an air of superiority. He works in air conditioning in Saigon while we sweat it out far from that center of power. Since he works in Saigon, he thinks his job is more important than ours."

Bromhead laughed again. "We think of you the same way. Sitting around in your air-conditioned comfort while we toil in the heat and humidity."

"You're treading on thin ice, Captain."

"All the time, Major."

As the entered the communications bunker, Gerber asked, "What did you learn from that reporter?"

"Not much. His name is Kendall Stacy. He's a freelance and supplies copy to various outlets, though from the way he talked, I don't think he's considered top of the line. He heard about the missing general and hopped on a helicopter."

"You were talking to him for quite a while."

Bromhead laughed. "Yeah. He was telling me all about his hard luck stories. He has delusions of grandeur. He's trying to find a big story that everyone will want rather than the press handouts they get in Saigon. I think that Chuck Tatum is his hero. Manipulating the facts for the big byline."

Gerber walked over to the situation map posted on one wall. There wasn't any classified information on it. Just a general overlay of what was known about the enemy in the area. That information, as such, was not considered classified because the VC knew where they were.

Bromhead pointed to an area to the north of the camp, and to the west that was near the Cambodian border. "I think their infiltration route is somewhere in this general area. They should be passing north of here, using the jungle as cover."

"You didn't mention any of this to him, did you?"

"Of course not. I told him that there was nothing going on here. We were just supplying the landing strip for the helicopters. They're not under our control and while we are supplying a strike company if needed, we just weren't involved in the operation."

Gerber said, "I don't like having that reporter here, if he's looking for a big story that will elevate his career."

Bromhead sat down in one of the lawn chairs facing the map. "Between you and me, I don't think he's all that smart."

"Even the dumbest reporter can take a few observations, twist them around, and we end up holding the dirty end of the stick. We are interviewed by the brass; other reporters show up and things get out of hand."

"What are you suggesting we do about him?"

"Well, we can't kill him. But we can do our best to keep him isolated. Keep him away from the strikers. Assign one of your NCOs to escort him around."

"He's going to think we're hiding something from him."

Gerber grinned. "All we're trying to do is ensure that he doesn't twist the situation around so that we look bad. If there was a way to get him out of here, that would be best. Get him chasing a story that requires he go to Tay Ninh or even back to Saigon."

"There's really nothing going on here," said Bromhead with a straight face. "I'll just have someone with him all the time. It'll pay off in the long run."

"Keep him away from me."

Bromhead shrugged. "Sure. Why not?"

Fetterman had explained to Nguyen that he, Nguyen, was in charge of the patrol. Fetterman said that his role was that of an observer. Although American soldiers, especially those in the Special Forces, had been called advisors at first, their role had expanded. There were rules about that role, including what weapons they were allowed to carry and that they were never to be in charge of the Vietnamese soldiers. But all that had changed unofficially as the war expanded and American soldiers and Marines were brought in. All it meant to Fetterman was that he could carry a concealed weapon, and that Nguyen would take his advice as if it was an order.

The pace set by the point was not as fast as Fetterman would have liked. He wanted to get across the killing zone quickly so that they would be inside the tree line where there was some protection from the enemy. That would make it harder for the enemy to spot them and take them under fire if there were any enemy still around after the rocket attack.

Once they had reached the relative safety of the jungle, the pace slowed. Now it was all about stealth. Noise discipline was the most important. They spread out, keeping the man in front in sight, but not getting so close that they all could be cut down quickly.

After an hour, just as Fetterman was wondering if they would ever take a break, the point dropped to one knee. He looked back at Nguyen, who nodded. Fetterman crouched, facing away from the platoon, watching the jungle in front of him. He was listening but only heard the sounds of the animals, birds and the insects. If there was anyone else in the jungle around them, the noise would have been different.

Fifteen minutes later, they were on the move again, in the general direction of where the rocket launchers should have been. After another hour, they came to a slight clearing and found that the launchers were still there. It didn't mean that the enemy would be coming back to use them again. These were makeshift launchers and not worth much. They were easy to erect from a few thick sticks. The rocket would be set on them and could be launched by a crew or by a long fuse.

Fetterman caught up with Nguyen, leaned close and whispered, "We could set a mechanical ambush here in case they come back."

"Danger to farmers. Much danger."

"Farmers won't come close to this place. They'll know what it is here, and they will avoid it so that they don't run into the enemy. Or one of our patrols. Only the enemy will come close."

Nguyen nodded, as if he was considering the suggestion. He stroked his chin and closed his eyes, as if deep in thought. Finally, he nodded and said, "Yes. Mechanical ambush. Good idea, Sergeant."

Fetterman didn't bother to correct him. The Vietnamese military didn't recognize the importance of a sergeant major. Instead, he said, "Shall I supervise the installation?"

"Yes. You supervise. Be quick. We go."

Fetterman tapped two of the strikers and motioned for them to follow him. The trick was to place the grenades with the pins pulled, but with the safety spoon held in place by pressure against the side of the launcher and the grenade. If it was jostled, the grenade would fall, and the spoon would be released. The grenade would detonate in about three seconds. Fetterman thought about replacing the grenade fuse with one from a smoke grenade. There was no delay with the smoke grenade fuses. They fired the instant the safety spoon was released. Smoke grenades were not explosive.

Fetterman found a good place for a grenade, partially concealed by the launcher, and set the trap, showing the strikers what he was doing. One of them nodded and found another place. He pulled the pin and began trying to set it.

Fetterman took a deep breath and watched carefully. If the man made a mistake, Fetterman would not have much time to either correct it or take cover. He stepped back, close to a fallen log. If the spoon flew, he'd have three seconds to dive over the log. That should protect him from the shrapnel and the overpressure of the blast. He thought about stopping the striker, but didn't want to discourage his initiative.

But the striker was careful and set the grenade so that it was wedged between two of the supports for the launcher. It wasn't the best position, but the grenade would not detonate by accident.

Nguyen approached and asked, "We ready?"

"Yes, Lieutenant."

They continued, moving toward the northwest. Although Fetterman hadn't provided the direction of march, it was the way he wanted to patrol. The enemy had been infiltrating that area, at least according to the recent intel reports. There was some sort of buildup, or rather that was what the intelligence suggested. Fetterman wanted to verify that, if he could.

He noticed a great deal of aviation activity overhead. There were single airplanes, jet fighters, single helicopters and flights of Hueys. The jungle canopy blocked his view of the sky, but he could hear the aircraft, identifying them by the noise from their engines. Some were low, overhead, but others were in the distance or flying higher. He wondered if they were all involved with the search for the missing general. He figured they were on the wrong side of the border.

The point stopped, holding up a balled fist as he dropped to a knee. The patrol spread out and then crouched. Their weapons were ready. Both Nguyen and Fetterman worked their way forward. The point man didn't say a word to them. The problem was obvious. There were human shadows moving in the jungle ahead of them. These were somewhat disciplined men. They weren't making much noise; they weren't talking, but Fetterman could hear them over the normal jungle noise.

He counted twenty enemy soldiers, which meant they were about evenly matched. Fetterman and his patrol had the advantage of surprise, but Fetterman didn't want to engage. That would tell the enemy that they had been spotted.

Nguyen was crouched nearby fingering the selector switch on his M-16. He wanted to fire but didn't do it. Before he could act, the enemy was out of sight. They weren't far away because they were still making noise, but they were moving away.

Fetterman moved around and leaned close to Nguyen. "We should withdraw to the south."

"We surprise them?"

"Our mission is to observe but not engage. We need to report to your captain and to Captain Bromhead. We have the advantage of seeing them but not being seen ourselves."

They fell silent but there were no more enemy soldiers in the area. Just that one patrol that had passed by them at about a hundred yards. Fetterman was impressed that none of the strikers had opened fire without permission. Nguyen, and Bromhead, had taught them well.

After an hour, when they were sure that the VC were far away from them, they began to withdraw. They moved slowly and listened to the jungle around them. It would take them several hours to return to the camp. Fetterman had learned what he wanted to and thought the intelligence would be valuable to Bromhead. The movement of the enemy in the daylight told him all that he needed to know. The enemy was not afraid of being seen.

Warrant Officer Terry Becker had picked up the map in Operations. He had studied it and saw that his search sector was getting very close to the Cambodian border. He wasn't sure that the threat of triple-A worried him. That was designed to take out fighters and high-flying airplanes. It was not directed at low-flying, single Huey helicopters that might be flying too low for them to effectively engage.

He walked out, into the revetment area where the helicopters were parked. He wondered why he always ended up at the farthest corner of the area, no matter what aircraft he was assigned. The crew was assembled, sitting in the cargo compartment, though the door gunner was lying on the deck using his chicken plate for a pillow.

Becker put his helmet and chicken plate on his seat in the cockpit and then spread his map out on the cargo compartment floor. The door gunner sat up so that he wasn't in the way, and he could see the map.

When the crew chief and the Peter Pilot, WO1 Randolph Smith, joined him, Becker said, "Okay. This isn't exactly an easy mission for us, but it shouldn't be too dangerous. Our search area is here, away from the border." He circled the area with his finger. "Okay. Here is the Cambodian border and the jungle in the area is from scraggly trees and bushes to almost opaque triple-canopy jungle. If that crew has survived, I would expect them to throw a smoke grenade to mark their position if we get near. If they didn't..." He didn't finish the sentence.

"What are we looking for?"

"Okay. If we're over the triple canopy we need to look for a place at the tops of the trees that have been broken. If the helicopter burned, there might be a blackened hole. If we're not over the jungle, then we look for the wreckage. There won't by many wrecked Hueys around. Okay, remember, the rotor blades have been painted with one black and the other white to help us see them, thought I don't really know if it does any good. The synchronized elevators are dayglow orange and if the aircraft is not inverted, we should be able to see them."

"When do we take off?"

Becker looked at his watch. "Just as soon as I fold this map and we can get cranked up. I understand the fuel trucks are being positioned at the fire support bases and Special Forces camps in the area so that we can refuel without having to return here."

He turned his attention to the crew chief, Spec Five Jason Grant. "I will assume that you followed your instructions and secured C-rations for us?"

"Yes, sir. Got the whole box."

"Whose turn is it to get the pound cake?"

"I believe it is yours, sir."

"Okay. That's what I thought. Let's not discover that it has disappeared."

"How long do we search?"

"For the pound cake?" asked Becker.

"No, sir. For the helicopter?"

"We look until I'm satisfied that we have done a thorough job of searching our area of responsibility. Okay, let's get cranked and get this bird in the air."

Becker climbed into his seat, strapped himself in and put on his helmet. He quickly surveyed the instrument panel and said, "Clear?"

Both the door gunner, Spec Four Greg Navarro, and the crew chief looked to the rear from their seats and yelled, "Clear."

"Okay, I'm lighting the fire." Becker set the throttle and pulled the trigger under the collective. As the turbine caught, he rolled the throttle up slowly, until the engine reached operating rpm. The rotor was in the green. Becker said, "Okay. Coming up to a hover."

Carefully, he moved the aircraft out of the revetment and then hovered toward the active runway. He stopped short and called the tower, telling them where he was and what he wanted to do.

"You're cleared to the active."

"Roger." Becker turned the nose of the helicopter and then pushed the cyclic forward as he slowly pulled up on the collective. Over the intercom, he said, "Okay. Here we go."

As soon as they passed over the perimeter and reached four hundred feet, he turned to the west. The sky was clear, and the sun was bright, but the sun didn't bother him. He worried about clouds, but not sunlight.

"Okay. About ten minutes to our search area. Let's stay alert."

They had climbed to two thousand feet, well outside the small arms range that was normally directed at helicopters. Becker knew that at a lower altitude they would be able to see better, but at the higher altitude they could cover a larger area faster and were slightly safer.

They had been flying a linear search pattern but there was nothing on the ground that interested them. Becker had switched the ADF over to the commercial broadcast band so they could listen to the music on AFVN. He knew most of the pilots used the ADF for entertainment rather than navigation. He knew the area well enough that he just needed his compass to find his way around, but he liked to use the ADF for directions for part of the day.

Becker had just turned them back to the north when there was a ripping sound from an AK-47. Over the intercom, he asked, "Anyone see where that came from?"

"Off to the right."

There was a second burst from something larger than the AK. Navarro said, "Got it, on the right."

Becker felt the rounds hitting the aircraft. He jerked the cyclic over to the left and dived. It would put the trees between him and the enemy. He saw a glowing green tracer flash by the nose of the aircraft, but didn't feel any more hits.

"Can you engage?"

"No, sir. I don't have a good line of sight."

"Okay. Put out some rounds anyway."

Other enemy weapons joined in, but none of the rounds hit the aircraft. Becker believed the problem was that the VC hadn't been taught how to lead the target. They fired directly at the aircraft. Those rounds passed behind them.

Becker rolled over, pushing the aircraft to the red line. He knew that there was an extra twenty to thirty knots available above the red line if he needed it. That was for emergencies. They were flying out of the kill zone, and it was no emergency. He wouldn't need the extra speed. He just wanted it.

"I think we've crossed the border." Smith had the folded map in his hand. We're four of five klicks into Cambodia."

Becker was about to turn back, into Vietnamese airspace, when he had a thought. If the general's aircraft had been engaged in the same way, the pilot might have turned west to avoid more of the enemy. If he had been hit, they wouldn't have flown too deep into Cambodia. He was now outside their official search area but he didn't change direction.

"We're in Cambodia," repeated Smith.

"I know where we are, but we're close enough to the border that we can claim ignorance. Besides, we have bullet holes in the aircraft to prove we took fire and evasive action."

"How do you know we've taken hits?"

Becker's first thought was to call Smith an FNG. He hadn't been around long enough to know better. Becker had his feet on the pedals, and he could feel the vibrations as the rounds hit the tail boom.

"Fire on the left," said Grant.

Becker broke slightly to the right, away from the enemy fire. He began a climb back to two thousand feet. He wondered if that might be a mistake. More of the enemy could see them, but it made them a harder target.

Just as he was about to turn back, flying to the southeast, Grant said, "I think I saw something."

"Okay. Don't keep it to yourself. What the hell did you see?"

"Sorry, sir. Looked like a burned area in the jungle. Treetops sheared off."

As Becker rolled out of the turn, he too could see the blackened area. Once over the top of it, he slowed to nearly a hover. If there was anyone on the ground, the aircraft was now an easy target. They'd fill the helicopter full of holes before he could react. It was a dangerous maneuver.

Looking down, through the chin bubble, and through a gap burned in the trees, was the wreckage of a Huey. It had burned. The magnesium in the fuselage providing hot fuel for the fire. The only recognizable part of the Huey were the rotor blades. The black and white paint made it easier to spot the wreckage.

"You see anybody down there?"

"No, sir," said Grant. "No movement."

Becker was going to ask Navarro but realized that if there had been anyone still around, they would have popped smoke.

"No sign of survivors."

"Okay. If anyone had survived, they probably would have hotfooted it out of there." Becker was unaware of the pun.

As he turned back, toward South Vietnam, Becker asked, "Randy, you get a fix on the location?"

"Yeah. I think so."

"Okay. Now all we have to do is survive another crossing of the border back into Vietnam."

"How you going to explain how we found the wreckage?"

"If that's the wreckage of the general's aircraft, I don't think that question will come up. If it does, we have the bullet holes in the aircraft to explain what we were doing."

"I think we're back in Vietnam."

Becker climbed back to altitude and keyed the mic. "Search control. I think we might have found the general's aircraft." He knew what they'd ask. He added, "The aircraft burned and no sign of survivors."

CHAPTER 10

Colonel Evens was not sitting behind his desk. Instead, he was pacing from one end of his office to the other. He walked to the window but saw nothing other than the parking lot filled with jeeps and a few highly polished staff cars belonging to various generals and even a few senior colonels. Evans, although a colonel himself, was outranked by time in grade, based on date of rank of those colonels blessed with a staff car. He was stuck with a jeep, though it was a newer model and washed almost daily by a specialist assigned the duty.

At the other end of his office was the door that looked out on an office where his staff waited for instructions. He tried not to open the door, but every five minutes he couldn't help himself. He knew that General Dekker wanted to know what happened to General Patterson and Dekker expected him to find the answer immediately. Every hour, almost like clockwork, Dekker's aide would appear to ask for an update. It was Dekker's way of keeping the pressure on and it annoyed Evans, as it was supposed to.

When he could stand it no longer, he would open the door and ask, "Any word from the search teams?"

The senior NCO, an older sergeant, which meant he was in his late thirties, would rise and then shake his head. "No, sir. We'll be sure to let you know as soon as we hear something."

Evans had accepted that answer but also knew that Dekker's aide would be back soon to ask the same question. "Make a few phone calls and check with Operations. See what they have. Check with the bases and camps out in the search area, if you can get through."

"Yes, sir." The sergeant didn't like the order because he knew that if anyone had any information, they would have let them know. But he also knew about the pressure being exerted by Dekker and he didn't want to lie to Evans. He tasked one of the Spec Fours to make the calls, if the lima lima was still working.

Evans closed his door and walked to the window. It was sunny outside. Brightly sunny. So bright that it hurt his eyes just to look out, into the parking lot. Even though it was only late morning, the heat was shimmering off the concrete, giving the parking lot a slightly psychedelic look.

He sat down at his desk, picked up a folder marked secret and tried to read it. He just couldn't concentrate. He wanted a drink. He had a bottle of bourbon stashed away, but was afraid that Dekker would show up asking for information about the time that he finished the drink. The last thing Evans needed was for Dekker to see him drinking long before noon.

There was a knock on his door. "Come."

The NCO entered and laid a sheet of paper in front of him. "Just got this from communications." He waited, standing at a position of attention.

Evans glanced at the paper. "This all they've got? The crash site, or maybe just a crash site has been discovered but not the one we're looking for."

"Yes, sir."

"No mention of survivors?"

"No, sir. Just they found the crash site."

"Why didn't they land to inspect the site?"

"I wouldn't know, sir. The sergeant that brought the message didn't know anything. He was just the messenger."

"See if you can follow up on that."

"Yes, sir. Will you be calling General Dekker?"

Evans stood up and said, "No. I'll take this to him personally, though he probably already has a copy."

"Yes, sir."

As Evans walked to the door, the sergeant stepped aside. Evans told his staff, "I'll be back in twenty minutes or so."

"Yes, sir."

Evans reached the outer office where Dekker's immediate staff worked. He looked at the aide, a young captain, and asked, "General Dekker in?"

"Yes, sir. You have word?"

"Not much."

The aide tapped on the closed door to Dekker's inner office, opened it and said, quietly, "Colonel Evans is here, General."

Evans saw Dekker gesture for him to enter. He knew that Dekker was a stickler for military protocol, so he marched to within three feet of Dekker's desk, saluted and said, "I have a communication."

Dekker returned the salute. "About time, Colonel." He took the message from Evans.

He read it quickly. "This all you have? Someone, somewhere might have found the crash site?"

"That was all that communications had. I've already started to make inquiries to find out more but that will take a little time. We don't have commo with some of the bases, given their distance from here and the unreliability of the land lines. I thought this preliminary message would be of interest to you."

Dekker tossed the paper down onto his desk. "This is practically useless. All it says is they found a wrecked helicopter, but they don't say where. They didn't land, they say nothing about survivors or bodies. Hell, there are wrecked Hueys all over the place. This could be one of those. It just doesn't tell me anything."

"Yes, sir. The message was in the clear and I don't think the pilot wanted to compromise the intel. We have to wait for him to reach some place with secure communications."

"Why aren't you on your way out there to find out what in the hell is going on?"

"There is really nothing I can do, sir. We don't even know which base is closest to the wreck and I don't know where the pilot is going."

Dekker slammed a hand down on his desk. "I don't understand these incompetents. Nobody got his call sign. That'll give you his home unit. They find something but they don't investigate. They just tell us they found something. Where is that captain we were dealing with? What's his name?"

"Cooper, sir. He's at one of the Special Forces camps."

"Get him on the horn and ask him some questions. I better get some answers pretty damned soon or there'll be some unhappy people around here. No, strike that. They'll be unhappy somewhere else."

As he left Dekker's office, Evans wondered what Dekker was going to do to them. Send them to Vietnam?

Out of the corner of his eye, Becker spotted the star-shaped Special Forces camp with a flight of Hueys sitting on the runaway just outside the perimeter wire. Without a word, he turned in the direction of the camp. He lined up on the runway, shooting his approach to land well short of the flight.

"Why are we landing here?" asked Smith.

"I'm hoping that that flight is part of this search-and-rescue operation. We have information that is relevant to them."

They landed close to the end of the runway and then hovered forward. When they were close to the main entrance to the camp, and away from the flight of Hueys, Becker put the skids on the ground. He then lowered the collective. He started through the shutdown procedures.

As the blades slowed, two men began to walk toward them. "Here comes the reception committee," said Smith.

"I see them." Then to the rest of the crew, "Okay. You remain here. I'm not sure how long this might take. We'll get a chance to relax here for a few minutes anyway, okay?"

Becker climbed out of the cockpit and headed toward the two men. He noticed one was a major and the other a captain. He did not salute them for two reasons. First, they were in the field where enemy snipers might be waiting to shoot an officer and second, because they were, technically, on a flight line.

The major asked, "What can I do for you?"

Without thinking about it, Becker waved a hand at the flight behind him. He said, "I assume that this is part of the search-and-rescue operation?"

"I'm not sure that is any of your business."

"Sir, I was flying one of the missions searching for the downed aircraft."

"So?"

"I might have found it. I thought this flight might be standing by for the rescue operation."

The major grinned. "And if we were conducting search-and-destroy operations instead?"

"I just figured that this close to the border and the search area, that it was a better than even bet that this might be part of the search."

The captain said, "Maybe we should stroll over to the team house for a private discussion."

"My crew is still on the aircraft."

"Following the tradition that you have just established, I will assume that your crew also knows what is going on?"

"Be hard to keep it from them. They have been briefed, and it was the crew chief who spotted the wreckage."

"Then invite them in."

Becker turned and saw that Navarro was sitting on the deck of the cargo compartment, watching. Becker waved a come-on gesture to them. Navarro said something and then pushed off. Smith climbed out of the cockpit and joined him as they walked toward the gate. The crew chief came from his side of the aircraft.

Becker said, "Okay. I'm Becker. The AC." He did not hold out a hand.

"Gerber and Bromhead. Captain Bromhead commands here."

When the crew joined them, they headed toward the team house. Bromhead asked, "You need something to drink?"

"Whatever you have, sir."

Bromhead put bottled water and Pepsis on the table. "Take your pick."

As they settled in, Gerber asked, "Now, why are you here, exactly?"

"I think we might have found the downed helicopter. It burned. We saw no sign of survivors."

Gerber nodded. "So, what's the problem?"

"The aircraft is in Cambodia." Becker hesitated and added, "I think they took some heavy fire and tried to evade it. They dodged it, but took damage and crashed in Cambodia. They're not all that deep into Cambodia — four or five klicks."

"And the aircraft burned?"

"Yes, sir. Since we were in Cambodia, we didn't hang around. I didn't know why it burned and there were no signs of bodies, but if they had been in the aircraft when it burned, we wouldn't have been able to see them."

"Why do you believe they took fire?" Gerber grabbed one of the Pepsis and pulled on the tab. He dropped the tab on the table.

Becker picked up one of the Pepsis, took a drink, and said, "Because we took fire when we were close to the border. I dived and evaded to the west, into Cambodia. We took some hits, but they didn't hit anything vital."

Bromhead looked at Gerber. "I need to get more information on that. Give us some clues about the infiltration of the enemy."

"We can get him over to the communications bunker for a proper debriefing," said Gerber.

"Maybe we should recall Nguyen and Fetterman."

"Yeah. But a couple more minutes won't make much difference."

The conversation stopped when the door opened. Cooper, who had been waiting with the flight on the runway, entered. He looked around, as if trying to memorize the scene. "Is this a private conversation?"

"Just exactly what is your role here, Captain?" Gerber asked.

"Colonel Evans tasked me with gathering information about the loss of General Patterson. If there is nothing new here, I probably should try one of the other camps."

"Maybe you should wait outside," said Bromhead.

Cooper held up his hands in mock surrender. "I'm on your side. I'm not here to find fault or direct the operation. I'm just gathering information for General Dekker."

"Mr Becker, tell him what you observed. Cooper, you are not authorized to communicate this to anyone without my permission," said Gerber. "I'm providing this as a courtesy and once I have all the information, I'll get it to Dekker."

"Yes, sir, but I do have instructions from a higher authority and information gathered here might be of value to others. I have an obligation to report all that I learn."

Gerber rubbed his face with both hands as if tired. "I will point out that Captain Bromhead controls access to the communications facilities here. Our problem here is to check out some new information and our chain of command does not run through the same organizations as does yours. Over to you, Mr Becker."

When Beker finished, Cooper said, "I need to communicate with Colonel Evans and tell him that we've found the general's helicopter."

"How do you know?"

"Whose else would it be?"

"Let's slow down," said Gerber. He glanced at Bromhead and then Becker. "All we know is that we have a wrecked helicopter and no sign of life around it." Before Becker could interrupt, Gerber added, "That doesn't mean there weren't survivors. They might have burned the aircraft themselves and then escaped, or they might have been captured, but our first order of business is to check out the wreck to make sure that it is the general's helicopter."

"It's in Cambodia," protested Cooper.

"We know that, but that is also irrelevant. It isn't deep in Cambodia. Besides, we need to check it out."

"How are you going to do that?"

Gerber leaned back in his chair and grinned. "We put in some people on the ground. Mr Becker, were there any clearings around the crash site?"

"Not really. There were some spots where a Huey, a single Huey, could get in and out but it would be tricky. The clearing isn't all that large. We could carry ten men, but if we find survivors, trying to get them out would be difficult. We might have eighteen passengers if we send in ten men."

"How far from the border?"

"Several klicks."

"I wonder what the orders given to the leader of that flight out on the runway were?"

Becker said, "I don't think he has a lot of options. He'd be in communication with his C and C. But I don't think he could just launch part of the flight without permission, especially if we aren't sure that it is the missing general's aircraft."

"Yeah," said Gerber. "I don't want to be broadcasting this all over South Vietnam."

"What are you planning?"

"Get some people in there, on the ground, to take a look around. Before we do anything, we need to scope out the situation and be sure this is the right place."

Bromhead said, "Well, you won't have trouble getting soldiers. I command here and I can issue orders for a recon. No one would question that, and we have the airlift capability if we can get permission to use it."

"Except that you're going to cross the border."

"Well, there is that."

"We need to talk to the lead pilot and ascertain his exact orders. We need to get people to the crash site."

"When's Fetterman due back?"

Gerber looked at his watch. "Shouldn't be all that long. Captain Bromhead, who on your team do you want to throw into the mix?"

"Wait a minute," protested Cooper. "You can't actually be thinking of engaging in a cross-border operation without getting permission from MACV?"

"Of course not. They'll cross the border by accident, find the wreckage and get the hell out. Even if there are some chairborne rangers at MACV who are horrified, if we have answers about Patterson's fate, they'll overlook that innocent mistake."

Fetterman had seen enough. In front of him was a reinforced company of enemy soldiers that included a platoon trained in the use of mortars. They were establishing a camp, which suggested they would be there for several days. No one was patrolling the jungle around them. Fetterman thought they felt safe where they were, close enough to the border to offer a haven if they needed it. They might have been able to call on other units just across that border if they needed help. They'd begin patrolling at some point but that wasn't a priority.

He slipped to the rear and leaned close to Nguyen. He said, "I think we need to fall back. We should leave a team here to watch but not to engage. If the NVA come toward them, they should escape and return to the camp. Their job is to observe only and if there is any chance they'll be discovered, they need to get out."

Nguyen, as he usually did, thought about it and then agreed with Fetterman's plan. Both moved through the platoon, giving instructions. Nguyen selected one squad to remain behind, giving them the same explicit instructions that Fetterman had given him. That done, the rest of the platoon slipped back quietly, deeper into the jungle. After ten minutes of slow progress and far enough from the NVA, they began to move faster.

Fetterman took the point. That wasn't his responsibility, but he wanted to get back to the camp quickly and while the strikers were good in the jungle, he was better. The intelligence they had gathered was important, but he didn't believe it represented an imminent threat.

They didn't stop to rest but kept going. Since they knew the destination, rest stops were no longer that important. The jungle had thinned and made travel easier. They still stayed away from the paths and animal trails and saw no sign of the enemy anywhere around them. Fetterman knew that they could walk into an ambush at any time, and it was the lazy and the careless who did just that. He was neither, but he was in a hurry. The information was important.

When they reached the tree line outside the camp, Fetterman saw that another helicopter had landed. He had rarely seen so many aircraft sitting on the ground outside a Special Forces camp. Helicopters were such a high-value target that they tried to avoid having the aircraft shutdown and waiting in a relatively unprotected area.

Fetterman led them quickly across the killing ground and into the camp. He waited as Nguyen gave the instructions to the strikers, telling them to take care of their weapons, get some water, and that there would be a weapons inspection in twenty minutes. Once that was all completed, then they could relax for the rest of the day.

With that, Fetterman left them, heading for the team house. The door was closed, which was unusual. He knocked, walked in and saw that a meeting was underway.

Gerber looked up when the door squeaked open. "Ah, Sergeant Major, you have returned."

Fetterman stood there somewhat confused. The information he had was important, but he suspected what they were doing was also important. He said, quickly, without preamble, "We found a reinforced company, but it looks as if they're going to stay where they are for a few days. They're just getting settled in. We have a squad watching them with orders not to engage and to flee if it looks like they're about to be spotted. What's happening here?"

"You don't know Warrant Officer Becker. He believes he found the wreckage of the general's helicopter and we are the closest of the bases. He saw no sign of survivors at the scene."

Becker said, "But we don't know for sure that it was the general's aircraft."

"That's our problem, but not the only one. The aircraft is down inside Cambodia."

Fetterman went to the refrigerator and grabbed a cold Pepsi. He leaned his weapon against the wall but kept it within easy reach. "We have a plan?"

"Mr Becker can fly us over the crash site. I'm thinking a half dozen of us could repel down to see if we can verify that we have the general's aircraft."

"Who is going to repel into this?" asked Fetterman suspiciously.

"We haven't decided yet," said Bromhead, grinning.

Fetterman looked at him and then back to Gerber.

"This is an American mission. I'm going," said Gerber.

"And who have you volunteered to go with you?"

"Why, Sergeant Major, I thought you'd want to be part of such a wonderful, clandestine mission."

Fetterman took a long pull at the Pepsi. "How soon?"

"I have to talk to the Flight Leader to see what his orders are. We'll want to have a platoon or two on several aircraft for support if we need it. I think he's supposed to remain here, but then, he's part of the search effort, so we might be able to use those aircraft, given what we have."

"How deep into Cambodia?"

"Not far. All things being equal, we could walk out in a couple of hours if we had to."

Fetterman grabbed a chair and pulled it around so that he could sit down. He was still close to his weapon. "Major, I'm getting too old for this shit."

Gerber was surprised by that. "What are you saying, Tony? You want to opt out?"

"I was just wandering around in the jungle. I haven't had a chance to decompress from that last mission and now you want me to head out on an unauthorized cross-border operation and repel from a hovering aircraft."

"Well, this is a volunteer mission. I take it that you are not volunteering."

Bromhead said, "Smith will go with you, Major. Sully would jump at the chance to see lovely downtown Cambodia."

Fetterman sighed. "I was looking forward to an afternoon off. Take a nap with a fan blowing on me. Maybe a cold beer later if that decrepit refrigerator is up to the task of cooling a beer."

"Well, we should be back by the time the sun crosses the yardarm so that you could have that beer."

"When do we go?"

Gerber didn't miss the acceptance of the mission. He glanced at his watch. "Probably in about an hour. Time to brief the flight crews and the strikers."

"You have permission to use those helicopters?"

"I thought of it as asking for forgiveness rather than permission."

"I was afraid of something like that."

CHAPTER 11

Cornett crouched in the corner of the ruined, stone building for the little protection it offered. The jungle surrounded him, as it did the rest of them. They had been hiding there for a couple of hours. Cornett was not sure for how long. He only knew that a platoon or more of the enemy had set up camp a hundred yards south of them in an area of light jungle. The enemy didn't seem interested in patrolling. They were in Cambodia and no American or South Vietnamese forces were supposed to be operating there.

He sat with his back against the wall, looking to the north. He sat holding onto an M-16, the butt sitting on the ground in front of him. The problem was that for the two M-16s — the other one held by Masters — there was a single bandolier of twenty-round magazines. In any firefight, they would be out of ammo in the first five minutes.

They had escaped with the M-60 machine guns but didn't have the manpower for them. Weaver had a broken arm, and the general had never been trained on machine guns. He hadn't been an infantry officer, stuck instead in supply where skill with a firearm was not required. Dealing with a mountain of paperwork was the real enemy.

They had abandoned one of the machine guns, stripping the parts from it and scattering them in the jungle. Cornett was sure that even if Charlie or the NVA found some of the parts, they wouldn't get them all. The weapon would be useless to them.

It meant that their only viable strategy was to hide from the enemy, hoping that they would vacate the area without exploring their surroundings. Since this was Cambodia, Cornett believed that the enemy would feel safe and ignore military protocol. They wouldn't patrol their surroundings.

Cornett thought it might work because an Army helicopter had flown over the area a couple of hours earlier. Had the enemy not been so close, he would have popped a smoke grenade. Now, his best hope was that they had seen the wreckage and concluded all had died in the crash. He also knew that hope was not a viable strategy.

Brigadier General Patterson crawled close. He looked hot and sweaty. In a quiet voice, he said, "Shouldn't we try to move away from the enemy?"

Before Cornett could answer, Sergeant Major Stein said, "No sir. Our best option is to remain chilly."

"Meaning?"

"We stay here," said Cornett. "We can't move fast and frankly, I'm not all that good in the jungle. We have an injured man. Our position is somewhat defensible, though anyone trained in small unit tactics would quickly outflank us as we ran out of ammo."

Patterson turned to Stein. "Sergeant Major?"

"He's right, General."

Patterson fell silent. Cornett did not want a lot of chatter. Sound didn't travel all that well in the jungle and the noise of the animals covered some of it. But any talk could bring the enemy down on them.

"How long do we wait?" asked Patterson.

Cornett didn't answer for a moment. "Probably until two or three in the morning." He remembered someone telling him that it was the time when most people were sleepy and not as alert as they were earlier in the evening.

Patterson crawled away and took up a position near Weaver, who was asleep. Patterson wondered how he could sleep given their circumstance. Maybe the broken arm had sapped his strength to the point where he could do little else but sleep. Maybe it was a way to dodge the pain of the broken arm.

"You think that helicopter was looking for us?" Stein asked.

"I don't know. The NVA has some helicopters, but I don't think there are any this far from Hanoi. It sounded like a Huey, but I don't know why they would be looking for us in Cambodia."

"Yeah. I wondered that too."

"Sergeant Major, we should keep it down."

Stein almost said, "Yes, sir." But Cornett was only a warrant officer, which meant he was barely an officer, at the very bottom of the officer corps. Stein was a sergeant major at the very top of the NCO corps with more than two decades of experience. He realized that he had gained a great deal of respect for this kid, who was something more than a helicopter pilot. Cornett had put down the helicopter that kept most of them alive. Now he was leading them in their escape from enemy territory. Stein couldn't fault him for his decisions.

Instead, he just moved away and tried to hide himself a little deeper in the jungle around him. He didn't think they would get away. The best he could expect is that they would be taken prison rather than being shot outright.

Major Edward Gore was sitting in his office on the Tan Son Nhut airfield, his feet up on the desk. From his window, he could see the ramp area where the aircraft assigned to his unit were parked. These were twin-engine, high-wing OV-10 airplanes used by the forward air controllers. They had been impressed into service in the search for General Patterson.

Many of his aircraft were involved in the search and the remainder were engaged in their original mission. The point was that Gore had nothing to do at the moment. He could relax now. He was thinking about finding a cup of coffee and maybe a copy of the *Stars and Stripes*.

One of the senior NCOs, Master Sergeant Nick Brown, tapped on the door and entered. "We had a communication from Sidewinder Two Seven."

"And?"

"He said that he thinks the Army found that missing helicopter. He heard a Fox Mike report to some Army Operations radio in the clear."

Gore held up a hand to stop him. "How did he happen to hear this message?"

"I don't know, sir. He didn't say that it was on Guard, only that he heard it. They landed at some Special Forces camp near the border and south of Tay Ninh City."

"That's it?"

"Yes, sir. We tried to get some more from the pilot, but he said that was all he knew. He said that he had been flying along near the border. He didn't see anything. Just heard that bit of the message."

Gore dropped his feet to the floor and sat up. "I want you to whistle up a jeep for me. I'm going to find General Dekker and let him know what we have."

"He's Army."

"So what?"

Brown was confused by the question. He didn't know what to say about that. Instead he asked, "When do you want to go?"

"Now."

"Yes, sir. We've got a staff car and a driver you can use."

Gore grabbed his hat but didn't think about a weapon. He assumed the driver would be armed, but they'd be in the city, surrounded by all sorts of people. Driving the road between Saigon and Long Binh wasn't as dangerous as it once had been. He just sat back and watched everything going on around him, amazed at the number of motorbikes weaving in and out of the traffic. Many of them had young women on the back, clinging to the young men driving. There were dozens of military vehicles, from a few staff cars to military trucks and jeeps. Lots of traffic for a city that was involved in a war.

The reached Long Binh about thirty minutes later. Gore thought that he should have requested a chopper to move him around. The driver pulled up in front of a large building that looked as if it had been designed by a military architect rather than a civilian. The driver leaped out and hurried around to open the door for Gore, surprising him. Such courtesy was usually reserved for those at a higher pay grade.

As he got out of the car, he said, "Please wait here. I doubt this will take very long."

"Yes, sir."

Gore found his way to Dekker's outer office and entered. He was stopped by a sergeant who said, "May I be of assistance, Major?"

"I need just a few minutes with the general."

"Do you have an appointment?"

"I have information that he is interested in. Just came in."

The sergeant hesitated but then stepped back and tapped on the door before opening it. He leaned in and said, "There is an Air Force major here that needs a few minutes, sir. Says he knows something that you want to know."

Dekker sat still, as if thinking about it and then said, "Let him in."

Gore entered and saluted. "I don't want to take much of your time, but one of my pilots has reported that General Patterson's aircraft has been located."

"And?"

"That's all I have. The message was broadcast in the clear. I don't believe the pilot wanted to compromise the mission. I have requested additional information."

"Maybe you should now direct more assets into the search. Now that we have a location."

"I don't have the location. Only that the aircraft has been found. No word on survivors. Just the wreckage has been found."

Dekker nodded. "That's all that you have?"

"Yes, sir. I thought it important to let you know that the general's aircraft was found. I have no other information."

"Thank you, Major. Please keep me in the loop."

Gore saluted and left.

Gerber entered their temporary quarters. Fetterman was sitting on his cot, looking at his unlaced boots. His weapon had been set on his cot, near him, but the magazine had been removed. There was a single round on the cot, telling Gerber that Fetterman had cleared his weapon. He just hadn't put the ejected round back in the magazine.

"Tony? You all right?"

Fetterman didn't move, other than looking up. "Mack, I'm just tired."

"I don't remember you ever admitting to being tired."

Trying to change the subject, Fetterman asked, "This new mission a good idea?"

"We must learn if the burned helicopter was the one that Patterson was in and if his body is in the wreckage. It's an American aircraft and it shouldn't be in Cambodia."

"I know, but I just spent the morning in the field, and now I'm going into Cambodia."

"You don't have to go, Tony. We've got some very good soldiers here. Sully and Travis, to name two. You know them and how good they are. And most of the strikers are very good as well."

Fetterman took a deep breath. "We're going back across the border. There's only so many times you can do that before the odds catch up to you. Either the bad guys get you or the brass hats find out about it, and that's the end of your career. We just can't keep beating the odds."

Gerber sat down on his own cot. He carefully set his rifle on the cot and then leaned back, against the plywood wall. The ceiling fan was spinning slowly but it was doing little to stir the air.

"Maybe you need to take an R and R. This whole thing will be over in a couple of days at the most. With the resources they're pouring into the search for Patterson, they'll have an answer one way or another. Then you can head out to Australia or Hong Kong or wherever you might want to go."

"I don't need an R and R."

Gerber laughed. "We all need an R and R."

Fetterman stood up and walked over to a small refrigerator. He took out a bottle of water and drank deeply. After a moment, he said, "I'll ask you again. Is this a good idea? Should we, you and me, be taking this risk? There are many others. There's that LRRP team that started some of this that's basically on call. And Captain Bromhead can handle it. He can send in a platoon of strikers."

"But we're here, Tony. Shouldn't we be leading by example? We talk about those chairborne rangers in Saigon who are living in comparable comfort while we repel into a jungle crash site in Cambodia. Tony, you are not obligated to go on this mission. I sort of volunteered you even though I didn't know if you would get back in time to go. That wasn't fair of me."

"That's not the problem, Major. We've been together long enough that you know what I would want to do. I don't want to be left behind. But I'm slowing down. I don't recover as quickly, and I was in the field all morning."

Gerber was becoming worried. Fetterman had always been the first in line, had done more than his share and had worked his way to the top of his profession by being better than anyone else. "What are you suggesting?"

"Time to pull the pin, I think. Retire. I have more than twenty-five years in, and my pension is earned."

"You want us to pay you for not showing up?" Gerber was trying to lighten the mood.

"Yes."

"This isn't the time for this conversation. I need to talk to that flight leader and get with John to figure out how we're going to run this operation."

Fetterman finished the water and tossed the bottle at the trash can. He missed but didn't bother to pick it up. "I just need to rest for a few minutes. I'll be ready to go in about an hour, I think."

"If you're sure you want to make this mission."

Fetterman sighed deeply. "Major, it's my job. It's what I signed up for. It'll be a nice helicopter ride, a little bit of walking around on the ground, and then we're out. Back here before dark."

"Then take it easy for a while, Tony. I'll look in on you in about an hour."

Gerber found Bromhead in the team house, where he had left him. He leaned in the door and said, "Let's go talk to the flight leader."

They drove out to the lead aircraft sitting next to the runway. The strikers were sitting off to the side, waiting. Gerber said, "They should be doing something useful."

"Such as?"

Gerber suddenly realized what he had said. He was becoming one of those lifers that he had always disliked. There was a time when he would have let the soldiers relax because there would be times when they wouldn't have the opportunity.

"I was thinking that they could be cleaning their weapons and being drilled on small unit tactics," said Gerber.

"But we can't break down the weapons while waiting for orders to take off and they know small unit tactics."

"John, I was just thinking out loud. Idle soldiers are something that I have learned to accept but always think there is training that can be accomplished while they're waiting. But I do remember, as a young soldier, that I enjoyed these hurry up and wait opportunities. All we had to do was just sit quietly for a few moments."

They stopped by the lead aircraft. The crew was sprawled in the cargo compartment or on the troop seat resting. As Gerber got out of the jeep, one of the pilots saw him and asked, "Can I do something for you, Major?"

"You the AC?"

"Yes, sir." The pilot sat up.

Gerber thought for a moment. "I think we might have located the downed helicopter. Or rather, a downed helicopter has been located. We need to send in a small team to identify it if they can. Twenty-five or thirty strikers plus four of us."

"The Huey is designed to carry eight to ten American soldiers depending on the equipment, or twelve to fourteen Vietnamese. Looks like you'll need three helicopters for this."

"You authorized to make a decision about fulfilling the aircraft requirements for the mission?"

"No, sir. I'd need to check with C and C to do that."

"This mission shouldn't take more than two hours and if we're right, then no one will be calling for the flight. We have the helicopter located and I don't believe anyone else will find it."

"Major, I'm just a warrant officer. I fly helicopters. I don't make command decisions."

"You're flight lead, aren't you?"

"Yes, sir. But I just lead the flight where the air mission commander tells me to lead it. I don't make that decision myself." He climbed out of the helicopter.

Gerber put a hand up to shade his eyes. "The mission is to find General Patterson. We have the opportunity to do so without broadcasting that information all over Three Corps. I believe that security demands we are careful about what we say."

The pIlot rubbed his face with both hands and looked down the line, at the other helicopters lined up, waiting. Without thinking about it, he said, "Last three aircraft and I'll lead."

"No, we have another helicopter to lead us in. You'll be standing by with the strikers in case we run into trouble. You'll have the small strike force."

"I'm going to catch hell for doing this. If my CO learns about it."

"But you'll be protected by General Patterson, if we pull his fat ass out of the fire. And if we just discover what happened to him, then there are a couple of generals in Saigon who can fly cover for you."

"I'll tell the Acs in the last two aircraft. I'll fly lead for our team, following that other helicopter."

"Good man. We'll hold a quick briefing at the trail aircraft. Becker will take us in."

General Dekker was more than a little annoyed. It had been several hours, and he had no new information about the fate of General Patterson after the Air Force guy said they'd found a downed helicopter. He had ordered Evans to keep him informed but Evans hadn't done that. He had thought that Cooper would be on the ball, but Cooper had disappeared. No one in the Comm Center or in the Intel Office had anything to tell him either. He shouted for his aide.

"Yes, sir?"

"I want you to find Colonel Evans and have him report to me immediately."

"Yes, sir. He's not in his office?"

"If he was in his office, I would have talked with him. He is not there, and no one is sure where he is. Your job is to find him and not bother me with questions."

"Yes, sir."

When the aide left the office, Dekker walked to the window. The view wasn't much but he enjoyed it nonetheless. It was a parking lot filled with military vehicles, including jeeps and six by six trucks. On one side were several staff cars with the drivers waiting for the brass. But beyond that was the rest of the base with white two-story buildings. It was a peaceful view. No sign of the war, but sometimes there would be columns of black smoke signaling an ambush and burning vehicles. What he didn't know was that Evans had been looking at the same view earlier.

There was a tap at the door and Evans said, "You wanted to see me?"

Dekker turned and then moved to his desk to sit down. "Where have you been?"

"Checking on the status of the search for General Patterson."

"And what did you learn, or is it a military secret?"

"No, General. But there is no new information. The search is continuing and nothing has been reported. We have helicopters standing by at a Special Forces camp and at three Fire Support Bases. There are American infantry standing by if needed. There simply isn't anything more that we can do here."

Dekker didn't like that answer because he was hoping there was new information. He also believed there was always something more that could be done. He thought for a moment and then asked, "Have you checked with the airfields in that area to see if they heard any sort of a distress call?"

"It there had been a distress call, it would have been broadcast on Guard. Everybody monitors that frequency. We only have a rough idea of where they were flying. All I can tell you is that whatever happened, it happened fast. I don't know why there was no distress call unless the aircraft just blew up."

"Wouldn't someone have seen it?"

"I don't know, General. There are explosions around all the time. There are areas where we don't have many soldiers. We just have no information."

Dekker picked up a pen, as if he was going to make a note, and then tossed it down. "That is not acceptable. I want some answers, and I want them before the sun goes down."

Evans took a deep breath and said, simply, "Yes, sir." He didn't know what else to say.

Dekker was not happy with that response. "How are you going to find out what has happened?"

"The only thing that hasn't been done is sending officers out to the various bases and question them personally. We've done that over the radio, and I don't see how sending people out will speed up anything."

"It's not as if we are lacking the personnel to do that. But I'll give you a hint. Sidewinder Control has learned that someone found a downed helicopter. It could be Patterson's. Did you know that?"

"No, sir." There was nothing else that he could say. He added, "Captain Cooper is out in the field, but he hasn't reported in."

"He's one man. There are several bases out there. Get someone out to all of them. I don't know why I must tell you this. You should have been on top of it from the beginning. I shouldn't have to learn the status of the search from an Air Force major."

"Yes, sir."

"And when addressing a general officer, the correct response is yes, General. I am tired of having to supply basic military knowledge to senior officers around here."

Evans didn't know what to say to that. He was getting angry himself and didn't need the pressure. He gave the only response he could think of. "Yes, General."

"Get some people into the field and find me some answers. You are dismissed."

Evans took a step back, came to attention and saluted. "Thank you, General."

When Dekker returned the salute, Evans spun and hurried out of the office.

Cooper spotted several of the Green Berets standing near the lone helicopter surrounded by several others who had to be flight crew. Something was going on and they were working to keep him out of it. He didn't understand why. He was a soldier, he was out in the field, and he wanted to be included. He needed to be Ied. Besides, Dekker wanted him there and that should have been clear to them.

Just as he reached the group, they split up. Cooper said, "Major Gerber? A word."

Gerber stopped and turned. "What can I do for you, Captain?"

"What is going on here?"

Gerber smiled. "Nothing that concerns you."

"I am representing Colonel Evans and General Dekker."

"I don't know any Colonel Evans. I don't believe he is in my chain of command, so I am uninterested in anything he might have to say."

"He's a full colonel and has the ear of General Dekker."

"Are either of these officers Special Forces?"

"No."

"I'm sure you meant no, sir. We are following our orders from our chain of command, and you are not a part of that."

"I can radio Saigon and have General Dekker talk with your commanding officer."

"Is that a threat? Do you really think that I care what your General Dekker has to say about anything?"

Cooper was surprised because nearly everyone in the Army feared generals. He knew of senior NCOs who avoided talking to anyone over the rank of captain and who had never interacted with generals.

"Major, we're on the same side here."

"I don't have time for this, Captain. You come find me after we return, and we'll settle this. Beyond that, you have no real function here, other than to get in the way. Have I made myself clear?"

"Yes, sir."

As Gerber walked away, several of the helicopters started up. To Cooper it looked random, but he was sure there was a reason. He watched as the strikers climbed into three of those that had been part of the flight. Gerber, along with several others, boarded the single helicopter.

That helicopter lifted to a hover. The rotor wash caused a swirling of dust and dirt, and Cooper had to turn away until the aircraft began to lift off. He watched as it climbed out and then the other three helicopters followed. They disappeared to the north. Cooper had no idea where they were going, but he did know what he was going to do.

Cooper found his way to the communications bunker. It was easy to spot because it was the one with all the antennae on it. It was partially buried and heavily sandbagged up to the top. These were the green, rubberized bags that were designed not to rot away quickly in the tropical environment. The older, cloth bags hadn't lasted very long.

No one stopped him as he walked down the four steps into the bunker. It was air-conditioned because the radios demanded a cooler environment. It was almost cold inside. The senior NCO present saw him and asked, "Can I help you, sir?"

"I need to make radio contact with my unit in Saigon."

"We're on radio silence, sir. No outgoing messages."

"I need to make contact with either Colonel Evans or General Dekker."

"I have my orders, sir. Captain Bromhead was quite clear on that. We are not to make contact with anyone until he returns."

"Who's your superior?"

"That would be Lieutenant Carson, sir. But he's going to tell you the same thing."

"I'm sure that he'll understand the situation. Where might I find him?"

"Either in his quarters or in the team house."

"You people keep strange hours around here."

"Yes, sir. We respond to the mission requirements. We take our rest when we get the chance and sometimes it is several days before the mission requires our full attention."

Cooper felt himself getting angry. It wasn't the sergeant's fault. He had his orders, and he was obeying him. Cooper wondered if he outranked Bromhead. His date of rank might be earlier than Bromhead's, but he didn't think that would make any difference around here. These Green Berets seemed to have their own rules.

Instead of carrying on the conversation, because he knew he was about to lose his temper, he said, "Thank you, Sergeant."

Carson was in the team house eating a bowl of Cheerios. He didn't stand when Cooper entered even though Cooper outranked him. He just kept eating his breakfast.

"I need to contact Saigon," Cooper said without preamble.

Carson finished chewing and set down his spoon. "We're on radio silence."

"So your sergeant said. But I do need to contact Saigon."

"Sorry, sir, but that's not going to happen."

"Do I need to remind you that I outrank you?"

"No, sir. I can plainly see that you're a captain, and I'm a lowly first lieutenant with very little time in-country but the camp's senior American officer has ordered us not to break radio silence. That's the way it's going to be."

"I could have a general countermand the order."

Carson smiled. "That you could, and I have to admit that a general ordering me to break radio silence would certainly influence my decision. However, to do that, I'd have to break radio silence to allow you to communicate with your general, so, I guess we're at a stalemate." He picked up his spoon to finish his breakfast.

"I'll see that you're are court-martialed for this."

"No, you won't. You might try, but anyone looking at the facts, one of which was that I was obeying the last order of my commanding office, would dismiss any charge you brought. That would make you look foolish for attempting to countermand an order that was lawful at the time it was issued by an officer of the same or superior rank. Now, is there anything else?"

Without a word, Cooper left the team house.

CHAPTER 12

Gerber had known that Fetterman wouldn't miss the flight. It was not in Fetterman's nature to miss a mission. If he had not been ordered to be on the flight, and that hadn't happened here, he would have found a way to be there anyway. He felt it was his duty to join his fellow soldiers on a dangerous mission.

Before they had reached the border, Becker dived toward the ground to low-level across. That way, they avoided the more dangerous anti-aircraft artillery. They were too low for it to be affective, but were now exposed to the small arms of the enemy. But they simply weren't visible to the ground forces for long and often, by the time the enemy had the weapon ready, they were out of sight.

Low-level flight was not something that Gerber enjoyed. It seemed to him that the pilots were tempting fate by flying so low that they had to climb slightly to clear fences or animals and hootches. They just flew along at ninety or a hundred knots, much like a race car driver on a track. The difference was that there were no obstacles on the track, and the countryside was loaded with them.

Fetterman, sitting on the troop seat, the butt of his weapon on the floor and the muzzle pointing upward, had closed his eyes. Gerber wondered if it was his way with dealing with the crazy pilots who were just barely avoiding disaster, or if he was relaxing. He'd had the thought before, but had never asked Fetterman about it.

Once across the border, they climbed to fifteen hundred feet, which took them out of effective range of the small arms.

Now, out to the right was thick jungle that petered out into a series of rice paddies, though they looked to be abandoned.

The crew chief tapped Gerber on the shoulder and leaned close to shout over the sound of the turbine and wind noise. "About two minutes."

Gerber nodded and then held up two fingers, telling the others that they were two minutes out. They began to arrange themselves so that they could get out of the helicopter as quickly as possible. Two men on the right side and two on the left.

The nose of the aircraft came up and they were hovering about twenty feet over the crash site. Without orders, Smith and Peterson stepped onto the skids, facing backwards, into the cargo compartment. They pushed off and dropped out of sight. The aircraft rocked with the sudden change in its center of gravity. A moment later, Gerber and Fetterman did the same. Bromhead remained on the aircraft as the ground mission commander.

Gerber reached the ground just before Fetterman. He unhooked the ropes. The jungle around him was blackened by the heat from the burning helicopter. It was little more than ash. The magnesium used in the fuselage, if it caught fire, was difficult to extinguish and burned hot. The fire consumed nearly everything.

The sound of the helicopter faded as Becker, and then the three aircraft following him, broke off to the south. They would orbit until the ground party finished their investigation of the wreckage and a search of the surrounding area. There was a clearing about a klick to the south where a single Huey could land. It was all they needed.

Fetterman joined Gerber. "Nothing here to tell us if it was the general's aircraft."

"No sign of bodies," said Gerber.

"Fire would have destroyed them."

They began to pick through the debris while Smith and Peterson provided security.

"You know what to look for?" asked Fetterman.

"Anything that might have been human."

Outside of the remains of the helicopter, Fetterman crouched. "Might be a leg bone here."

"I wish we could find something that told us if this was the general's aircraft. All the numbers are burned off."

"I wish we knew where the crew was. I don't think they were here when the aircraft burned. I think they set it on fire."

"Why?"

"Just a hunch. It doesn't really look like a crash. They were forced down but weren't killed then. They burned it."

"This bone." Fetterman pointed at it.

"One of them had been killed, but maybe they took fire, and he was killed then. Becker said that they had taken fire, and he avoided it by crossing the border."

"Major?" That was Smith.

"What you got?"

"Looks to me as if someone pushed his way through the jungle here. I don't think it was anyone coming to the site. Looks like they were moving away from it."

"Survivors," said Fetterman.

"Now involved in escape and evasion." Gerber turned his attention to Smith. "Can you follow the trail?"

"They weren't careful about leaving sign. If they don't change that, I can follow them."

Gerber took out his radio and keyed the mic. "This is six on the ground. We're going to follow a trail to the south…" He looked up, spotted the sun and added, "To the southwest."

There were two clicks in response, meaning that Becker had received the message and understood it.

Gerber nodded and Smith pushed aside a thick branch, ducked under one, and disappeared into the jungle. The rest of the team followed, with Fetterman bringing up the rear.

To the southwest of the crash site, near the stone wall that he had found, Cornett thought he heard helicopters in the distance. He wondered if it was a search party, looking for them. He hoped it was, but didn't think they would be searching in Cambodia. They would assume that Cornett and his party were down in Vietnam. Flights into Cambodia were forbidden by regulation.

Patterson crawled close. "Helicopters."

"Yeah, helicopters."

"Searching for us?"

"I would hope so. They sound like they are over the crash site, or at least in that area. Can't really be sure."

"Will they come looking for us?"

"I don't know. They would have no way of knowing if the crashed helicopter was ours even if they put a team on the ground to investigate. The fire would have destroyed everything other than it was a wrecked helicopter."

"We should have left a sign of some kind."

"For the NVA to find?"

Patterson was surprised by the comment. He wasn't used to having very junior officers ask such pointed questions, but then realized he'd let this extremely junior officer order him around for hours on end. The man couldn't be more than twenty-one or twenty-two but everything he had said and done was for the good of those with him. Patterson couldn't think of a mistake he had made.

"Then shouldn't we use smoke to attract their attention?"

"No, sir. We could also attract the attention of the enemy. They're not all that far away and smoke would give us away."

Masters dropped to the ground near Cornett and Patterson. "Sir, there are helicopters looking for us. I'm thinking, sir, that if I work my way back to the crash site, I might be able to attract the attention of the pilots."

Cornett turned his attention to the sound of the helicopters. He couldn't see them, but the sound suggested they were far away. There was no way to be sure exactly where they were. Cornett didn't want to split up his small group because it made them more vulnerable. He didn't want Masters to risk his life on the assumption that the helicopters were searching for them. If he was caught alone, he didn't have much of a chance.

"Sir. This might be our only chance."

Patterson, who had remained quiet, said, "I think it is a fine idea."

"General, it's not a good idea to split up at this point. There is a good chance the enemy will move out and then we can escape and evade toward Vietnam. That is our best course of action. Lay low and be patient."

"Mr Cornett, we are far from your wrecked helicopter and as the senior officer present, I want your man here to make the effort to contact those helicopters. That is our best course of action — no more sitting around hiding."

"I don't want to endanger the lieutenant's life."

"Admirable, but we must do something. We're running out of water and won't be in any shape to walk out of here in a day or two."

"I'm aware of the situation but the real danger, the immediate danger, is those soldiers a couple of hundred yards away."

Masters asked, "Sir, what am I supposed to do?" He was looking at Cornett.

"Stay in place." Then he added, "Give me a chance to think."

Patterson looked at Masters. "I can do a lot for you when we get out of here, if you can signal those helicopters. Think about that. Mr Cornett can't protect you if we get out of this, but I can."

"General, this is doing us no good and I don't think we should be talking about it now. We don't know if the enemy has patrols out. We need to be quiet."

Patterson rocked back on his heels, and for a moment it appeared as if he was going to say something. Then he crawled back to his hiding place. He disappeared into the undergrowth.

"Sir, are you sure you're right?" asked Masters.

"Christ, Hank, I don't know. I'm just trying to keep us all alive."

"But if they find the wreck burned, they're going to think we all died in the crash."

Cornett thought about that and then realized it might not be right. Those helicopters had been flying around that area for ten or fifteen minutes. If they thought everyone had died in the crash, then they should have flown back to Vietnam.

"We'll know soon enough. Just relax. If nothing changes, then maybe we should try to get out of here in the dark."

Sully Smith came to a fork in the trail. Not exactly a fork, but a point where the path they were following crossed an animal trail. He crouched down, trying to figure out which way to go.

Fetterman caught up to Smith and asked, quietly, "What you got, Sully?"

Smith pointed to his left. "Animal trail there, heading in the direction of Vietnam. The trail I was following continues off to the southwest, away from Vietnam. I'm not sure which way they went."

Fetterman examined the sign. "I think they continued to the southwest. They had been going in that direction and the sign indicates that someone pushed into the jungle here. I think they were trying to avoid capture. They'll eventually turn to the east, but any enemy looking for them will assume that they turned east."

"You sure?"

Fetterman just looked at him. "Sully."

Smith stood up and turned to the southwest. Gerber and Peterson followed while Fetterman hung back, taking up the last position.

Overhead, the helicopters circled like buzzards over the freshly dead. Gerber wished they would slide off a klick or two, but they needed to stay close in case those on the ground ran into trouble. He couldn't see them but could hear them, and he knew that meant any NVA in the area could hear them too.

Sully stopped about thirty minutes later. He'd found a wide spot where it looked as if whoever had made the trail had stopped to rest. Branches were bent, some of the smaller vegetation was crushed, and there was a pristine footprint that looked like it was made by an American boot and not a Vietnamese sandal. Smith hoped the foot in that boot was an American.

This time it was Gerber that crouched near him. Smith pointed at the footprint. "American?"

"Looks like. How long ago?"

"It's fresh. No more than twenty-four hours. Maybe less. Means we're close."

"Let's take ten and then get going."

"Yes, sir."

Gerber fell back, close to Peterson, who asked, "What's going on?"

"Think we might have found a footprint from the crew. Seems like such a long shot, but it does add to the evidence that some of the crew survived."

Gerber took out his canteen and drank. The water was warm and tasted of plastic and chemicals. It didn't taste very good, but he knew that he wouldn't ingest any microbes or bacteria that might cause health problems. It seemed that every time he tasted the chemicals, he had the same thought.

They pushed on for another twenty minutes. Smith stopped again, held up a balled fist and looked at a stone wall. The vegetation around it had been trampled. He was about to say something to Gerber when there was movement to the left. He spun, slipped off the safety of his weapon and was ready to fire.

"Don't shoot!"

"Shit."

Gerber pushed forward. "Who are you?"

"Warrant Officer Wayne Cornett."

"What are you doing here?"

"We were shot down."

Gerber thought of several other questions, but another man appeared. "I'm General Patterson."

Gerber didn't answer. Instead, he took out his radio and spoke into it. "Search leader. This is Gound Six. We've located the crew."

Cornett said, "There are NVA close by."

Gerber nodded and said, "We'll head for rendezvous one. You copy?"

There were two clicks in response.

"We have a PZ about a klick from here," said Gerber to Cornett.

"There's a company or so of NVA about a hundred, two hundred yards to the south of here."

"Patrols?"

"Haven't seen any."

"Then let's get out of here."

"I have an injured man."

"Can he walk?"

"Yes, sir."

"Then let's get out of here. Sully, you take the point?"

"Not really."

Fetterman said, "I'll take point."

Peterson was crouched near the wall. He whispered, "Someone is coming."

"Tony, get going," said Gerber. "You people fall in behind him. Leave everything you don't need. We'll follow in a minute or two."

Cornett and his crew scrambled around the corner of the wall. Two of them were supporting a third, whose face was pale and covered with sweat. There was nothing wrong with his legs but there was a makeshift splint on his arm.

When they were all behind Fetterman, Gerber tapped Peterson on the arm and nodded. Before he could move, there was a single shot.

"Think we've been spotted," said Peterson.

"Go."

Peterson spun and trotted after the others. Gerber knelt and watched the jungle. He didn't see anything moving. He was about to follow when there was a flash to his left. Without hesitation, he fired at it. There was a burst of return fire.

Gerber slipped the selector to full auto and pulled the trigger. He fired two bursts of five rounds. Then, without hesitation, he leaped up and ran after Fetterman and the group.

He didn't hear any pursuit. He thought he had stopped them for a minute. They would spread out and try to flank him, but he wouldn't be there. He wished there had been time to set a mechanical ambush, but the enemy was too close, and he didn't have the time. He had to put some distance between him and them.

There was more shooting behind him, but he didn't hear any of the rounds coming close. They were shooting at shadows. Gerber thought they might not be combat-experienced enemy. Maybe supply soldiers whose function was to transport arms and ammunition from the north and then join a unit operating in Vietnam. They'd gain combat experience there.

He almost stumbled over Peterson. "Let's go," he said. "I've got rear guard."

Together they headed followed the path made by Fetterman and the others. They came to a wide spot in the jungle. There was a large tree laying off to the right that would offer some protection from rifle fire. Gerber headed for it with Peterson right behind him.

Gerber knew that he had a few minutes before the enemy caught up. He decided to deploy a mechanical ambush. He took a grenade, pulled the pin but held the safety spoon. He carefully set the grenade on the ground, leaning it against the tree. He braced it so that the safety spoon was held in place. As the enemy approached, he hoped that one of them would dislodge the grenade. The explosion would slow them down.

The enemy appeared five minutes later. They were moving slowly, cautiously, but no longer shooting. That made Gerber smile. They were nearing the area where he had set the ambush. He picked out a target but before he shot, he said, "Take out someone on your right."

Peterson fired almost simultaneously with Gerber. Two of the enemy fell and the rest dived for cover. They opened fire but it was poorly aimed. They were just spraying the area, hoping to hit something. Rather than return it, Gerber said, "Let's get out of here. That should hold them for a while."

Now they slipped away, staying low as the enemy shot up the jungle. Gerber led the way, moving faster. He didn't say anything to Peterson, but he thought they had to be close to the PZ. Overhead, he could hear the helicopters.

Behind him there was an explosion. The mechanical ambush had been tripped. That would slow the enemy. They would be looking for additional hidden grenades or maybe searching for the soldier who had thrown the grenade. He didn't care which, as look as it slowed the pursuit. There was a wild burst of shooting, as the enemy tried to eliminate the threat, unaware that Gerber and Peterson were now heading for the pickup zone.

Up ahead, there was a shaft of sunlight. That was the PZ. Gerber halted and then tried to spot the enemy, but they were still shooting up the fallen tree and the jungle around it.

As he reached the edge of the clearing, he saw Fetterman toss a smoke grenade out, into the tall grass. An instant later a helicopter dropped out of the sky, flared and then touched the ground.

Cornett was the first to reach the helicopter. He stepped on the skid and nearly launched himself into the cargo compartment. He turned and helped the injured man into the helicopter. Patterson ignored everyone as he climbed into the helicopter. He sprawled out on the cargo compartment floor as if exhausted by the ordeal. He didn't move as the others struggled to get on board.

Fetterman came back. "You okay, Mack?"

"Let's empty a magazine or two into the jungle behind us. I don't think they're very close but let's give them something to think about if they are."

Fetterman raised his weapon and pulled the trigger. He didn't let up until all twenty rounds had been fired. Gerber shot in short bursts, as did Peterson. Together they backed up, toward the helicopter. There was return fire, but it was still poorly aimed. It didn't sound as if the enemy was close. They were just shooting up the jungle.

As Gerber stepped on the skid, Becker pulled pitch, lifting the aircraft to a three-foot hover. Fetterman and Peterson were already on board. The nose of the helicopter dropped as they picked up speed. They cleared the trees and as they did, Becker banked to the right, flying over the enemy. They didn't fire up at the helicopter, but both door guns shot down, into the jungle.

Gerber slapped Fetterman on the shoulder. "We're clear. We'll be back in time for dinner."

Patterson sat up. He looked at Gerber and Fetterman, but neither was wearing any insignia. "Who in the hell are you people?" Patterson asked. "Who is in charge here?"

"I am," said Gerber.

"I'm General Patterson and I need to get to Saigon as quickly as possible."

"We'll get transport arranged once we land."

"Where?"

"Special Forces camp. We need to refuel but there is a flight of Hueys there, as part of the search-and-rescue operation. They'll be able to get you to Saigon quickly."

Patterson considered that and nodded. "You have anything to eat? It's been a while."

Gerber tapped the crew chief on the shoulder and when the man leaned close, he asked, "You have any C-rats here?"

"Under the troop seat. Nearly a whole box."

Gerber reached around and pulled it out. Over the roar of the engine, he pushed it toward Patterson. "Take your pick."

As Patterson pawed through the carton, Gerber shouted at Fetterman. "You still feel too old for this shit?"

"Yes, sir. I certainly do."

CHAPTER 13

Kendall Stacy was wearing jungle fatigues, but they were bright green, identifying him as a recent arrival in Vietnam. He wasn't called an FNG by the soldiers because they knew he was a reporter and, therefore, not one of them. He wasn't worth even being called an FNG. No one knew whose side the reporters were really on, but soldiers sometimes believed that the reporters were more dangerous than anything the VC could throw at them.

He wondered why he had bothered to catch a ride out to this Green Beret camp because none of the men there would answer his questions. Most of the strikers either didn't speak English or claimed they didn't, which was the same thing. And as he tried to engage the helicopter crews in conversation, they just said that all they knew was that they were to wait where they were unless called out for some sort of mission. Stacy suspected they knew what that mission was, but they weren't talking to him.

He was sitting in the team house, drinking a Pepsi that he'd taken from the refrigerator without permission. He was watching Bromhead, who was reading some document that was classified. Bromhead had been polite but had made it clear that he was busy and was monumentally uninterested in answering questions about anything, especially from a reporter.

Stacy turned when the door opened. Another officer entered, went to the refrigerator and grabbed a Coke. He popped the top and looked around. Stacy said, "Over here, Captain."

"Who are you?"

"Stacy. Came in on a supply chopper this morning."

"What is your function?"

Stacy looked at him and asked, "Why so hostile?"

The man sat down but didn't take a drink of his Coke. "Sorry. I'm Cooper. I'm with MACV. I came in with the flight."

Stacy reached across the table to shake his hand. "I didn't see you."

Cooper stared at the man. "Just what is your function here?"

Bromhead grinned to himself. He enjoyed watching the two interlopers going at one another. He decided to stay out of the fight and let them spar with one another, though he thought about berating them for taking the soft drinks out of the refrigerator without asking.

"I'm chasing a rumor about a general being down somewhere out here. His aircraft is overdue. No one will tell me shit."

Cooper laughed. "Well, I might be the senior officer here right now, but no one will tell me anything either."

"I might remind you gentlemen that certain things are classified, and we don't discuss them in the open," said Bromhead without looking up.

"We're all friends here, Captain. No one is listening."

"I might remind you, Captain, that you are here only because neither Major Gerber nor I thought you would cause trouble. However, I can have you on a helicopter in five minutes heading to Tay Ninh. You can find your way home from there."

Stacy lowered his voice. "Well, I guess we know who's in charge."

"Doesn't matter. There isn't much to talk about anyway." Cooper sipped his Coke and then added, "You didn't tell me your function."

"It's no military secret. I'm a reporter and here to find out if there is anything to the rumor."

"What rumor?"

"That we've lost a general somewhere around here."

Cooper leaned forward and whispered, "It's true. They clamped the lid down on this in Saigon. Don't want the VC looking for the general."

The door opened again and one of the Green Berets entered. He leaned close to Bromhead and whispered. "Just heard from our…" He looked at the other two, lowered his voice, and then continued. "I think we've recovered the general. They'll be here in about thirty minutes."

"They tell you anything else?"

"No, sir. I don't think they wanted to say much in the clear. All I know for sure is that the strike team never landed. Extraction took some small arms fire, but no one was hit."

"Thanks. Keep this to yourself."

"Sir. They've also issued a recall for the flight that has been standing by here. They're to take off as soon as they can and return to their home station."

Bromhead laughed about that. "They're only going to get about an hour of flight time today. Not very good."

The sergeant straightened up. "I don't think they care. They had a poker game going on in one of the helicopters. Some of them are asleep. Guess they're used to these sorts of missions."

Bromhead closed the folder. He stood up. "Let's go talk with the lead pilot."

"He's with Major Gerber on the, what? Retrieval flight."

"Right. Well, we'll find who is next in the chain of command."

As Bromhead reached the door, Cooper asked, "What's going on?"

"Let you know when I know more."

Cooper caught up with him and said, "I need to communicate with Colonel Evans and General Dekker."

"No."

"Look, Bromhead…"

"That's Captain Bromhead to you. I have things to do."

"What's your date of rank?"

Bromhead laughed. "You're not going to pull that old chestnut, are you?"

"What's your date of rank?" Cooper repeated.

"It makes no difference. I command here. My chain of command does not run through MACV but through Special Forces. If we get to the point where I must justify my actions to anyone, you're going to be the loser. In fact, I can order you off this camp on the first available transport, which I'm on my way to talk to."

Cooper stood there looking at Bromhead. He didn't know what to say. He held a hand up to shade his eyes but didn't speak.

"If you're through, I've wasted enough time here." Bromhead turned and headed toward the runway.

They were nearly two klicks into Vietnam when Becker began a quick climb to fifteen hundred feet. Gerber finally relaxed because if anything happened now, it would happen in Vietnam and there were all sorts of resources that could be called on for help. There wouldn't be questions about cross-border operations now that there were back in Vietnam.

Patterson put down the canteen that he had emptied. He handed it to the crew chief and yelled, "Thanks."

He then twisted around so that he was facing Gerber. "How soon before we reach that camp of yours?"

"Not my camp. Just a staging area for the search. Captain Bromhead commands there."

"I really don't care to hear these details. You didn't answer my question, Major."

"No, General, I suppose I didn't." He looked at his watch, glanced at the instrument panel and saw they were cruising at eighty knots. "Probably no more than half an hour. Maybe sooner."

"I need to get back to Saigon," said Patterson.

"We have aviation assets available. Something can be worked out. I'd like to talk to you before you go."

"About what, Major?" Patterson wasn't particularly interested in the answer.

"On the ground, sir. Too difficult shouting over the turbine."

Fetterman, who had been sitting with his back against the armored seat of the aircraft commander, asked, "What was that about?"

"I want to let him know that we were in Cambodia, and it might be best if no one mentions that."

"Yeah."

Gerber grinned and asked, "What do you think about our little operation?"

"Well, there wasn't much shooting, and those people have to be VC or they're scraping the bottom of the barrel for soldiers in the north." Fetterman rubbed his eyes and then took a drink from his canteen.

"Maybe their mission was to carry stuff south before they head home to get some more."

"Whatever. It was momentarily exciting."

Cornett, who was close enough to hear some of their conversation, leaned closer. "There going to be trouble from us going down in Cambodia? It couldn't be helped, given the situation."

"I don't know, but I'll have a word or two with the general so that he understands the score. Since we're all clear now and there doesn't seem to be any foreign outrage that we were a few klicks into Cambodia, I doubt there will be any trouble."

"I've been a little worried about that. I wasn't sure that anyone would be looking for us in Cambodia."

"We figured it out. We took some fire near the border and our best evasion took us to the border."

"Yes, sir."

Colonel Evans was sitting at his desk, a classified assessment of NVA anti-aircraft capabilities in front of him. While the subject was of great interest, Evans was distracted. Dekker was on his back about the missing General Patterson, and Evans didn't know what else he could do. Sitting at MACV provided him wIth a great many resources, but none of them provided any insight into the location of Patterson.

His sergeant major burst into his office without knocking. He waved a sheet of paper to catch Evans' attention. "They've got him."

"Who?"

"Patterson. We received a short transmission that claims to have found Patterson and recovered him."

"Where?"

"Right now, they are approaching a Special Forces camp."

"How reliable is the information?"

The question caught the sergeant major by surprise. He hesitated and then said, "Came over the guard frequency. Sometimes the pilots make unauthorized transmissions..."

"What do you mean by unauthorized transmissions."

"The Army helicopter pilots sometimes just say, 'Short.' That causes others to comment on it. Sometimes they pass along information."

Although Evans wasn't all that interested in what Army pilots might be saying on guard, he needed to know about the reliability of the information. "What do you mean, short?"

"Everyone in the Army, hell, everyone in Vietnam knows exactly when he will DEROS. As the number of days count down, especially when they have less than one hundred days left in-country, they say they're short. This calls for a response by others who are shorter and —"

"Forget it," said Evans, cutting him off. "I don't care about the games the Army plays. How reliable is the information?"

"I think that because the information about Patterson was closely held, there is little chance of some sort of joke or mistake. I think we've got him back."

"Give me that paper."

Evans examined it but it didn't tell him much, other than the call sign of the pilot reporting that they had Patterson. The call sign was the big clue. If it was a joke, the pilot wouldn't have used his call sign. "Do we know who the pilot is?"

"We have traced it to his unit, and he was one of the pilots involved in the search. I'm sure this is legit."

"I'm going to see General Dekker."

"Yes, sir."

Evans nearly ran to the door and out into the corridor. He slowed his pace, took a deep breath, but the excitement of an answer caused him to nearly shake. He entered the outer office, ignored Dekker's aide and sergeant major. He pushed open the door to Dekker's office without knocking. There were two other men in there, sitting with the general.

"We've got him," announced Evans, waving the paper.

"You're about five minutes too late, Colonel," said Dekker. "I already know that and have verified the information."

Evans felt deflated. He lowered the paper. "We wanted to verify the information before passing it along."

"What happened to that captain you had tasked with gathering information about the search?"

"Cooper? He is in the field but has not reported in. He might have been at the wrong forward base or has been unable to verify the report."

Dekker turned his attention to the other two men. He waved a hand and said, "This is Major Gore from Sidewinder Control and Master Sergeant Lopez. They have been aiding in the search. Are you gentlemen satisfied that General Patterson has been returned to our control?"

"There is no question that the search has been completed, and General Patterson is alive," Major Gore replied. "He is on his way to one of the American camps."

Evans had a spark of insight. "My information is that he had been found and recovered but there is nothing in it about his state of health."

Dekker cocked his head. "Are you suggesting they recovered a body rather than a living person?"

"No, sir. Only that we don't know the state of General Patterson's health. My message said that he had been recovered. He could be injured, in good health, or we just recovered the body."

"Those are all very good points, Colonel. Maybe you should follow up with your man in the field and let me know when you have an answer."

Evans realized that he had been dismissed as unimportant. "Yes, sir. Thank you, sir."

As he left Dekker's office, he heard the general say, "How is it that neither of you thought of that?"

"Because the message said they had recovered him and not that they had recovered the body. Had he been injured or dead, that would have been noted. The important point is that the general had not fallen into enemy hands and that crisis has been averted."

"Excellent point."

Gerber jumped from the aircraft as soon as they landed and hurried to the lead helicopter. He stepped up on the skid, outside the cockpit, and said, "We need to have a debriefing with the pilots who went with us. Can you round them up?"

"Not a problem, sir. Where will we debrief?"

"Team house inside the redoubt in about ten minutes. Gives everyone a chance to relax for a moment."

Gerber walked back to Becker's aircraft. Patterson was standing by it, looking out at the jungle. Patterson wondered how far they were from the edge of the jungle and if there were VC hiding there.

"Major, are we safe standing around out here?"

Gerber shrugged. "As safe as we can be. If you're worried about snipers, we're about five hundred meters from the jungle edge to this point. Unless there is a trained sniper out there, the odds are that any shot fired at us will miss. They probably wouldn't shoot unless they could identify a high-value target."

"I don't really care about any of that. I need to get to Saigon."

"Yes, sir, I understand that, but we need to chat about some things with the flight crews and we'll need your observations during your evasion. If you'll follow me, we'll go to the team house."

"I need something decent to eat."

"Then follow me to the team house. We can find you something there, even if it's only C-rats. Might be able to get something a little better."

"I had some of that on the chopper. I'm interested in real food."

"Yes, sir. As I say, we can get something at the team house, take care of business, and then get you on your way to Saigon."

In the team house, Gerber announced, "The general would like something to eat."

Bromhead, who had followed them in, asked, "And what about the flight crews?"

"They're probably hungry, too. What have you got that is quick and easy?"

"Sandwiches? Maybe a hamburger, and we did just get in fresh eggs that we can scramble."

Patterson collapsed into one of the chairs. He'd been based in Saigon for so long that he just didn't think about the needs of the soldiers. As a young officer, he had often heard that a good officer took care of the men first and then worried about his own needs. But all he had thought about was to get something to eat for himself and not for those who had been with him in Cambodia or the men who had pulled him out.

"Where is the flight crew?" he asked.

"Coming along with the others. They thought they might hit the latrine before they got bogged down in a meeting," said Bromhead.

The door opened and Cornett walked in, followed by his crew and Sergeant Major Stein. Patterson was embarrassed that he hadn't even thought about Stein. He knew the sergeant major could take care of himself, but he should have thought about him.

"We were about to scramble up some eggs," said Bromhead. "That satisfy all of you?"

Cornett, who looked tired, sat down. "Whatever is convenient. I'm not all that hungry right now."

"It's going to be a little crowded in here," said Gerber. "Let's have those who are hungry have seats at the tables."

Becker, leading the other pilots, entered. "Okay. We're here, but we've been recalled and need to get back to our base."

"Have a seat and we'll get this started." Gerber turned his attention to the flight lead aircraft commander. He looked at his nametag. "Chambers, you're in command of the flight?"

"Technically, Major, I am flight lead. Not quite the same as being in command. Major Whittier is the air mission commander who has overall command that includes the guns ships and smokey, if we need him."

"Where is he?"

"You mean Major Whittier?"

"Yes."

"I believe that he is still airborne. I haven't heard from him, which is strange, given the amount of time we've been gone. I suspect with nothing going on, he returned to home to refuel and get something to eat. I suspect we'll hear from him soon."

Patterson said, "Pardon me for interrupting. Smokey?"

"Yes, sir. A Huey that has a ring near the turbine exhaust. It injects oil into the exhaust that creates a cloud of smoke. We sometimes use it to conceal the flight or to shield single ship missions where there has been enemy activity. You know, medevacking wounded and that sort of thing."

"Thank you," said Patterson.

While the Vietnamese cook was preparing the food, Gerber stood up. "Let's get this show on the road. First question goes to you, Chambers. Do you know where we were when we extracted the general?"

Chambers, who was a twenty-one-year-old helicopter pilot, shook his head. "Given the situation and our proximity to the Cambodian border, I suspect we were several klicks inside Cambodia."

"Yeah," said Gerber, "I thought you might think that. Would it be a problem for you to forget the exact location?"

Although he was young and most of his Army experience had been in basic training, flight school and five months in Vietnam, Chambers understood what was happening. He stared at Gerber, then said, "We were close to the border, and I really don't know what side of it we were on."

"Mr Becker. You took us to the crash site."

"Okay. Is that a question, sir?"

"Without confirming where we ended up," said Gerber, "how is it that you found the wrecked helicopter?"

"We took fire when we flew over that cluster of hootches near the border. Given the location of the enemy guns, a turn to the west was the quickest way to escape that danger, okay?"

"Mr Cornett. Why did you crash where you did?"

Cornett looked at Becker, who shrugged. "We took heavy fire from a village. General Patterson was directing our route, but that fire crippled the aircraft. I just wanted to get away from the enemy position as quickly as I could. I turned to the west because that put the enemy behind us. Like he said, it was the quickest way to get out of the kill zone."

Patterson, who had just been served a plate of scrambled eggs with toast and orange juice, asked, "Is there a point to all this?"

"Do you know where the helicopter crashed?"

"Given the discussion here, and the clues I learned while running around in Cambodia, I can make an educated guess." Patterson took a bite, grinned and said, "Hey, these are quite good." He hesitated. "But I wasn't navigating, and I lost my map when we crashed. I don't believe my educated guess would be accurate."

Gerber nodded and realized that some generals were smarter than they looked. "Mr Cornett, do you know where you crashed?"

"Well, sir, I was pretty busy trying to evade the enemy fire and find a place far enough away that they wouldn't be in a position to capture us. I was close to the border, but I think we remained in Vietnam."

Becker looked at him, then Patterson, and finally Gerber. "Okay, Major. We weren't in Cambodia."

Chambers wasn't quite as quick as the others. "I'm fairly certain that we crossed into Cambodia."

"Were you plotting the course on the map, or were you just following Becker?"

"Following Becker, sir."

"Then you can't be sure exactly where you were. No lines on the ground to show the border. Just jungle that looks the same no matter which side of the border you're on."

Chambers finally caught on. "We were very close to the border, but I think we remained in Vietnam."

As more food was served, Gerber said, "Here's the deal. While we can argue that we were close to the border but don't believe we crossed into Cambodia, it is important to make everyone believe we stayed in Vietnam."

"Okay," said Becker. "I get it. But why not just tell us that the mission was secret and be done with it?"

"Because there are those in Saigon who just love to learn about mistakes made by the combat troops. They can raise a stink, and we just don't want to deal with the stink. You'd think that they would be happy that we found General Patterson."

As he said it, he realized there was another problem. "Where's Cooper?"

Bromhead said, "I forgot about him. He was bored here, and we have a patrol going out. He's with them, getting some of that combat experience that the chairborne rangers in Saigon don't get. He can now astound them with his tale of a combat patrol with the Green Berets."

"Well, if no one gets blabby, he won't know where we were." Gerber turned his attention to Patterson, who had almost finished his eggs. "General? Do you have a few words?"

Patterson put down his fork and stood up. "This is one of those strange situations that we encounter in the Army. A mission that is perfectly logical, one that saved lives, and I include myself in that, but we were not exactly where we were supposed to be through no fault of our own. We were avoiding enemy ground fire. I can't be sure about where we crashed but I do know that Mr Cornett was very good at avoiding the enemy."

Having told them that the important point was that they were fleeing the enemy, he then said, "But I don't believe we were in Cambodia. However, to make all this clear, as the senior officer present here, I have the authority to classify this operation, and I hereby declare the activities of today secret. They are not to be discussed with anyone outside the small group here. Aircraft commanders, you are to impress on your crews that no matter what they might think, we were not in

Cambodia. If anyone has trouble with that, have the offender get in touch with me at MACV. I'll straighten them out."

"Won't someone wonder if we could recover the wreckage?" Becker asked.

"I can certify that the chopper was consumed by fire. There is nothing left but ash. There is nothing that would be of use to the enemy."

That triggered a thought. Gerber said, "You aide was KIA. We didn't recover the body."

Patterson paled. "I had forgotten about him," he said quietly. "His body was consumed in the fire. There was nothing left to recover. I'll have to tell his parents about his loss." He hesitated. "He'll be awarded a Purple Heart. I think we can, *I* can authorize the award of the Silver Star to him as well."

"General," said Gerber, "I think that awards to the flight crews are justified as well."

"Of course, Major. Before I leave, I'll need the names of all those who had a significant role in our recovery. I'll take care of ensuring those people are recognized." He glanced at Cornett but didn't add anything.

Gerber waited for several seconds and then asked, "Are there any other questions?"

"What am I to tell Major Whittier?" asked Becker.

"You can tell him that we had located General Patterson, and I used part of your flight to transport a strike team to the crash site for the rescue operation. Which, by the way, was our mission in the first place. As far as you know, we were close to the border but did not cross it. If he has questions, you have him call General Patterson for clarification."

"Yes, sir."

"Has there been any word about the status of the flight?"

"At the moment? No. I will assume that they'll be recalled. I told Lieutenant Nguyen to release the strikers. They should be back on the compound."

The door burst open, and Lieutenant Carson entered. He walked straight to Bromhead. He leaned close and whispered something to him. Bromhead stood up. "Patrol's back and it's not good."

CHAPTER 14

Colonel Evans didn't like being summoned to General Dekker's office, especially when the call came from a low-ranking enlisted man. When that happened, it was always bad news. When he arrived at the outer office, the aide just said, "You may go right in."

This set up another problem. Was he to follow the parade ground protocol, or the informal agreement between senior officers that dispensed with all that. He walked in and saw Dekker sitting at his desk, pretending to study an important document. Evans decided that there was no point in playing the game. The problem, whatever it might be, wouldn't be made any worse by skipping the salute.

"You summoned me, General?"

It was almost as if Dekker hadn't heard him and didn't know that he had walked in. He waited a moment longer and said, again, "You summoned me, General?"

Dekker pointed at one of the chairs near his desk. "Have a seat, Colonel, I'll be right with you."

Evans sat down and watched as Dekker flipped to the last page of the document in front of him and then closed the folder. He looked up. "I have a single question. What was the name of the young officer you tasked with gathering information about General Patterson?"

Thinking that they had gone through this before, Evans said, "Captain James Cooper."

"Have you heard from him?"

"No. But given that General Patterson has returned to our control, I didn't think his silence was significant."

"He failed in his mission?"

"That I don't know," said Evans. "All I know is that he didn't provide any information to me. He might not know that Patterson had been found, or he might have arranged for the information to be transferred to you first."

Dekker scratched at the back of his head as if in deep thought. "I'm not sure that we need him to be attached to this headquarters. What is his background?"

"He has been through the Infantry Officers' Basic Course. He was assigned to us when he arrived in-country. Done an adequate job."

"Adequate?"

"He just never did anything that caught my attention. Solid officer who doesn't drink…"

"I'm not sure we need an officer who doesn't drink."

"General, he is not a regular drinker, but he is not afraid to have a cocktail or a beer on occasion. I was just saying that he isn't an alcoholic."

"When he returns, let's evaluate his performance on this task. I think he dropped the ball. He was right there but provided no intelligence about the search to us. That was his job."

"I'm not sure that's fair, General."

"I don't believe I asked you for your opinion. I want his performance reevaluated with the view to finding him a new assignment away from here. You might want to think about your decision to delegate this task to him. That reflects upon your leadership."

Evans felt the blood drain from his face. He saw his chance of obtaining flag rank disappearing into the distance. He was now on thin ice and wondered if he wasn't actually skating on warm water.

"General, Captain Cooper is not part of my staff. He is in the Army and has some connections that were important. I had others attempting to learn more about what was happening."

"It seems that those connections were not all that valuable, were they?"

"The location was so close to Cambodia and communications were sporadic at best. There was nothing I could do about it."

"And yet, I was able to get the information, wasn't I?"

"I was here within minutes with that same information."

"But the point is, I already had it. Doesn't matter how much earlier I got it; the point is that I got it before you reported to me."

"But, General, I would have been here sooner except it took me some time to get here. I had the information."

"You're whining, Colonel."

"I wanted to be sure that the information was accurate before I brought it here."

"You were supposed to bring the intelligence to me as soon as you received it. You were not required to analyze it. I have officers who are paid to do that."

"General —"

"That will be all, Colonel."

Evans jumped to his feet and said, "Yes, sir. I'll track down Cooper. I'll get to the bottom of his failure."

Dekker was not interested. "You do that."

Evans turned and fled the office.

The first of the mortar rounds fell short, hitting neither the camp nor the runway where the helicopters sat. Chambers leaped up and glanced at the door. "The flight!"

"Get them out of here. You are released. Do not talk about our rescue of General Patterson other than to say it involved three of your crews. You'll be connected later with additional information. Patterson will want to thank you personally as well, which should appease your CO."

There was a second explosion that was still far from the team house. Chambers ran to the door, hesitated and then exited. He was followed by the other pilots. There was a series of detonations, but they didn't seem to be walking toward the camp. He didn't think they were targeting the flight either. It was random, unaimed fire by the mortar crew somewhere north of the camp.

As he reached the runway, he was about to wave his hand, telling the other pilots of crank the engines, but saw some of the rotors were already turning. The crews had not abandoned their aircraft to run for the bunkers. They were more interested in getting out of the way and knew that it was safer to get the helicopters into the air than to hide in bunkers.

Chambers reached his aircraft and climbed into the cockpit. He didn't bother with the shoulder harness or seatbelt. He reached over the center console, and rolled the throttle to the flight idle detent. He backed off slightly and pulled the trigger under the collective. As he watched the gas producer he muttered, "Come on. Come on."

His copilot had just dropped into his seat. "Buckle up," Chambers yelled at him. "Everyone here?"

"We're ready back here," he heard the crew chief say.

Outside the aircraft there were more explosions, but they were aimed at the center of the camp. It was as if the enemy didn't know there were ten or twelve aircraft sitting on the runway. Destroying them would be quite the prize.

Chambers strapped himself in, put on his helmet and then keyed the mic. "Flight status."

Before there was a response, there was an explosion at the end of the runway. Chambers didn't know if that had been a long round or if they were beginning to target the flight. He rolled the throttle to sixty-six hundred RPM, saw that the gas producer was in the green. So was the rotor RPM.

"Lead is on the go."

He pulled pitch and dumped the nose as they came off the ground. He didn't gain much altitude, sacrificing that for speed. He stayed low, racing for the tree line south of the camp and out of the danger zone.

Over the intercom, he said, "Either of you guys back there see anything?"

"Flight is following. There is one aircraft on the ground."

"That one of ours?"

"No, sir. I think it was that other helicopter. You've got eight behind you."

Once over the tree line, and out of sight of the mortar crews, wherever they were, he slowed to sixty knots and began a slow climb to fifteen hundred feet. Once they reached altitude and weren't taking any ground fire, Chambers began to relax.

"Lead, you're joined."

"Roger. Anyone have any damage?"

When there was no response, he said, "Rolling over to eighty."

In another thirty minutes, they would be back at their base camp and did not have to worry about mortars or ground attacks. At least, the worry belonged to someone else.

"I'm getting too old for this shit," Chambers murmured to himself. What he really meant was that he was too young for it.

*

When the first round hit, Bromhead didn't move. He waited for the second round to determine which way the rounds were going. If the next one was closer, that would determine one reaction and if they weren't, then a second. When the second fell farther away, he leaned back and took a sip of his beer.

Gerber stood up. "I'm going to the fire control tower."

Fetterman didn't say a word. He followed Gerber out the door. They ran across the compound. Gerber grabbed the ladder and started up. There was another explosion, but Gerber didn't even duck. He hung on to the ladder for a moment and then climbed up and scrambled over the sandbags. Fetterman joined him quickly.

From the bottom of the tower, Bromhead yelled, "I'm coming up."

Gerber picked up the binoculars and began scanning the jungle to the north of the camp. He picked up the flash and pointed it out to the Vietnamese soldier in the tower. That man grabbed the field phone, spun the crank and began to speak in rapid Vietnamese.

The countermortar team returned the enemy fire. The first rounds fell short, as far as Gerber could tell. Bromhead asked, "You saw the flash?"

"Yeah. Your man directed the countermortar."

The next rounds were closer to the flash. Gerber thought they were close enough that the enemy would scatter. He thought it was a 60mm mortar, which was quick to break down. If they knew what they were doing, they were long gone.

Gerber continued to scan the jungle to the north, but there was nothing more to be seen. "I think we can cease fire," he said. "You're just wasting your ammunition."

"We have lots of it," said Bromhead. "That is the one thing that is never in short supply around here. The supply sergeant knows everyone and is great at getting us whatever we need."

Gerber lowered the binoculars. "I think maybe I'll get him transferred to me then."

"He'd desert rather than become a rear area wienie."

"Then he shows great sense."

Satisfied that the mortar attack was over, Bromhead said, "Changing the subject, that patrol that just came back said that the enemy was forming to the north. Thought it was a company-sized force. I suspect it's probably more battalion strength."

"You think they're going to hit tonight?"

Another enemy round fell short of the camp but blew up in the wire. It created a small gap in the wire but nothing the enemy could exploit.

"Damn. They're more persistent than I thought. You see where that came from?"

The striker shook his head.

They all searched the jungle, but there was nothing to tell them where the mortar tube had been hidden. It was just the one round, making it nearly impossible to find. Gerber had been lucky to spot the first tube.

Bromhead said, "I'm thinking of sending out a force to try to flank that battalion. Catch them by surprise by maneuvering rather than waiting for the attack. What do you think?"

"John, this is your war. I'm now here as an unwilling observer."

There was an explosion on the runway, short of where the helicopters had been. Fetterman said, "They missed a golden opportunity. That should have been their first target."

"Yeah," agreed Gerber. "They could have destroyed all those helicopters if they had been paying attention."

"That would have just given us forty more soldiers here."

"A bunch of pilots?"

"All went through basic training. Not to mention the weapons they would have added to our defense. Their door gunners have what, twenty, twenty-two machine guns. Quite the force multiplier."

Bromhead handed the binoculars back to Gerber. "I'm going to talk with Lieutenant Nguyen. I want to send one company out the south gate to set up that flanking force."

"Might I suggest, Captain," said Gerber formally, "that you cover their departure was a mortar barrage of your own?"

"We don't know the exact location of the enemy force."

"Doesn't matter. The point is to keep their heads down until your company can get to the jungle on the south."

"I don't think that will fool anyone," said Fetterman.

"Possibly not, Sergeant Major, but someone being shot at, even indirectly, tends to keep his head down. They aren't as observant as those who aren't worried about a mortar round dropping on them."

"Unless, of course, you are far off the mark, or the enemy knows that there is little danger from scattershot artillery."

Bromhead couldn't help laughing. "How many times have you two had this discussion?"

"Normally, we talk about other things. We are having this discussion for your benefit."

"I'll go out with that company, if you don't mind," said Fetterman.

"Tony, you don't need to do that," said Gerber. "Especially after all that you've done today."

All that Fetterman said in response was, "Yes, sir."

"If you want to go screwing around in the jungle at night, I have no objections," said Bromhead.

The camp's mortars fell silent. There were no more rounds from the enemy. Gerber said, "Might be a bit premature to send out that company. I'm going to the team house to find out what Patterson is doing."

"I forgot about him," said Fetterman.

"Well, we've still got Becker's helicopter sitting on the ground here. We can get him out on it if we have to."

When they reached the team house, Patterson was sitting there drinking a beer with Becker and the rest of his flight crew. Gerber said, "General, the flight has evacuated. Mr Becker's aircraft is the only one left and can get you out of here."

"You think that was the last of it?" asked Patterson. "The mortars, I mean."

Bromhead shook his head. "Harassment fire. Happens two or three times a week. They just do that to annoy us. They might drop a couple additional rounds later, or they might have just faded back into the jungle."

"If it was the precursor to a ground attack," added Gerber, "they wouldn't have stopped until they had knocked down the fire control tower and our communications, or have given it a good try. They know the tower is still standing and nothing came close to the commo bunker."

"Are they that good?" asked Patterson. "Charlie, I mean."

"No, but they can get lucky. They'll expend all their ammo and then try to breach the wire. That probably won't happen tonight unless they start up with the mortars and rockets later, sometime around midnight."

Becker, who was drinking a Pepsi, set the can on the table. "I'd better get ready to fly out of here. I don't care to watch a ground attack from the ground."

"General, we need to get you out of here, along with that damned reporter and Captain Cooper."

"Where is our distinguished member of the press?" asked Bromhead.

"I believe he was heading for a bunker the last time I saw him."

"You guys just stayed here?"

"Rounds weren't walking our way. I thought we were safer here than running across the compound to a bunker."

"I didn't know you flyboys were that in tune with mortar attacks."

"We find ourselves being mortared frequently. We quickly learned what we needed to do. Sometimes it just isn't worth the effort to head to the bunker when the rounds weren't close and didn't seem to be coming closer."

Patterson said, "A few mortar rounds don't bother me."

"Still, General, you are a noncombatant," said Gerber.

"No, Major, I trained as an Infantry Officer. I wasn't always a chairborne ranger. I have lived through mortar attacks that lasted an hour or more."

"Excuse me, sir, but I was thinking of your current assignment."

Patterson stared at him. "You have no idea what my current assignment is. And I'm not going to argue the point with you. I remind you that I am the senior officer present. I've had enough of you subordinates who have assumed more power than you have."

Becker stood up. "While you two hash this out, I'm going to check on the aircraft." He turned his attention to Patterson.

"General, all things being equal, we can be out of here in about twenty minutes." He gestured at the rest of the flight crew.

As Becker and his crew left the team house, Gerber said, "General, I don't mean to be rude."

"You just have to remember that I am a general and have been in the Army longer than you."

"Of course," said Gerber. He looked at the others in the team house and lowered his voice. "I believe that the search for the missing aircraft had greater importance than just the fact that we had lost track of it and there was a general on it. There was another component to it."

Patterson didn't say a word. He just sipped his Pepsi and acted as if he hadn't heard what Gerber had said.

Becker returned. "Okay. We're not going anywhere in my aircraft. Shrapnel through the rotor blades. I need to contact my operations to arrange to get it lifted out of here."

"How long will that take?"

Becker shrugged. "I don't know. Depends on what's available and where they are, but I'm guessing it won't be until after dawn tomorrow. Getting it out in the dark is a complication they're going to want to avoid."

Stacy walked into the team house. His uniform was dirty, as if he had been rolling around on the ground. He spotted Patterson. "General. I have some questions, if you don't mind."

Patterson shook his head. "You'll get no answers from me other than I'm relieved to be back here."

"You mean in Vietnam, General?"

Patterson stared at Stacy. "No, I mean out of the field and here, on this camp. I said nothing about Cambodia."

Bromhead pointed at the refrigerator. "Grab a beer or a soft drink and have a seat."

"You're not conducting a classified planning session?" asked Stacy.

"Not at the moment. If we decide to have one, we'll let you know."

Fetterman found Nguyen in his quarters. He sat on his cot and was sharpening his knife. Fetterman didn't think it needed to be sharpened, but that was one of the things experienced soldiers did when they had the time. They wanted to be sure that their equipment would not let them down if it was needed. During his career, Fetterman had sharpened his share of the knives and watched dozens of others doing the same thing.

"Lieutenant? A word?"

"Certainly, Sergeant Major. What may I do for you?"

Fetterman was surprised by the formal language. He ignored that. "You're going to lead the flanking force?"

"That seems to be the plan. I am awaiting the word of the commander."

"I thought that I would accompany you."

"That's not necessary, Sergeant Major. I don't believe that we will run into any trouble."

Fetterman leaned against the door jamb. He was holding his M-16 by the pistol grip, the muzzle pointed at the floor. "I just wanted to tag along as an observer. I'm interested in the tactics being employed by the enemy out here. They seem to be organizing for a larger attack."

"I am about to assemble the company. You may tag along, as you say."

"What is the plan?"

Nguyen slipped the knife into the scabbard taped to his web gear. "To attempt to get to the jungle south of the camp and then work my way around to the east and then to the north."

"Wouldn't it be better to attempt to engage the enemy to the west, before they get into position?"

"No, Sergeant Major. My assigned task is to hit their flank as they assemble for the ground assault. My best strategy is to use surprise. I believe that we will be outnumbered, but surprise should change that."

Fetterman grinned. "Just wanted to understand what is happening. Your plan sounds good."

Nguyen put on his web gear, grabbed his weapon and said, "Let's go see if the company is assembled and my commander is ready to give the word."

They had been broken into platoons and were using the buildings to conceal their movements from any spies who might be hidden in the jungle to the north. Nguyen gathered the senior NCOs in the shadow of one of the long hootches so that he could brief them.

Fetterman stood to one side with Staff Sergeant Oscar Reynolds. Fetterman didn't know much about the man, other than he was a small arms expert who was probably the best shot in the camp. They had spoken once or twice but had not engaged in any long conversations. Reynolds had joined Bromhead's team after they had been deployed, and the small arms expert had been medevacked due to illness. Reynolds was his replacement.

"How did you get stuck with this job?" Fetterman asked.

"My turn to accompany the Vietnamese into the field."

"I don't expect we'll run into much. We might be premature."

Reynolds wiped a hand over his face. "They're out there, somewhere, Sergeant Major."

"They're always out there, somewhere, but I don't believe they're coming this way, unless they begin to hit us with a mortar and rocket barrage soon. That's the key."

"Then we'll have an easy evening."

Fetterman listened to Nguyen giving instructions to the Vietnamese NCOs. He understood most of it, but Nguyen was keeping his voice low, as if worried that the enemy might overhear him. Nguyen said something that caused a laugh, and the meeting broke up.

Reynolds said, "Here we go."

"There is always someone who has to say that."

One squad left the shelter and pushed their way through the gate and the gaps in the wire. As they reached the outer strand, a platoon led by a senior NCO followed. Slowly, they worked their way through the wire as the point crossed the open ground between the camp and the jungle. There were no flares to give them away and the moon was a fingernail crescent that shed little light onto the field.

Fetterman fell in with the second platoon, following them out. The rest of the company then followed. In twenty minutes, they were reassembled inside the jungle, spread out almost like they were a blocking force. Looking back, at the camp, there was no evidence that anything unusual was happening there. Fetterman thought, for a moment, that the attack wouldn't come that night. It was then that the mortars began to fall again, this time hitting inside the redoubt, where the command and the communications bunkers had been built.

CHAPTER 15

"What in the hell do you mean that Patterson is still at that Green Beret camp?" shouted Dekker.

Evans stood at attention in front of Dekker's desk and was almost afraid to say anything. With Dekker glaring at him, Evans finally said, "All the helicopters had evacuated during a mortar attack. This was a flight that had been on standby in case they needed to airlift troops to the crash site."

"You're telling me that the pilots just took off without ascertaining if Patterson was on board?"

"They weren't responsible for transporting General Patterson anywhere. Their job had been to transport a strike force into the field if needed to rescue General Patterson. They had been recalled after the general had been picked up."

"This is incredible incompetence. They all just took off during a mortar attack without worrying about their passenger."

"General, with all due respect, they had no responsibility for the general once they had been recalled. There was another helicopter there, which General Patterson could use. They didn't leave him stranded."

Dekker scrubbed his face with both hands as if he had just awakened. "Then why is Patterson still on the ground in that camp?"

Evans knew they were about to engage in another round of say it again. Instead, he said, "I don't have that information at this time."

Dekker sighed. "I just don't get it. Patterson is out and is safe. Nothing has been compromised. But we can't get him back here."

Feeling he was on safer ground, Evans relaxed slightly. "The general was picked up by a helicopter crew. There was no contact with the enemy."

"Except for the machine-gun fire that brought down his helicopter in the first place."

"I meant that he had not been captured and is apparently uninjured."

"Okay, Colonel, here's what I want done in this order. I want you to make contact with those Green Berets and get Patterson on that helicopter. They're to tell the pilot that his orders, coming from MACV, are to bring General Patterson here as quickly as possible. He is not to go anywhere else until General Patterson is here. I don't want any discussion on that point. Make it clear that they come here no matter what other orders they have been given, and I don't give a crap who issued the order. I'll see to it that there are no repercussions from that. Understood?"

"Yes, sir."

"And I want Captain Cooper brought here, to my office, the moment — and I mean the *very* moment — he is back in Saigon. He's not to go to his quarters. He is not to shower or shave or change his uniform. I know that people in the field sometimes do not adhere to parade ground standards. They don't always have access to the facilities that we have here. I'm not worried about that. If he goes anywhere else, he is through. Understood?"

"Yes, sir."

"I want a complete written report of what happened here from the moment that we learned that General Patterson was down to the point he is returned, and then I'll want an analysis of the search procedures you employed to find him. I want everything in that report so that we can learn from our mistakes, so that we'll have a contingency plan if something like this happens again. And I want the names and ranks of everyone involved in this half-assed operation. That includes the helicopter pilots, the Special Forces soldiers and anyone else you think had a role."

"Yes, sir."

"Do you have any questions at this time?" It was clear that Dekker didn't want questions. He was just telling Evans to go to work. That he was dismissed.

"No, sir." He saluted, did an about face that was sloppy because it had been a long time since he had felt the need to do an about face when leaving such a meeting.

"And, Evans, don't think that just because you are a senior Air Force officer that is going to make a difference. There was enough wrong with this half-assed operation that many heads will roll."

In the hallway, Evans' sergeant major said, "I guess that didn't go all that well. I think they heard Dekker all the way to downtown."

Evans decided to ignore the comment. He just said, "We have some work to do."

The first round fell on the four-foot berm that protected the redoubt if a ground attack breached the outer defenses. The detonation was close enough that the shrapnel rattled on the roof of the team house, sounding more like hail than the bits of the mortar round. Patterson and Cooper hit the floor instantly. Both Gerber and Bromhead listened for a second explosion, smiling at the rear area commandos. The second round landed in the middle of the redoubt.

Bromhead said, "I'm going to the fire control tower. Coming?"

Gerber shook his head. He crouched down so that the sandbags on the outside of the team house would protect him from shrapnel, unless the round detonated on top of those sandbags or hit the roof.

Two more rounds hit but it sounded as if they were on the other side of the redoubt. They were walking away from the team house.

"Sounds like they have us locked in," said Gerber. "I'm going to the communications bunker to see what we can get for countermortar."

Bromhead grabbed his weapon but hesitated at the door. More rounds fell but these were outside the redoubt. He saw explosions that looked like an eruption of sparks from a fireworks display. He didn't know what the enemy was aiming at. He waited for a moment and when there were no more explosions, he pushed open the door and sprinted out. He reached the fire control tower, climbed rapidly and then nearly fell over the sandbagged protection there. The Vietnamese spotter was squatting against the north wall of sandbags, his head nearly invisible.

Bromhead was about to ask why he was not searching for the flash of the mortar tubes when machine-gun rounds raked the sandbags. The striker pointed to the north. "Shooting at us," he said.

Bromhead took the binoculars and knelt near the man. He swept the jungle and saw the flashes from several mortars. He counted six, but thought there were more. Unnecessarily, he said, "Incoming." He ducked down. When the last of the six rounds fell, he popped up.

When he saw more flashes, he dropped down, his back against the sandbags. He grabbed the field phone and spun the crank. "Countermortar. North, about half a klick. First rounds illumination. Then Willy Pete marking rounds." He didn't think it was necessary to tell the mortar team where the enemy was hiding.

"Yes, sir. Got it." Bromhead recognized Sully Smith's voice.

There were pops from the camp's mortars and the shells burst high over the jungle. From the fire control tower, it looked to be an unbroken sea of green. Bromhead knew there had to be clearings for the mortars. Those clearings didn't have to be very large. Just big enough for the tube and the crew. They might not have much room to make adjustments because of the tall trees, but they certainly could cause trouble for those in the camp.

Smith didn't wait for any more orders. He fired the Willy Pete rounds. They detonated in the jungle canopy; large, bright explosions that threw off clouds of white smoke and burning bits of magnesium.

Bromhead said, "Add fifty. Left fifty." He then dropped down again, behind the protection of the sandbags.

There was no response from Smith but an instant later, there was the sound of the mortar firing. Bromhead popped up to see more detonations in the jungle.

"On target. Six rounds HE."

As he waited for the flash of yellow-orange fire, more fire came from the jungle. One of the enemy tubes was close to the first detonation. Bromhead said, "Add one hundred. One fifty right."

More Willy Pete erupted from the jungle. Bromhead corrected the aim. "Right fifty." It looked as if the Willy Pete had hit the target.

More machine-gun fire hit the sandbags protecting the tower. Bromhead was sure that it was an RPD, a .30-caliber Soviet-made weapon. It didn't have the penetrating power of a larger weapon, but he still felt the impact against the sandbags.

"Glad they don't have a fifty caliber," he said to himself.

There was a momentary lull. Bromhead used it to sweep the jungle with his binoculars. There were no clues providing the location of more of the enemy mortar tubes. All he could do was watch for the flashes. He realized that this was more than the normal harassment of the camp. They were preparing for something bigger than a few mortar rounds or rockets.

Gerber had run to the communications bunker. He found Lieutenant Carson was already there, on the radio. Carson was trying to get a helicopter gun team out of Tay Ninh for countermortar. The problem was the distance. The pilots weren't standing by their aircraft, waiting for the call. It all took time to coordinate with the helicopter operations.

"Who do you have on the line?"

"First Cav. Call sign is Arrow Three Seven. I think the Rat Pack and the Stingers are busy somewhere else." Carson knew the Stingers were in Cu Chi and it would take an hour to get them on station.

"You have arty registration?" Gerber asked.

"Yes, sir, but I need the coordinates for that. Captain Bromhead has not provided those."

"Alert them, anyway, that we might have a fire mission. We might need them later if there is a ground attack. We'll have to be careful; we have strikers out there in the jungle."

The bunker shook and dirt cascaded down from the sandbags that covered the top of the bunker. It had detonated in the PSP that lined the top. There were sandbags laid over the PSP and more under. That caused the round to detonate before it penetrated deep enough to cause real damage or injure those inside.

"Direct hit," said Carson.

"I think it was a sixty millimeter. Eighty-two would have been louder and caused more damage."

Carson laughed nervously. "We had that in mind when we built the bunker."

There was a new radio call. "This is Arrow Three Seven. I have three gunships. Say situation."

Carson answered it. "We are under mortar attack." He looked at his watch. "Last rounds fell about four minutes ago."

"Can you spot for us?"

"We can try. Mortars situated north of the camp." There was a distant detonation. "We just took a few more rounds."

"We're on the way. Are you firing countermortar?"

"I can shut that off any time you say. We're firing to the north."

"Roger."

Gerber listened to the exchange. "You need any help in here?" he asked.

"No, sir. Captain Bromhead has held several drills, and we've coordinated with the aviation and arty assets in the past. I know what I'm doing."

Gerber left the bunker, heading toward the fire control tower. He wanted to get a better look at the lay of the land but knew that Bromhead would have done that already. Gerber was still operating as an observer, knowing full well that he would soon be a participant.

There was a nearby explosion and Gerber instinctively dropped to the ground since he was outside. It hadn't been close, but it was inside the redoubt. The enemy was targeting, as best they could, the command structure but the command structure was scattered all over the camp. They wouldn't be able to take it all out with their mortars unless they had a detailed map of the camp.

Gerber jumped to his feet and sprinted to the fire control tower, but rather than climbing the ladder immediately, he waited for another salvo from the enemy mortars.

Those rounds fell on the north side of the camp, away from the redoubt. They did not damage any of the structures. As they detonated, Gerber climbed the ladder. Once over the sandbags, Gerber said, "Gunships are on the way. About fifteen minutes or so."

"Call sign?"

"Arrow Three Seven. They'll come up on your freq."

Bromhead crouched, checked the PRC-25 and held the handset to his ear. He heard the carrier wave. The radio was on and was working. He didn't feel the need to contact the gun team at that moment.

From his position in the jungle, Fetterman watched the mortar rounds hitting the camp. It wasn't a precision attack. It looked haphazard and he didn't think it was doing much in the way of damage. There was a single fire burning among the hootches on the south side. He wasn't sure what was on fire, but it wasn't a large fire. No one seemed interested in putting it out.

Lieutenant Nguyen crouched near him. "We look for enemy now?"

"No, sir. They've got countermortar firing. We'd only get in the way. The VC aren't doing much damage anyway. We sit here and I don't want to give away our position if they launch a ground assault. If they do, we can hit their flank, which ought to surprise them."

Nguyen nodded but in the dimness of the jungle it was difficult to see the gesture.

"We have security in front of our line?" Fetterman asked.

"Yes. On right flank too."

"Good. Then our job is to remain chilly."

"Chilly?"

"Stay quiet and wait patiently," Fetterman explained. He was surprised that Nguyen didn't know what that meant. He was often surprised with Nguyen's command of English, though sometimes he spoke as if he hardly knew the language.

"We stay alert to midnight."

"No," said Fetterman. "Give the strikers a chance to rest. Half alert now. Full alert after midnight. If they are going to attack tonight, that's when they'll do it, around two or three in the morning."

"Eagle Six, this is Arrow Three Seven."

"Go, Three Seven."

"We are three minutes from you."

"Roger. We can mark the enemy locations with Willy Pete."

"Roger."

Bromhead switched from the PRC-25 to the field phone. "Reynolds. You have the coordinates where we had dropped the Willy Pete?"

"Sure."

"Do so now and keep it up until I tell you otherwise."

"Rounds on the way."

"Three Seven. Rounds on the way."

In the distance, in the jungle to the north, there was a series of explosions. The Willy Pete was bright enough that it lit up the area. Fires now burned, providing more aiming points.

"Eagle Six, we have your camp in sight."

"Roger. Shutting off the Willy Pete." Back on the field phone, Bromhead ordered, "Last rounds. Clear the tubes."

"Got it. Last rounds fired. Tubes clear."

"Arrow Three Seven. Last rounds fired; tubes clear."

The gunships passed over the camp and headed directly at one of the fires burning in the jungle. Green tracer rounds reached up toward the aircraft but missed.

"Three Seven taking fire on the right."

The trailing gunship rolled in, using the miniguns. Every fourth round was a tracer, giving the impression of an unbroken red ray. It looked like something from a science fiction movie.

"I'm taking some fire on the right. Fifty meters to the east."

Arrow Three Seven saw the muzzle flashes. "Got him. Rolling in." He used rockets. There was a series of explosions. There was no return fire.

He was followed by the second gunship and again the ray stabbed out. The enemy guns fell silent. He didn't know if he had eliminated the threat or if they were afraid of his minigun.

"Eagle Six, we're getting low on ammo. You have a backup team coming?"

"Roger. They're ten to fifteen out."

Bromhead had been watching the show. The enemy had stopped firing mortars. They were laying low. He said, "Three Seven, how long can you stay on station?"

"We can stay here about thirty minutes."

"Roger."

Three Seven spotted several fires to the northeast. "Eagle Six, I see fires."

"Hit them. Should be where the tubes are." As he said it, he realized that if the mortar crews knew what they were doing, they would have broken down their tubes and fled the area. Or they were already dead.

Three Seven turned to set up the run on the fire. As he rolled in, he saw the huge, glowing green tracers floating up toward him. "Jesus Christ! They've got a fifty."

"I see him. I got him." The second gunship rolled in and as he did, the fifty swung around to engage. "I'm taking hits."

Three Seven watched as his wingman broke off the attack, turning to the left. As he did, Three Seven rolled in and fired all the rockets he had left. The area around the enemy gun erupted.

"Eagle Six. I just took out a fifty."

"Roger that."

"Eagle Six, this is Rabbit Four Six. I'm here with a heavy fire team."

"Say ordnance." Bromhead glanced at Gerber, as if to ask about a gun team with the call sign rabbit.

"I have a forty-mike-mike and M-60s. We have one minigun ship and one rocket."

"You see where the other team has been working?"

"Roger that."

"There is a Twelve decimal Five that they might have taken out. The enemy is in the jungle to the north and northwest of the camp. They have been firing mortars."

"Roger that. Rabbits, I'm rolling through. Watch for enemy fire."

A line of white tracers came up at him, but they were poorly aimed. There were four or five men shooting at him with the AK-47s. It seemed they were attempting to drive him away rather than hit him.

The number two gunship rolled in, using the miniguns. As he opened fire, the enemy stopped shooting.

"I don't know if I hit anything but they're quiet now."

"Rabbit Four Six, target the fires you see burning."

"Roger that."

Rabbit Four Six adjusted his flight path and fired the 40mm gun in the nose of his aircraft. He walked the rounds up to one of the fires and dropped several rounds into it. That put out the fire and there was no evidence of anyone there shooting at him.

They attacked several other locations but didn't receive any return fire. Four Six announced, "Eagle Six, we're about out of ammo. Heading back to the barn."

"Thanks Rabbit Four Six. Next time you're in town, stop by for a beer."

"You don't have to ask me twice."

Bromhead watched the gunships disappear. To Gerber, he said, "I think that's got it for the night."

"You know better than that. The enemy was testing your resources. The gunships scared them."

"I can get fast movers in here, but that takes about an hour unless they're already airborne. Then it's a matter of minutes."

"It seems that you've got everything covered. You have anyone coming in to get those flight crews and Patterson out of here?"

"There is someone coming to get General Patterson tomorrow. That reporter, Stacy, doesn't want to hang around. He wants to be on the first aircraft out of here. He'd probably get a good story if he stayed, but I think he's scared."

Gerber chuckled. "He's not the only one."

"I think everything is going to remain quiet," said Bromhead. "Let's go to the team house."

"Fetterman's still out in the jungle. You going to recall the company?"

"Do you think I should?"

"I've said it before, John. This is your show. That company out there is vulnerable to attack, but then, if the enemy doesn't know they're hiding in the jungle, then you have a real advantage."

Bromhead turned to the Vietnamese soldier. "You stay here and keep watch. I'll get your relief sent up in about an hour."

"Yes, sir."

As he climbed over the sandbag wall, Gerber asked, "You going to consult with Captain Trang?"

"I find it best to let him come to me. That way, I don't have to deal with him all that much and his bizarre sense of military protocol. He thinks he's a general and not just a Dai Uy."

"You don't like him?"

"He's typical of too many of the South Vietnamese officers. Bought his position but didn't have enough money or pull to become a colonel."

As they reached the ground, Gerber said, "Then why is he stuck out here?"

"As I said, because he didn't have enough political pull or money. He wanted to be an officer, and this was the best deal he could get."

"Not a good officer?"

"No, sir. But Lieutenant Nguyen is very good. He's been around a long time and earned his rank." Bromhead chuckled. "There are times that he speaks English like a native, but I've seen him pretend that he doesn't understand some of the jargon."

They reached the team house. Bromhead pulled open the door and stood back so that Gerber could enter first. They found General Patterson and Captain Cooper sitting there.

"That was an exciting hour," said Patterson. "We finished for the night?"

Bromhead went to the refrigerator but rather than grabbing a beer, he took out a can of Pepsi. The others noticed but didn't say anything. Bromhead sat down at the table and took a deep drink.

Gerber turned his attention to the general. "We have evidence of a large enemy force operating around here, but I don't think we need to worry about anything other than a few more mortars."

"Are you sure?" asked Patterson.

"No, General, I'm not sure. Charlie sometimes fools us."

"Do they know that I'm here?"

Gerber thought the question was narcissistic but then realized that if the VC and NVA knew there was a general officer in the camp, they would probably attack in full force. Capturing an American general would be a political coup.

"I don't think so, General. I think this is part of a larger strategy. You just got caught here before we could get you out."

"So, what happens now?"

"We have gunships on call, with have arty on call, and Captain Bromhead tells me we can get fast movers in if we need them." Gerber looked at his watch. "If they're going to attack tonight, they'll start with another mortar barrage, bigger than what they've thrown at us so far. But it's getting late for that. They'd want to overrun us before dawn."

"Then we can relax."

"Oh, no, sir. We can't relax unless we can verify that they have left the field, or we destroy that regiment that is facing us."

217

CHAPTER 16

General Dekker slammed the folder on to his desk and turned his wrath on his sergeant major. "What in the hell is Patterson still doing on that Special Forces camp?" he shouted. "We need to get him out of there now. He needs to be here."

"There have been a series of mortar attacks. All the aircraft have been evacuated. There is no way for him to get out right now."

"He's a general officer. I'm a general officer. I want a special flight arranged. Task one of those assault helicopter companies in that area to pick him up. Hell, get a C-123 tasked with getting him out. I don't want excuses. I want action. If he's not here in the next hour, someone is going to be extremely unhappy."

"General, I don't think we can get him out that fast, even if everything works perfectly. Flight time from that area is about an hour or so and that's if he can catch a ride, well, right now. There is nothing available that fast. And there isn't a C-123 close to that camp. He'd have to come from Tan Son Nhut, or maybe even Nha Trang."

Dekker fell back in his chair. He lowered his voice and realized that he had lost his temper. The first thing he had learned in his officer training was to control his emotions. Never lose your temper. Shouting at subordinates served no useful purpose and was often counterproductive.

"Tell me again, what has happened?"

"Yes, sir. The helicopter company that was on standby at that base was recalled when it was clear that General Patterson had been located and was in our control. That flight was released for other missions. The aircraft that picked him up, short on fuel, landed at the camp. Not long after that, there was a series of mortar attacks resulting in damage to the single aircraft that remained. They couldn't fly it out. Bad luck, really."

"I suppose a convoy is out of the question," said Dekker, thinking out loud. "That would take too long, they would probably be ambushed along the way given the number of enemy in the area, and I'm not sure just how to form a convoy to get him here." As soon as he said that he wished that he hadn't.

Not knowing what to say, the sergeant major just said, "Yes, sir."

"I just don't know what is happening out there." Dekker ran a hand through his hair and sighed. He realized what he had just said and wanted to retract it too, but thought that would make him look even weaker.

"General Patterson has not attempted to share the intelligence he gathered with us, has he?" asked Dekker.

"No secure communications are available. I doubt he would have mentioned it in the clear."

"Thank you, Sergeant Major. My outburst was not directed at you. It is just frustration with the events of the last day or two."

"Understood, General. Is there anything else?"

"Just let me know if we have any communication from General Patterson. I'll be here for the next hour or so and then in my quarters."

"Yes, sir."

Kendall Stacy, who had been in Vietnam for a few months, had never been through a mortar attack. When the first rounds fell, he didn't know what to do. One of the rounds exploded close enough that he heard the shrapnel rattling against the metal roofs of some of the buildings. He had dived to the floor and oddly thought of the attack in terms of a Hollywood production.

When there was a lull in the mortars hitting the camp, Stacy raised his head and looked around. He saw the entrance to a bunker about twenty yards away. He didn't know what it was, but figured it had to safer than staying where he was. He climbed to his feet and sprinted toward the entrance. He dived through and found he was in a bunker with Vietnamese strikers and one Green Beret sergeant.

"Just who in the hell are you?"

Stacy, still shaking from being outside as mortars fell, sat down, leaning against the sandbag wall. "Stacy. Press."

"Press what?"

"I work for a newspaper."

"Well, Mr Stacy, of the press, stay the hell out of the way. Just sit right where you are and keep your mouth shut or you'll find yourself on the outside, looking in."

"What's going on?"

"Are you nuts? We're being mortared."

Stacy stared at the man. He looked to be about thirty, was wearing jungle fatigues that had faded to a light green and were stained with dirt and sweat. Although Stacy had been working near soldiers for months in Vietnam, he still didn't understand the rank structure. The man was wearing black stripes on his sleeves which meant he was a sergeant, but that was all he knew.

"Will there be more mortars?"

"Don't know and am not worried about it. This bunker can take a direct hit from an eighty-two-millimeter mortar. Probably the biggest they have. Rockets are a different story."

"Then I'll just stay here, if you don't mind."

"Stay out of the way and stop bothering me."

Stacy felt his fear drain away for the moment. No mortars were falling and he was now in a bunker, designed to survive a direct hit. He grinned, thinking of the stories he could tell back home. He was on a Special Forces camp that was being attacked by the VC. Well, they weren't storming the wire, but dropping mortars on them was about the same thing.

The sergeant said something in Vietnamese, but Stacy didn't understand it. "What was that, Sergeant?"

"Craig. It's Sergeant Craig. I told them to keep a sharp eye, though I don't expect a ground attack, and I told you not to bother me."

And the fear washed over him again. A ground attack was not something he wished to see. He didn't know what would happen in a ground attack. He had no weapon, and no training in how to use a weapon, though as a kid he had a twenty-two. That wasn't the same thing as an M-16. Worse, he didn't know if the VC would take him prisoner or just shoot him outright. These were things that he should have known but just didn't. The press briefings in Saigon hadn't touched on that subject.

"Are you going to be in here all night?"

"Or until we are told to go to half alert or a quarter alert. We are at the mercy of the enemy and our officers."

Now completely frightened, Stacy asked, "Mercy of the enemy?"

"I mean, we are going to stay here, and it is now up to the enemy to change the situation. They have to launch the attack.

There is nothing that we can do to provoke it and we can't go out in search of them."

"Why would you want to do that?" Stacy was horrified by the suggestion.

"We wouldn't, though we hold the advantage of a defensible position, interlocking fields of fire, including artillery, on-call helicopter gunships and all the fighter support we can get."

Feeling better, Stacy nodded. "I'll just remain here."

"Then please stop diverting my attention."

"Okay. Is there any water around here?"

Craig looked at him and then took his canteen from its pouch on his pistol belt. "Take a sip, swirl it around before you swallow. If you empty the canteen, you're going to have to refill it and there is no source of water in this bunker. You'll have to go outside to get it."

"Thank you, Sergeant." He took the canteen and did as he was told.

Both Becker and Cornett were in the team house with the others when the first rounds detonated. They had been through mortar attacks in the past, knew what to expect and weren't very worried about this one. They listened for the points of detonation.

"Not coming at us," said Becker, meaning the rounds weren't walking toward the team house.

Just as Becker finished saying that, a round fell much closer. Everyone, with a few exceptions, dropped to the floor. Becker grinned. "My fault. Shouldn't have tempted fate."

Cornett, who was now sitting up, laughed. "Maybe we should try to get a flight out of here. Surely one of our companies will send a helicopter to retrieve us."

"Can't hurt to try."

There were more explosions, but they sounded as if they had fallen outside the camp. Becker stood up and asked, "Should we head for the communications bunker?"

"Probably safer than here." Cornett stopped for a moment and then added, "Weaver is being looked at by the medic. I'm not sure where he is. He should have been flown out with the flight. I'd say to get proper medical attention, but I think their guy here is very good."

Becker moved toward the door and looked out. There was nothing to see in the redoubt. He wasn't sure where the one round had landed. Nothing had been damaged.

Becker said, "I'll go. The rest of you stay here."

"If your company can't get in, or has other orders, then we'll have to try mine. I'll go with you."

"Wait a minute," said Owens. "This isn't exactly a bunker."

"We don't know how much space there is in the communications bunker. We'll make the calls and then come back here. We should stay together as much as possible in case they send someone." Cornett turned to Becker. "You ready?"

"Sure."

They dropped the two feet to the ground and ran across the redoubt, looking for the bunker that had the radio antennae on it. That had to be the communications bunker. Cornett waited while Becker entered and then followed.

A buck sergeant came toward them. "We don't need a bunch of people in here. You'll have to leave."

"You sure don't," said Cornett, agreeing. "But we need to make contact with our home units."

Becker looked at the bank of radios. "Okay. Which one can I use?"

The sergeant hesitated, as if weighing his options. He finally decided that there was no reason for them not to contact their units. He pointed to a radio at the end of the line. "Probably have the best luck on the uniform."

Becker twisted the dial on the UHF radio, setting it on his company frequency. He made the call quickly, explained the situation, giving as little tactical information as possible so the operations officer would understand, and waited.

The response was quick. "We can dispatch an aircraft. Take about thirty minutes."

"Roger. I have another crew here. We need to get them out. They can call their company once we're on the ground."

"Roger that."

Becker looked at Cornett. "Okay. Anything you want to add?"

"Just that we have an injured man."

"Right." Becker keyed the mic. "Be advised that one of the other crewmen has a broken arm."

"Do you need a medic?"

"Negative. He's getting first aid here."

"Roger."

Cornett said, "That seems to be too easy."

"Your guys wouldn't come to get you?"

"Well, it wasn't them who got us out of the jungle, was it?"

"Good point. Okay. Did you expect them?"

"We didn't expect anyone given our location, which shall forever remain nameless."

Becker handed the mic back to the sergeant. "Thanks for the use of the radio."

"No problem, sir. Good luck on getting out of here. I wish I could go with you."

Becker was going to comment but then decided he didn't want to know what the guy meant. To Cornett, he said, "Let's get back to the team house."

"Lead the way. I'll be right behind you."

General Patterson, who had been at the bottom of a pile of soldiers when the first mortars fell, understood the situation. That he had been a little faster than the younger men, which explained why he was on the bottom, was based on his experience in another Asian war. In Saigon mortar attacks were rare. There had been rockets and mortars used in Saigon during the TET offensive, but that was the exception and not the rule. Patterson had learned about mortars when he was a young officer in Korea.

Even after the first wave of mortars had fallen and there was a lull in the attack, he stayed on the floor, sitting with his back to the plywood wall and his head below the level of sandbags stacked outside. If a mortar hit the roof, he might be in trouble, but the aim of the enemy mortarmen had been poor so far.

Patterson still had his pistol in a holster attached to his web gear. When he had been promoted to brigadier general, he had been presented with a special pistol and the accoutrements that went with it, such as a highly polished pistol belt and holster. The problem was that it was a .32-caliber semiautomatic. He thought of it as practically useless, especially in a combat environment, which explained why he had left that pistol at home, gathering dust, and had a Colt .45 ACP in the leather holster that was not polished. He knew the .45 had the power to knock down a person and in combat, that was an advantage.

He saw there were three members of the Special Forces team in the room with him and the others. He asked, "One of you guys the armorer?"

"Yes, sir. Sergeant First Class O'Neal, sir."

"Well, Sergeant O'Neal, I'm wondering how I might be issued, on a temporary basis of course, an M-16. You do have unassigned weapons?"

"Yes, sir. The armory is locked."

"But as the armorer you would have the key, wouldn't you?"

"Yes, sir. So does Captain Bromhead. He likes to control the unassigned weapons. We lose an M-16 and there is a lot of paperwork explaining what happened to it even if it was lost in an ambush."

Patterson grinned. "And usually, it was destroyed in a mortar attack?"

O'Neal looked uncomfortable. "Yes, sir. That sometimes happens."

"Well, I don't want to take it with me when I am evacuated tomorrow, but I sure would like to have one tonight, just in case. And a bandolier. An M-16 is much better at longer ranges and I would like it for those close-combat situations."

"I can arrange that. Would you like me to get a weapon for you, sir? I can bring it here."

"If it wouldn't be too much trouble. I'll even sign a hand receipt for it if that will make you happy."

O'Neal cocked his head to one side, listening. Quietly, calmly, he said, "Incoming."

Patterson didn't move. Others crouched, one or two of them trying to get under the table.

There was another series of explosions, but none of them near or inside the redoubt.

"Where's the countermortar?" asked Patterson.

Almost as if to answer his question, there was the quiet sound of the camp's mortars opening fire.

"There it is, General."

"So I noticed."

They heard another two detonations of mortars. They fell silent. O'Neal crawled to the door and peeped out. There was nothing to see, though there was a flickering outside the redoubt that meant one of the buildings was burning. The armory hadn't been touched.

O'Neal looked back at Patterson. "Here I go," he said unnecessarily.

"Be careful."

O'Neal disappeared through the door. Cornett, who had returned with Becker, watched him go. "I think I would have waited to be sure that nothing was going fall on me."

"They're not very good," said Patterson. "I mean the VC mortar teams. The random pattern of impacts tells me that they don't have adequate training."

"Golden BB, General," said Cornett. "Sometimes they get lucky and hit something vital. They just throw out rounds and hope for the best."

"You get anything arranged?"

"Yes, sir. We've got a helicopter or two coming in, or rather, I should say trying to get here in about thirty minutes. If there are no mortars falling and we're waiting on the runway, they should be able to get here. Whether or not they land depends on the situation on the ground."

"I don't like the idea of risking the lives of the flight crew. We're not in a great deal of danger here," said Patterson.

"Unless they launch a ground attack."

Before anyone could answer, O'Neal was back. He dived into the team house, like he was attempting to steal third base headfirst. He grinned and held up an M-16. He had another slung over his shoulder, along with a half dozen bandoliers. There were grenades in his pockets. He'd switched his Green Beret for a steel pot.

"You expecting trouble?" asked Patterson.

"Always, General. Always."

Fetterman crept around the line, checking on the strikers. There was no reason for him to do that. They had been well trained, and they knew their job. They were on quarter alert, which meant that the majority of the force was resting or trying to sleep. He wished they were at half alert, but he wasn't going to challenge Lieutenant Nguyen's order.

He settled into his place at the base of a tree. He had a partial view of the camp and saw the mortars hitting them there. To Fetterman, that was harassment fire. It was designed to annoy the soldiers, to keep them awake and on edge. But he also knew that soldiers who had survived mortar attacks became complacent during them. They didn't really fear a mortar attack. They might head to a bunker, or they might just stay where they were. The number of rounds and the random nature of them were not frightening. If they were worried, or Charlie used a few rockets, then they might head for a bunker. But the random nature of the attacks made that problematic.

Nguyen found Fetterman and whispered, "Should we try to take out the mortars?"

Fetterman shook his head, knowing that Nguyen wouldn't see the gesture. "No. Don't want to get in the way of the countermortar. Be tragic if the countermortar killed one or two of our own."

"Do you think this is prep for a ground assault?"

"No. It's not the type of barrage you would expect prior to an attack. This is just harassment."

Nguyen crawled away then. Fetterman thought that he was a good man. He understood what he was doing and was not afraid to ask for advice. He believed he was fighting for the freedom of South Vietnam. He wasn't political. He wasn't connected. He was just a soldier. If South Vietnam had more like him, then the policy of Vietnamization, as Washington liked to called it, would be working much better. The fighting could be turned over to the Vietnamese and the Americans could go home. But given the current situation, the South Vietnamese Army required the direct guidance of the American forces, as they had done for a decade.

Fetterman became aware of movement in front of him. He stared at it but saw nothing. He turned his head slightly, using his peripheral vision. That sometimes allowed him to see shadowy shapes better. He thought it might be a bush, or maybe an animal. He closed his eyes and opened them. He caught the movement again. It was man-shaped and not one of the strikers.

Fetterman slung his weapon and pulled out his knife. He had blackened the blade so that it wouldn't glint in the star or moonlight, though there wasn't much of either. The man was coming right at him. Fetterman thought he might be a farmer, but the man was moving like a soldier searching for the enemy. A farmer would not be out this late and probably wouldn't be in the jungle.

Fetterman wanted the man to walk by but that didn't seem to be an option. He had stumbled onto their position, and even if he didn't see Fetterman, he would probably find one of the other strikers.

Fetterman moved slowly, making no noise. Just before he collided with the enemy, Fetterman reached out, grabbed him, and spun him around. Fetterman grasped the man under the chin and lifted, exposing the neck. With a quick motion, he slit the man's throat, cutting deep enough that the man couldn't shout a warning. There was a spray of blood and a copper odor. It wasn't a textbook move, but it was effective. It was deadly.

As he lowered the man to the ground, there was a single shot to his right. Fetterman knew that it was an M-16 and not an AK-47 or an SKS. Two more shots were fired. Fetterman looked to his right. There was another man standing as if surprised. Before Fetterman could get his weapon, there was a third shot and the man collapsed.

From behind, Lieutenant Nguyen approached. "I come," he whispered.

"Got you," replied Fetterman.

Nguyen, in an almost normal voice, said, "We have been compromised."

"We need to stay right here. That was probably a patrol."

"The VC know we're here."

"Their response depends on what they plan for tonight. They might not even respond. We just have to go to full alert and be ready."

"My soldiers are all awake. They are ready."

CHAPTER 17

Colonel Tri Minh Nguyen had watched the mortars fall on the Special Forces camp and was disappointed by the results. He was sure that the enemy, in that camp, had not been frightened by the attack. It had been too random to be of much use and caused too little damage. It was not the prologue to the ground attack that he had planned for. He wished it had been more accurate. The only positive was they had damaged the helicopter on the runway. They would destroy it later, as they overran the camp, but it was not the main target.

He now stood at the edge of the tree line, confident that he was invisible to the puppet soldiers of the Saigon regime and the American imperialists that assisted them. He couldn't see much activity inside the camp. He didn't know if that was good or bad. Maybe the enemy was too frightened to fight back, or maybe they were just waiting in ambush.

His aide, standing next to him, holding Nguyen's binoculars and who was also his bodyguard, asked, "Do you attack tonight?"

"Yes. Later. Give them a chance to relax and let their guard down. Just when they least expect it, we'll attack."

Nguyen turned when he heard several shots that came from the jungle to his left. "What is that?"

"Patrols are out. One might have contacted the enemy."

Nguyen stared at the darkened jungle but could see nothing. He didn't like that. If one of his patrols had been in contact with the enemy, in the jungle, it might have alerted those in the camp, though the mortar attack had already done that.

"Do you want to dispatch a platoon to find out what happened?"

Nguyen thought about it. "No. When our patrols return, find out who engaged the enemy. Let them tell me what happened." There had only been a few shots, which suggested that one of the patrols had shot at something in the dark. Those few shots didn't mean much, given all the circumstances.

"Yes, sir."

He held out a hand and the aide put the binoculars in it. Nguyen surveyed the camp again. There was a fire burning on the far side, but no one was trying to put it out. That could mean that what was burning was of no importance to the defenders, or that they were too frightened to leave the safety of their bunkers. If asked, Nguyen would have said the fire was of no importance to the enemy.

He didn't see any movement in the camp. That surprised him. Soldiers should have responded, but the only response had been a few mortar rounds from them into the jungle. They hadn't been well aimed and had injured none of his soldiers. He had expected to see something more, including the puppet soldiers firing into the jungle.

There had been gunships working over the jungle, but they were after the mortar tubes. They had not attacked any of the companies of his regiments. It was an interesting exercise. A few mortar rounds to annoy the defenders and a response that was ill-timed and virtually ineffective. They hit the wrong places and now they were all gone.

"Are the regiments standing by?"

"At dusk, they had moved forward, crawling the last fifty meters to their positions. There are two companies ready to attack. They will be followed by two more, and finally by the entire regiment as you ordered."

Nguyen handed the binoculars back and then retreated deeper into the jungle. He passed a platoon, the men lying on the ground, their weapons ready. Each also had a canteen, first aid kit and a chest pouch that held three spare magazines loaded with thirty rounds of 7.62mm ammo. It was the same size as the ammo for the American M-14 and M-60 machine guns. The AK-47 ammo was shorter than the American round.

"We will open the assault with all mortars and rockets firing for ten minutes. As we lift the barrage, our first companies will attack the northern side of the enemy camp. At the same time, I want the second regiment to move to the left so that it might attack the east side. They will cross the runway, destroy the helicopter there and prepare to repel any air assault if one should be mounted against us."

Nguyen knew that giving these details to the aide was unnecessary. He felt the urge to confide in someone and his aide was his best choice. The man was loyal to him and no one else. Besides, there wasn't any chance of a compromise now that they were in the jungle near the camp. Who could the aide tell?

He looked at his watch, the hands glowing faintly. He smiled because the watch was American. It would help him determine when to attack and it was almost time to begin the first phase of the attack. Of course, he had developed the plan so that he could order the attack whenever he wanted. Everything was timed out carefully, based on the beginning of the artillery barrage of mortars and rockets.

"Bring me Colonel Ky."

"Yes, sir."

Bromhead, crouched in the fire control tower, said, "Fetterman's engaged."

Gerber, who held the binoculars, swept the jungle where the strike force was concealed. He saw a muzzle flash, but there was no prolonged firefight. It was one or two weapons and then everything fell silent. He watched for another two minutes, but the fight was over.

"I was going to contact him but realized that it might not be the best tactic to have his radio suddenly announce their presence while the enemy is near."

"Fetterman will call us when he has the situation figured out," said Gerber.

"I hate this," said Bromhead. "We hide up here in the tower while the fight swirls around us in the jungle."

Gerber had to laugh. "There is no fight swirling around us right now. Think of those up in the C and C helicopters overlooking battles. They do this on a daily basis while the fight swirls around below them. I don't think they're upset by that situation. They're doing their job, and we are doing ours."

"I know. I just want to know what is happening here and now, and if the strikers need assistance."

"Fetterman, or your lieutenant, will let us know if they want help from us. Patience."

"It's hard to be patient when it's your guys in the jungle."

"I know that. I've known it for a long time."

Bromhead looked at his watch. "Getting late. If they're going to attack, they're going to have to launch it soon or dawn will screw them up."

"I suspect that they think they have the force to overrun us. I'm not sure that dawn scares them. Maybe it's time to alert the fast movers and put the gunships back on standby."

To the north, the jungle began to sparkle. Even at the distance, he heard the mortars being fired. Bromhead picked up the field phone. "Incoming. Everyone take cover. Spread the word."

"This could be the big push."

The first of the rounds landed short. Gerber's first thought was that the mortar crews were inept but then he saw that the rounds were detonating in the wire and walking toward the camp. They were trying to destroy the wire. It was an obstacle for their attack, and they were opening a path through it.

"They're going to hit us on the north."

Bromhead, using the field phone, ordered, "Mortar crews, they are coming from the north. Drop you rounds at the edge of the jungle to the north. HE rounds. Fire when ready and keep firing until you run out of ammo or I order you to stop."

The mortar crews did as instructed. There were thirty seconds between the order and when the rounds began to drop near the jungle, some into the trees. If there was an attacking force there, that would disrupt them. If the mortars were on target.

On the field phone, Bromhead said, "Strikers, get ready on the north. Open fire as soon as you have a good target."

The mortar barrage from the enemy continued. Rounds fell on the bunker line but did little damage. They needed heavier artillery, but they didn't have it. Their only artillery was their mortars, most of them only 60mm. If they had anything heavier, they had yet to deploy it.

Bromhead watched as the enemy targeting shifted from the wire to the redoubt. They seemed to be aiming for the communications bunker and the team house. That meant that someone in the camp had provided information to the enemy. It couldn't have been given to the enemy recently because there had been no chance for that.

"Are you going to stay up here?" Gerber asked.

"Yeah. I can direct the fight better from here."

Gerber smiled and thought about those in the C and C helicopters circling the battlefield and thinking the same thing. "I'll be on the north side of the camp." He scrambled over the sandbags and nearly ran down the ladder. On the ground, he dropped to a knee and watched the line of detonations from the enemy mortars as they walked out of the redoubt. The target was now the striker quarters on the south side of the camp. It was intended to keep the strikers there, but they had already manned the bunkers, most of them on the north side.

As Gerber ran by the entrance to the redoubt, several soldiers appeared. Gerber didn't stop. He fell in behind them. He realized that General Patterson, carrying an M-16, was one of them. He wondered where Stein was. He figured the old soldier would want to be in on the action and be where he could keep an eye on his general.

They reached the bunker line on the north side. The men spread out, some taking cover on the berm and others dropping into the bunkers. Patterson had joined them. No one had fired yet. The enemy hadn't begun the ground assault. This was just the arty prep designed to soften the defenses. It wasn't doing much damage. There were only a few men clipped by the shrapnel.

Keeping to the timetable, their mortars fell silent after ten minutes. Colonel Nguyen used his binoculars to scan the camp. "First wave, go," he ordered.

Although there were still mortar rounds coming from inside the camp, there was a rising shout from the soldiers as they filtered out of the trees. The soldiers ran forward, screaming as they crossed the open ground. There were whistles and bugle calls urging them forward. Shrapnel from the camp's mortars cut down thirty or forty in the leading ranks, but the rest kept running. They were soon too close to the wire. The American mortars were now ineffective. The enemy was too close to the berm but the mortar crews keep firing, aiming for the edge of the jungle.

His aide returned with Colonel Ky. "You sent for me, sir," said Ky.

"What happened?"

"One of my patrols ran into several enemy soldiers. I have not had a chance to interrogate the members of that patrol. They have not returned to my control, and I didn't want to send more soldiers into that unknown situation. There was a chance that there would be a new engagement that might tip our hand."

A burst of machine-gun fire raked the trees above them. Ky and the aide ducked, but Nguyen did not. He ignored that. Instead, he said, "I want you to hit the east side of the camp as quickly as you can get into position."

"We're ready to go now, sir."

Nguyen pointed at the helicopter still sitting on the runway. "Hit them at that point. Make your approach as quietly as possible. Once your lead element is engaged, then send your battalion into the fight."

"No reserve?"

"No. Hit them with everything you have. Their attention will be directed toward the assault on this side of the camp. You'll have the chance to breach their defenses quickly. If you can get inside the berm, the defense on the north will collapse. Go now. Launch the attack."

Ky, the excitement obvious in his voice, said, "Yes, sir." He turned and ran off.

Without an order, the bunker line erupted in a solid wall of yellow-orange fire. It came from both the individual weapons and the crew-served M-2 .50-caliber and the M-60 .30-caliber machine guns. The front of the attacking force stumbled and fell. The initial attack was failing. But the second wave, with more men, spread out as it rushed from its hiding in the protection of the tree line. They were firing from the hip, without waiting, without aiming, sometimes hitting and killing their own men from the first wave.

Those in the first wave who had survived to reach the edge of the wire, dropped into a prone position. They engaged the soldiers in the bunkers and those along the berm with small arms, attempting to suppress the firing. They were drawing the fire of the defenders, giving those in the second wave a chance to cover the open ground without taking heavy casualties.

The two waves joined and now they were threading their way through the holes in the wire the mortars had created. They were shooting, attempting to suppress the defender's firing. They were getting closer to overrunning the berm.

For a reporter, Kendall Stacy had a sudden lack of curiosity. He had found what he thought of as a safe haven. He was sitting on a floor of rough planks, his back to a sandbag wall. There was a firing port where the Vietnamese strikers and a single Special Forces NCO were watching for the enemy. There was a single M-60 machine gun mounted so that it could cover an area of about 120 degrees. Stacy didn't know that because he was trying to calm himself.

No one in the bunker was paying any attention to him. He was interested in staying out of the line of fire and wondering what had possessed him to work so hard to get here, to this camp. Of course, he hadn't thought about the danger because of all the activity in the search for General Patterson. He had thought it would be a safe story to chase and could be his ticket to the big time.

He pushed himself up and was about to look out the firing port when the attack began. First, there wasn't much going on. There were bugles and whistles and a raising shout as the enemy attacked. Sergeant Craig was behind the M-60 and opened fire. Stacy couldn't believe the noise it made as it burned through the ammunition. The man was firing short bursts and Stacy didn't understand that. He was just aware of the increased noise as the strikers, using their M-16s, began to shoot.

He fell back, against the sandbags. He was vaguely aware of bullets hitting the sandbags but none of the rounds penetrated the wall. No rounds came through the firing port. Since he was near the rear of the bunker, he believed that he was safe, at least for the moment. He just wished the shooting would stop and that the VC would return to the jungle. He hadn't bargained on this. It was just too much for him.

He thought he might be safer if he wasn't in a bunker on the firing line. There had to be a better place for him. The exit for the bunker, an L-shaped open area, was near him. He thought about getting out and running for the team house, or maybe the dispensary. That was where he should be and if he needed information for a story later, he could talk to the Green Berets and maybe even General Patterson. The thought of writing a story from the scene of the battle, even if he wasn't an active participant, would certainly boost his career.

Gerber was in the bunker with the .50-caliber machine gun that was supported by two M-60s. The firing was a continuous roar with the fifty chugging away, cutting thought the attackers.

Gerber was standing back, out the of way, watching the assault through the firing port. He reached for the field phone, spun the crank and said, "Illumination on the north."

There was a slight delay and suddenly there was a yellow-green glow overhead as the flare rounds detonated. He could see the enemy attack was filtering to the point where the wire had been destroyed by the mortar barrage. "Move to the right!" he yelled. "Move to the right."

The gunners understood. They concentrated their fire on that point. They were using short bursts, trying to give the barrels time to cool down between bursts.

Gerber could see the tracers converging at the point where the wire was breached. Others, in the surrounding bunkers and along the berm, did the same thing. In seconds, the attack broke with the survivors attempting to flee.

"Hold your fire," said Gerber. He wasn't concerned about the enemy getting away. He was worried about the machine guns in the bunker. He grabbed a canteen and poured water on one of them, trying to cool it before the second attack started.

General Patterson was crouched behind the berm. His weapon was aimed over the top as he popped up and fired a short burst, then ducked back down. It had been a long time since he had engaged in close combat. The last time had been in Korea when it looked as if the United Nations forces might be pushed into the sea. In Vietnam, because he was now a senior officer, he found himself either directing the fighting from a helicopter circling the battle or assigned to a staff job in Saigon, where he directed the war from behind a desk. He rarely fired his weapon and then only on the pistol range to qualify as regulations required.

Now, he was in the thick of it again. The enemy was pouring out of the jungle, rushing toward them screaming. The firing increased until it sounded like the roar of several jet engines. It was continuous. He couldn't hear the individual weapons firing. Too many men were trying to kill each other and firing wildly. Patterson had been trained, so many years ago, in fire discipline. He didn't pull the trigger and burn through the magazine. He attempted to hit a target, firing one shot at a time.

Around him the strikers were engaging the enemy on full automatic. Out of the corner of his eye, he saw one of them fall and knew he was dead by the way the man fell. All strength seemed to have left his body. He just dropped in a loose, boneless way. He'd seen that before. The man was dead.

Patterson's attention was drawn back to the attacking force. They were trying to push through the wire, but the path was too narrow for so many of them. A few tried to open a wider path, but they were cut down immediately.

The first of the flares went out and they were in momentary darkness. The strobing of the muzzle flashes gave movement the look of a silent movie. It was nearly impossible to see the enemy now. Patterson held his fire. He knew that he didn't have much ammo and didn't want to burn through it too quickly.

Flares exploded into brightness. The enemy had not made much progress in the dark. Patterson thought that there were fewer of them standing in the wire, trying to get into the camp.

Patterson aimed at a man that was now only fifty meters away. Before he could pull the trigger, the man dropped, hit by someone else. The rest of the attackers had turned and were trying to get out the wire and back across the killing field. Patterson fired a few shots to encourage their retreat.

Around him the strikers were cheering. They had beaten back the first ground assault with only a few casualties. That was the way it should be. The attacking force had been inadequate for the job.

Patterson, who was the senior officer present but had no official duties, felt like the oldest, highest-ranking private. He had done what he had to do, what he had been trained to do. It would provide an interesting story when he got back to Saigon. He had forgotten the adrenaline rush of combat. He hadn't realized that he missed it.

Colonel Ky believed that the place for the commander was in front of his soldiers, leading them as they attacked the enemy. This wasn't an attack, yet. They were moving swiftly through the jungle, working their way around to the east side of the imperialist camp. Once in position, he would launch an assault, hoping to catch them by surprise while their attention was concentrated on the north.

Their movement slowed as they got into position. They were fifty or a hundred meters deep, into the jungle, using it to mask their movement. In the dark, it was difficult to see anything. The trees and bushes were black smudges against a charcoal background. The light from the enemy flares was too far from them to provide any useful illumination.

They tried to move silently, but in the dark, that was nearly impossible, and Ky didn't think that it mattered. One man might be able to slip silently through the dark jungle, but a company could not. As the size of the force increased, the ability to mask their noise was decreased. Men tripped, walked into bushes covered with thorns, bumped into one another and stepped in the wrong place and fell. They now moved slowly, but that didn't help.

The firing from the assault on the north had tapered. That had been one thing that masked their noise, but that sound was dying. Ky reached a point that he thought was due east of the camp and tried to halt his battalion. These were quiet orders, and the command to halt was passed along.

They began to spread out in company order and move closer to the tree line. Ky wasn't going to launch his assault until Nguyen ordered another attack on the north side. Hitting the enemy from two directions simultaneously would confuse them. It might provide the opening they needed to breach the berm protecting the camp. Ky was sure that they outnumbered the defenders by three to one, at least. He knew, from his command school classes, that an assault that size would have a very good chance of success. The theory was sound in school, but maybe not in the field.

He moved to a point where he was right at the edge of the trees. He could see down into the camp. There were fires burning now, most of them on the north side. But he didn't see much movement. The enemy was in his bunkers and lining the berm, waiting for another attack on the north.

Ky leaned forward slightly and touched the shoulder of the company commander closest to him. "When the new attack begins, we will move out," he whispered. "No one is to fire a round until the enemy fires. We should be able to get close before they see us. Have your senior NCO contact the company next to you and pass the word. Let's hope we can surprise them."

"Yes, sir." He moved off to pass the word.

CHAPTER 18

With the retreat of the enemy on the north side of the camp, Bromhead climbed down from the fire control tower. He sprinted across the compound toward the communications bunker. He ignored the fires that were burning and the one body that lay in his way. He dropped into the communications bunker. The lights were still on and the radios still working. The enemy mortar attack had failed to take out their communications or their generator. The radios had backup batteries.

The bunker had been divided into four segments, though only the corner with the radio was closed off from the others. There were fans blowing inside to help cool the electronic equipment. He stepped inside and said, "Get Tay Ninh arty on the line. Tell them we need flares. Tell them to fire when ready. That the illumination is necessary because we are under heavy attack."

The Communications NCO, a large Black man who had been in the Special Forces long enough to be on his second tour, knew the procedures better than anyone on the camp. He asked, "You want me to tell them we will be giving them coordinates for an arty prep?"

"No. Find out the call sign of any fighter squadron that can get here inside an hour. We'll want napalm. And tell them to contact Tay Ninh arty to make sure they're not flying through any gun target lines."

"Yes, sir."

Bromhead turned, raised his voice. "Anybody know where Major Gerber is?"

"Haven't seen him since he checked in here. Thought he was in the fire control tower with you."

As Bromhead was about to leave the bunker, the bugles started again. There was limited firing from the north berm. He'd left only the striker in the fire control tower. He could spot for the mortar crews, but he couldn't provide analysis of the assault.

Bromhead turned back. The lights flickered, but didn't go out. There was an explosion inside the redoubt. That had to be an enemy mortar round. The enemy was trying to suppress the fire from the berm to cover the beginning of the new assault.

He hesitated and made up his mind. "If anyone asks, tell them I returned to the fire control tower."

He left the bunker, crouched on the four steps up to ground level, listening. There had only been one mortar round. He didn't understand the purpose of that. He took a deep breath, leaped up the steps and ran back to the fire control tower. As he reached the ladder, he heard several rounds flash overhead. He was surprised that he could hear them. They had been much too close.

Once back in the tower, he surveyed the area. High overhead, the flares flashed into existence. In the strange green light, the flares were swinging under their parachutes. That caused shadows that danced around. The whole battle on the north side was laid out in front of him in that unreal green light. This was not just a company coming at them. It was a whole regiment, and if they got a few breaks, they'd reach the berm and swarm over it.

The sudden illumination supplied by the flares revealed the enemy force in detail. It was larger than Fetterman thought it was. Twice the size of his. Maybe three times. He had a defensible position, but in the jungle environment, he wasn't sure that made any difference.

The instant the enemy was exposed, the strikers opened fire, weapons on full automatic. It was a single crash that ripped through the enemy lines with devastating effect. The enemy was confused for a moment by the sudden onslaught of rifle fire. They didn't know who was shooting at them or where they were hiding. They didn't know how to stop it.

Fetterman, not wishing to reveal his exact position, grabbed his grenades. He pulled the pins and threw them as far as he could into the middle of the enemy formation, such as it was. The explosions looked like eruptions of a sparkling fountain incased in fire. At night, in the jungle, it had an immediate effect on the enemy.

He saw one man in a khaki uniform attempting to rally his men. He was waving at them, pointing into the jungle and yelling, but Fetterman couldn't hear the words. He was trying to turn his soldiers to where Fetterman's strikers were hidden. Trying to organize an attack on them. Fetterman aimed carefully and pulled the trigger. The first round struck the man in the shoulder, spinning him. The second hit him in the middle of the back. He fell, disappearing into the underbrush. He didn't get up. Two or three of the soldiers near him crouched, as if trying to give him aid.

There was a burst of firing from the attackers. They were out of position because they had formed with the idea of hitting the camp. Fetterman's force surprised them. Their shots were wild, slamming into the trees overhead. There was a rain of leaves, falling like confetti.

Without orders, the strikers had opened fire. They had better targets. The enemy was partially silhouetted against the flares over the northern end of the camp. They had good targets because they knew where the enemy was, and the enemy hadn't located their position.

The enemy firing around the strikers began to taper. The enemy soldiers were now trying to get away. Any thought of attacking the camp's east side was lost with the death of their commander. Several of the strikers stood up to get a better shot at the enemy. Lieutenant Nguyen pulled the closest man to him down so that he wouldn't get hit.

Fetterman stopped shooting. There was no need for it now. The enemy force was in full flight, defeated and in disarray as they tried to escape. Sometimes it was better to hold the ground they had than chase the enemy deeper into the jungle and back toward the larger force.

Nguyen appeared beside him. "They run."

"Yes, they do."

"We follow?"

"No. We hold here for a few minutes, but then we'll want to move. A little deeper into the jungle and to the right. We don't want them to find us here if they counterattack with a larger force."

Nguyen nodded and grinned. "We beat them good."

"That we did, Lieutenant. Surprised the hell out of them."

Nguyen turned and shouted in Vietnamese. The firing slowed and stopped.

Fetterman pulled a couple of the strikers aside and said, in Vietnamese, "I want to search some bodies. Take any insignia they have and any papers you can find. If you take any personal items such as a watch, remember that your fellow soldiers have not had the opportunity to look for booty. Conceal anything you find that is not of intelligence value."

He knew they would take anything of value from the dead, but that was the way of war. As long as they didn't cut off their ears or fingers, Fetterman didn't care what they did. He just didn't want to cause dissension in the ranks because some of the strikers had the opportunity to search the dead and others did not.

"We need to move quickly and watch for wounded soldiers. We won big. Let's not give them a chance to even the score."

Gerber had wanted to see what was happening on the north side of the camp. He could see it from the fire control tower, but being up there lacked perspective. He wanted to see how the strikers reacted as the enemy reached the berm.

Gerber ran out of the redoubt, turned to the left and found a position between two of the bunkers. There were strikers on both sides of him. They looked to be ready and if they were nervous, they didn't show it. One of their officers was walking behind them, giving them orders in Vietnamese. Gerber understood enough of the language to know what he was saying. They were told they could hold and in minutes there would be help coming from Saigon. To select their targets and not to waste their ammo.

He knew the enemy was hidden in the jungle in front of him. They had launched their assaults from there. He ignored the fighting on the east side of the camp. Fetterman was there and Gerber had complete confidence in him. If something had gone wrong, Fetterman would have alerted Bromhead and asked for help.

Now he saw movement in the trees as if some of the enemy was sliding to the right in an attempt to mask the coming assault. He crawled to the top of the berm so that he could see better. He was lying with his shoulders on the top and torso protected by the berm. It was not exactly the safest position, but he wanted a good look at the coming assault force. Had he been in the fire control tower he could have been sure what was happening around him.

As he watched, he was sure that they were forming up for a flanking attack. While the main body followed the same path to the openings in the wire, this group would either be able to get close and then cause trouble or draw attention away from the main body, giving them a chance to get over the berm.

Gerber slid back down. He pulled one of the senior strikers close. "They will come from the northwest. Be ready."

The striker nodded. "Yes, Major. I see."

"Keep your eyes on them. If they leave the jungle, take them under fire immediately."

"Yes, Major."

Gerber looked around carefully. He didn't want to micromanage the Vietnamese. He had to rely on them and to this point, they hadn't let him down. Bromhead had done a good job assembling the strike force.

Bending slightly so that his head was not visible above the berm, he ran to one of the bunkers. It held a Browning M-2 .50-caliber machine gun. Inside, the crew was Vietnamese, but one of the Special Forces sergeants was with them. He was using binoculars, sighting through the firing port.

"You see the movement to the right?" asked Gerber.

Turning, the sergeant answered, "Yes, sir. I was waiting to engage them."

"Use the fifty. Aim a little high to account for the drop. Engage them but watch your fire discipline. Don't overheat the weapon."

"Yes, sir." He switched to Vietnamese and gave the order.

The fifty opened fire with the slow chug of the large caliber weapon. Gerber didn't wait for the results. He picked up the field phone, spun the crank and said, "Mortar pit."

"Mortar pit. Sergeant Craig."

"Gerber. We need some HE to the right of the main body of the enemy."

"Yes, sir. Can you spot."

"Roger that. Fire when ready."

Gerber turned so that he could see out the firing port. Two rounds fell short. Over the field phone, he said, "Add fifty. Fire for effect. Give them half a dozen rounds."

The next rounds fell among the trees. He didn't see any more movement, but it could be that the enemy had flattened out, trying to avoid the mortars. He said, "Keep it coming."

Bromhead interrupted. "We have fighters coming in. Hold your fire."

Gerber wasn't sure that the mortar trajectory would take the rounds high enough to hit any of the fighters. He wasn't going to take the chance. He confirmed the order. "Hold your fire."

Colonel Nguyen decided to throw a whole regiment at the north side of the camp. He thought that Ky, causing trouble on the east, would draw off some of the defense. The strategy was to dilute the power of the defenders on the north.

He didn't like the flares overhead. His soldiers were exposed, making them easier targets. Once they reached the berm, the fight would be determined by numbers. If he had more soldiers than the enemy, they could overrun the camp.

The men ran forward, using fire and maneuver. That meant those in the lead would drop down, firing until those in the rear passed them. When the second wave began firing, the first leaped up and ran. It was a way of keeping up a wall of fire and inhibiting the defenders.

And then the flares began to go out one by one. The ground was now bathed in the soft light of a fingernail moon. Not much in the way of light. The NVA and VC were all on their feet, running forward, screaming as they worked their way through the holes blown in the wire.

From the west came the fighters. There were four of them, and they flew low, over the jungle. The napalm tumbled from under the lead jet, but it was short of Nguyen's position. He grinned at the miss.

But the second jet was nearly on target. The explosion of the jellied gas covered the jungle and part of one battalion in fire. There were screams, some of which were cut off sharply. Nguyen didn't know how many men had been lost. It might have been more than one hundred.

In front of him, the battle still raged. His men were getting close to the berm. He thought they might be able to overrun it. They looked close to doing just that. But then that attack faltered. A series of explosions came from the base of the berm and Nguyen knew what it was. Claymore mines had been detonated. Thousands of ball bearings shattered the attacking force.

The last of the jets made their runs. His men fired on them as the fighters flashed overhead. They hit nothing as the jungle burst into flames around them, eliminating that threat.

There was a moment when General Patterson thought they might not be able to hold. It was just a moment, as the enemy sprinted across the open ground to the wire and as they maneuvered through it. There were more of them coming this time. It looked as if the entire NVA was on the attack. He had already used most of his ammo and would be left with only his pistol. That was a last-resort weapon during a human wave attack, not suitable for stopping such an attack.

As the flares went out and there was more shooting from the attackers, he thought they might be overrun. But whoever held the controls for the claymores punched them off, and the enemy disappeared in a cloud of steel ball bearings from the mine. The only problem was that once they were fired, they couldn't be reloaded.

Patterson had closed his eyes, trying to save his night vision, but there had been too many bright flashes. Closing his eyes didn't do any good. He thought he heard someone scrambling up the other side of the berm. The soldier appeared above him and Patterson pulled the trigger on the M-16, but nothing happened. He dropped the rifle and clawed at his holster, knowing that he would not be able to draw and fire in time.

There was a single shot from his right and the enemy fell backwards, down the berm and out of sight. Patterson held his pistol in his right hand, but the enemy was still on the other side of the berm. Somehow, some of them had survived the claymores and reached the berm.

And then the jets roared in, and the jungle erupted in flames. Those few who had reached the berm turned to flee, but there were too few of them now and too many strikers. The enemy just couldn't get away fast enough and many were cut down long before they reached the safety of the jungle and the remainder of the regiment.

In the light of the fires started by the napalm, Patterson watched as the enemy tried to avoid the shooting from the camp and the napalm being dropped on them. He turned his back and sat down at the base of the berm. It had been close for a few seconds. That was enough time for them to kill him and the defenders, had there been more of them. But there weren't. They reached the top of the berm but no farther. Patterson didn't know that it was the high tide of the assault.

Patterson realized that he was still in great danger and while everyone else in the camp was in danger, he needed to get out. He looked left and right. There were dead and wounded around him. A few were the enemy who had penetrated the berm, the rest were strikers. It wasn't that he was afraid but that he had strategic information that he needed to get to Saigon.

He stood up, then, bending low like a man in a high wind, he ran back into the redoubt. He saw very little damage. This is where they would make the last stand, if it came to that. Patterson didn't think it would now. They had already turned two attacks. The enemy couldn't have much left for any sustained assault.

Colonel Nguyen had been pushed back, deeper into the jungle to avoid the fires created by the napalm. He had lost nearly a whole company to that attack. Two others had been shattered in the ground assault. He didn't know what happened to Colonel Ky, but his attack had never materialized. If he was going to win, he would need everyone still standing. One huge assault involving nearly a thousand NVA soldiers and VC. More than enough soldiers that they could cross the berm and get into the camp.

The jets were the motivating factor. If they came back, they could destroy his division without much trouble. He hadn't counted on that. He worried about helicopter gunships, but not jet fighters. He thought his soldiers would be in the camp before the jets arrived. That would have negated their value, but his soldiers were still not in the camp.

To his aide, he said, "Have the commanders meet me here. Use the senior NCOs to spread the word."

"Yes, sir."

When the aide disappeared, he turned back and faced the fires. They were slowly dying. The jungle was wet and although the napalm had been hot enough to start the fires, as it burned off and the fuel was now in the jungle's rotting vegetation, it hadn't been dried out enough to sustain the fires.

He couldn't see many bodies. Most of the dead had been incinerated. The twisted remains of their weapons, the metal parts, hadn't burned. They were barely recognizable, but he knew what they were. He thought it wasn't as bad as it could have been.

The remaining commanders assembled near him, none of them saying a word. They waited for his orders. He decided to give it to them straight.

"My mission was to overrun this camp to open a path to Saigon. They have put up a better fight than I thought they could. We are now going to mass the soldiers into a single assault to overrun them. We need to complete this before dawn because that is when they'll call on all their air power. We need to hold the camp and destroy their communications."

He looked around at the group. "I believe that you all know what to do. Are there any questions?"

"Colonel Ky?"

"We must assume that his mission has failed. We attack in fifteen minutes. First regiment will lead the way. Return to you units."

With the jets gone, there was a lull in the fighting. Gerber left the bunker but rather than return to his position on the berm, headed to the fire control tower. He climbed the ladder, and then over the sandbags.

Bromhead nodded to him. "Welcome back."

"Things seem to be going our way for the moment."

"Fetterman reported that they had engaged a company-sized unit, maybe larger, and scattered them."

"What's his plan?"

"They're going to stay out there. The main force is still to the north."

Gerber took the binoculars from Bromhead. He turned to the east but there was nothing there for him to see. It was quiet. To the north there were fires burning. There were shadows moving around the jungle.

"Should we drop some mortar rounds into the north?"

"There are gunships coming in for us. That will light them up."

Gerber smiled. "You think that you have this won?"

"I think there will be one more big push and if they don't breach the berm, then we've going to win. They'll have to get out of here."

"Are there any soldiers on standby to come in?"

Bromhead took the binoculars back. "There is a battalion alert at Tay Ninh ready when we call for them. We can get them in, but it would be best to wait for dawn. Night operations in this situation are a little hairy."

Bugles sounded and whistles blew. Bromhead pointed. "Here they come again."

Both Bromhead and Gerber knew this was the big push.

CHAPTER 19

Fetterman had moved forward about a hundred meters, beyond the area where they had engaged the enemy in a brief firefight earlier. If any of the NVA soldiers were still alive, they were either badly wounded or hiding. A single soldier, or even two or three, posed no real threat to them, but Fetterman assigned two strikers to check the bodies and collect the weapons. Fetterman and his small force continued, working their way slowly to the right, toward the main body which was massing for another assault on the camp.

He found Lieutenant Nguyen kneeling behind a large, fallen tree trunk. Nguyen was aiming into the jungle, where the enemy had been, but wasn't firing. "Lieutenant," Fetterman said, "we need to establish a firing line here. We need to deploy the majority of the strikers facing down, toward the north side of the camp. We need to form the remainder facing the enemy, so that we have an L-shaped position."

Nguyen didn't move or look up. He simply said, "Do it."

Fetterman nodded and in Vietnamese, gave the orders. He placed pickets behind his line and on the right flank so that his force couldn't be surprised from behind or the side. When the lines were formed, Fetterman walked along it, encouraging the strikers, telling them to hold their fire and to stay alert. Although he didn't say anything, he was sure that there would be one last attempt to overrun the camp.

Finally, he took a position in the angle of the L so that he would be able to turn his attention to whichever side needed it. He could look across the open ground to where the enemy had staged the first attack. The fires from the napalm still burned.

In the flickering of the firelight, he saw shadows. They were five or six hundred meters distant, at the outside effective range of the M-16s the strikers carried. They could engage, but the chance of doing any damage was remote. The problem was that any shooting now would give away their position. Fetterman wanted to surprise the enemy if he could, because surprise was his best weapon.

The firing had died away until it was only an occasional single shot. The strikers were holding their fire, waiting for the next attack. Gerber had been studying the south side of the camp. There were several fires burning there, but no one was fighting them. Beyond the berm, the ground was open for a klick or more. A platoon of strikers was holding the berm on the south. The force was large enough to slow an attack long enough that they could reinforce it. Crossing that much open ground would not allow for a surprise. The strikers' advantage was that they could run through the camp, but the enemy had to make a wide circle to get into position.

He turned back to the north and used his binoculars to sweep the area. "I think they're forming for another attack."

Bromhead used the field phone. "Mortars. Put HE to the north in the same place as before. I will spot if needed."

There was no verbal response. The mortar crews fired and Bromhead saw the detonations. Over the field phone, he said, "Add fifty and fire for effect."

The rounds fell among the trees, scattering some of the attacking force. Gerber said, "Nice work by the mortar crews."

"We practiced for that."

Below him, on the north side, one of the M-2s opened fire. The weapon had the range to easily reach the trees and do real damage. The red tracers flashed across the open ground. Some hit trees and spun off into the air. But the other rounds cut through the jungle. The first was joined by a second. Gerber hoped they weren't burning through their ammo too quickly.

"Those guys are going to force them to attack," said Gerber.

"Do we care?"

"Actually, I just wish they would withdraw. That would make life easier."

"We'd just have to give chase in the morning, or call for an arc light," said Bromhead. "Those bombers can really do some damage if they have a good target."

Gerber said, "I'm going back down to the north side."

"I thought you'd want to stay here to direct the fight?"

"John, this is your camp. You direct the fight. I'm just another soldier who can add his weapon to the defense."

When he had the chance, he climbed over the sandbags and down the ladder. He jogged to the north, took up a position between two of the bunkers, leaned forward onto the berm and waited for the attack to begin.

General Patterson had nearly burned through all his ammunition during the last assault. When the enemy was about a hundred meters away, he had switched to full auto. He was careful, aiming at the torsos of the enemy as he had learned so long ago. Center of mass. Might not kill, but it would put the enemy down. He remembered an instructor on the firing line say, "A sucking chest wound is God's way of telling you to slow down."

He saw one of the strikers with a bunch of bandoliers moving among the soldiers, handing out the additional ammo. He called to him, got his attention and waved him over. He saw the striker's eyes widen when he saw the stars on his collar. Patterson grinned at him and then took two of the bandoliers.

He draped them over his shoulders so that they hung, one on each side. "Thanks," he said, but he didn't know if the striker understood him.

Sergeant Major Stein, who had been in the communications bunker on orders from Patterson, left that area of relative safety. He moved along the north side of the berm. "General Patterson? Where are you?"

Patterson saw him and raised his weapon. "Over here, Stein," he yelled.

Stein hurried over. He was wearing a flak jacket, a steel pot and carrying a Colt .45 ACP in his left hand. It was the first time that Patterson had noticed that the sergeant major was left-handed and then wondered if Stein had injured his right hand. Stein knelt by the general, attempting to keep his head below the top of the berm.

"General, you have to come to the communications bunker."

"Why? Has there been a message from MACV?"

"No, sir. You know the reason. You have intelligence that is critical to planning a future operation."

"My place is here, Stein. You can monitor the radio communications. One of us should be there in case there are some specific questions."

There were sudden, loud explosions and both men ducked instinctively.

"They're about to attack again."

"Yes, General. Please come with me."

"Sergeant Major, either return to the commo bunker or grab a rifle." Patterson pointed to several M-16s that had been dropped by wounded soldiers. "Take one of those."

Stein holstered his pistol and picked up one of the weapons. "I haven't zeroed it."

"Doesn't matter. We just have to put out enough rounds to make it impossible for them to reach the berm. Find some extra ammo. There should be some spare magazines lying around."

"Yes, sir." Stein crawled off and found a dead soldier who had a bandolier next to him. Stein picked it up and then returned to Patterson. "General, you really should get out of here. You job is to get the intelligence to Saigon."

"Don't quote me, but I feel more alive now than I have in years."

"Yes, sir. Begging your pardon, sir, but you sound like an asshole."

"Good thing you're a sergeant major, Stein, otherwise you'd never get away with talking to me that way."

"Yes, sir."

Cornett sat in the anti-mortar bunker with his rifle set between his knees. His head was bowed, almost as if in prayer. He had listened to the mortar attacks and then the ground assault. He hadn't liked sitting in the bunker, but he was a pilot and not an infantry soldier. He'd had basic training and had been engaged by the enemy in hot LZs. The combat there lasted only two or three minutes. He'd had rounds smash the windshield or destroy part of the instrument panel. But his job had been to either pick up soldiers or drop them off. Once that happened, he lifted off and was out of range of the enemy quickly. He did not fire a weapon at them. His job was to fly the aircraft and not shoot at the enemy.

Now, he was in the bunker and not in the seat of a helicopter. He was waiting for those soldiers to hold the berm and turn the attack. If they failed and the enemy entered the camp, then his weapon would be one more in what he thought of as a last-ditch defense. In the dim light of the single light bulb dangling from the roof, he saw that his crew chief was getting antsy and didn't blame him.

"What's on your mind, Masters?"

"Sir, I don't like it in here waiting for the sky to fall on us."

"What do you suggest?"

"Sir, I think we should join the fight outside. On the berm."

Cornett grinned. "You looking for a Combat Infantryman Badge?"

"No, sir. I just want to join the fight."

"How about you, Owens?"

"I went to the Infantry Officer's Basic Course before flight school. But I'm thinking that I could contribute to the fight out there."

"Well, since we're on the ground and the helicopter is smoking debris in Cambodia, that's your decision."

"I don't think it's still smoking," said Masters.

There were only a few people in the bunker who were noncombatants. Cornett and his crew were not among them. He stood up and said, "Let's go see what we can do to help."

He moved to the small entrance, ducked, and climbed out of the bunker. He was surprised that the air was hotter than in the bunker. There was smoke drifting on a light breeze. That was from the burning buildings, from the explosions, and even from some of the old gunpowder fired by the older weapons used by the strikers. Cornett thought everyone had smokeless powder.

Once outside, the three of them ran to the entrance of the redoubt. They passed three bodies and one wounded man who was groaning. Masters slid to a stop and saw that the wound wasn't bad. He helped the man to his feet.

"I'm taking him to the dispensary. Where will you be?"

"On the berm somewhere. Find us if you can."

"Yes, sir."

Masters and the wounded man turned and ran deeper into the redoubt. The dispensary was built in a sandbagged hootch that had screens from about halfway to the roof. It had been built for the comfort of those inside. It was not built to withstand an enemy assault, but the roof was flat and covered with sandbags that would stop a mortar round.

The berm and part of the camp was bathed in the green light of the flares. The men on the berm were black blobs that were vaguely human shaped. Cornett ran to a point that looked as if it was poorly defended.

"We should hold here," said Owens. "Good field of fire and we're not the center of the attack if they attempt to use the broken concertina." He was looking at the number of bodies around the holes in the wire.

Cornett hit the berm, half diving for cover. He looked over the top and saw the bodies in the wire and the open kill zone. He didn't count but thought there were nearly a hundred of them. The fight was not going well for the enemy.

"We'll defend this little portion of the wall." He pointed to the right and Owens knelt there.

As Owens crouched near him, he said, "I went to flight school to avoid this sort of thing. I wanted a fight that I could get out of quickly if things went wrong, and a helicopter let me do that."

"Yeah, well, sometimes the war just gets in our way."

Kendall Stacy had left the bunker protecting the berm and found his way into the redoubt where he thought he would be safer. He'd taken refuge in the dispensary. To him it was one of the safest places on the camp. He crouched in a corner, a chest protector covering him from waist to chin. He'd found a steel pot and put it on. He didn't know where it came from, only that it had a strange odor of copper.

There was little light in the dispensary. The Special Forces sergeant, whose name he didn't know, was working by candlelight. He had bandaged the shoulder of one Vietnamese striker and was now examining the lower leg of another. That man was groaning, and the noise was beginning to unnerve Stacy.

Finally, he realized that he should be making notes and getting the names of those around him. He thought of the story it would make. He was in the middle of the defense of a Special Forces camp, right there with the Green Berets. He tried to think only of the story he would write, but the thought of some VC bursting into the dispensary and shooting everyone inside kept intruding. He couldn't concentrate on the idea of gathering information for a story.

He heard the sergeant suddenly curse. "Shit!" He threw the bandage he held on the floor. Stacy knew that the soldier had died. He didn't know why, but it was just another example of the fate that awaited him if the VC penetrated the berm. He didn't think about finding a weapon to defend himself. He had wrapped himself in the mantle of a noncombatant.

The sergeant looked around, but there were no more wounded to treat. The lull in the battle had reached the dispensary. Stacy hoped it was over but knew that it was not. They would be coming again, and he was sure that they would overrun the camp, killing every American they could find. He couldn't think beyond that scenario.

Captain James Cooper had stayed in the team house for the beginning of the fight. Since he had arrived believing that the major activity was the search for General Patterson, he had only brought a revolver with him. It held six shots, and he hadn't bothered to gather more ammo than the standard issue. In a firefight, his pistol wouldn't be of much use.

Although he hadn't thought about it, the pistol was a personal defense weapon. If one of the VC was to burst into the team house, he could engage him with his revolver. He didn't think about the enemy's advantage, which would be an AK-47. Cooper would just have to be quicker on the trigger. He didn't think about someone just tossing in a grenade.

With a couple of others, he sat on the floor so that no part of his body was exposed above the sandbag wall. The only danger he faced, as long as the enemy was outside the camp, was from the mortars, and they had stopped falling.

But Cooper was a soldier and part of the Army philosophy was that every soldier was a rifleman. No matter the source of the commission, every officer had some sort of basic rifle training. Prior to deployment to Vietnam, Cooper had qualified with both the .45 ACP and the M-16. He might not be an expert in the use of these weapons, he did know the basics. He could make himself useful outside, on the berm.

There was a lull in the fighting. The first assault had been beaten back, which was to be expected. The defense had not been degraded enough by the mortars and rockets. That first attack was more of a test of the camp's strength, and it had degraded the defense more.

He got up, moved to the door and opened it. There was a single body lying about ten yards away. Cooper thought there was a rifle near it. He dropped to the ground, ran to the body and grabbed the weapon. He didn't think about additional ammunition. He had a loaded rifle, and he was needed on the berm.

Sticking close to the redoubt for the protection, he ran to the entrance and then out into the main compound. There were scattered bodies and a fire or two burning, giving a flickering light. He halted there and then decided he'd head to the north.

He found more bodies and even a bandolier. He grabbed it and continued to the berm. He found a position between two of the bunkers and crouched there.

"Glad to see you made it, Captain."

He looked up and saw Patterson. "Surprised to see you here, General."

"Just doing my duty."

Cooper didn't have an immediate response for that. He had thought that the general, after his ordeal of the last few days, might have holed up in one of the bunkers. He just said, "My thought exactly."

Colonel Nguyen of the People's Army of Vietnam knew that he either had to overrun the camp with this attack or disengage until more soldiers could join him. There were other elements of the division moving south into Cambodia and then Vietnam. They were taking up their positions for the assault on Saigon, but Nguyen's assignment had been to destroy this obstacle that was in their way as they approached Saigon.

The companies and regiments were taking up their positions for what would be the final all-out assault. Some were still in the jungle but had to slide to the left to avoid the small fires that had been started by the napalm attacks. Those were dying and wouldn't have caused too much trouble. Nguyen didn't want his soldiers to see the burned bodies of those killed in the attack. He knew that discouraged heroism.

His aide returned. "All units are in position and ready, sir. They await your orders."

Nguyen nodded and looked right and left. There wasn't much for him to see. He had to take the word of his aide and the information given to him by the commanders. But he was hesitant to launch the attack. The American camp was stronger than they had thought. The intelligence provided in Hanoi wasn't as complete as it could be.

A bugler was standing behind him. Nguyen finally gave the order. "Signal the assault."

The bugler lifted his instrument and blew four notes. That was picked up by others and joined by whistles and a cry from the men. They leaped up and began the rush toward the camp. They stormed out of the jungles and flowed across the open ground, ignoring the American defense.

They were about halfway to the wire when mortars began to fall among them, tearing holes in their ranks. Even with their fellows falling around them, they continued, screaming as if trying to frighten the defenders with noise. Those in the front ranks began firing their weapons from the hip, ripping through their magazines. Some held the trigger until the weapon was empty but didn't think about reloading.

To them it looked as if the berm erupted in fire. Some were firing on full automatic while others were using single shots. The heavy machine guns protected by the bunkers raked the attackers. But taking heavy casualties, they came on. They reached the first strand of concertina. They filtered into holes ripped in it and the soldiers ran past it. It channeled them into lanes of concentrated fire.

Nguyen, watching from the safety of the jungle, wanted to cheer his soldiers on, but that would have looked undignified. They were getting closer to overrunning the berm and once that happened, the camp would fall, he was sure of it. All they had to do was breach the berm and the camp would be his.

His aide, a young captain, was not that restrained. He pumped a fist in the air and yelled, "We've got them. That can't stop us now. We going to win!"

Nguyen had been around long enough to know that the battle wasn't won until the enemy was utterly defeated. The battle would be lost or won in the next twenty or thirty minutes. It depended on how well trained the strikers inside the camp were and what tricks the Americans could pull out of their large bag of tricks. Nguyen now believed that he was going to win, but he was not going to let anyone see him celebrating until the last shot was fired and his flag flew over the camp. He would wait until he walked through the remains of the camp to ensure that the victory was complete.

CHAPTER 20

Bromhead didn't like standing in the fire control tower because he thought it removed him from the action on the ground. The other problem was that the fire control tower left him exposed to enemy fire. They could use it as an aiming point for their mortars and they knew the purpose of the tower. They had tried several times to destroy it with their 12.7mm heavy machine guns. Bromhead wanted to be on the ground, where the action was, rather than twenty-five feet above it in an exposed position.

In the light of the fires started by the napalm attacks at the edge of the jungle, he saw the shadows of the enemy as they assembled for the next attack. Using the field phone, he called the mortar pits, ordering them to fire HE rounds at the edge of the jungle. He wanted to disrupt the NVA formations and cause as much confusion as possible.

There were bugle calls and whistles and a sudden roar as the NVA soldiers rushed out of the jungle and over the open killing ground. Those in the front of the wave were firing their weapons as they ran, but it was haphazard, unaimed, and ineffective.

The response from the strikers on the north side of the camp was sporadic. They were allowing the enemy to get closer to the wire where the enemy would be slowed, and they could be engaged effectively. One, then the other M-2 .50-caliber machine guns opened fire, raking the attackers. The red tracers flashed out, some hitting the ground and bouncing high into the night sky.

There were more flares overhead, their strange green light creating dancing shadows on the ground. For just an instant, Bromhead was captivated by the fireworks-like displays of all the weapons firing, the green tracers of the enemy weapons, and the yellow of their muzzle flashes.

A burst from an enemy heavy weapon again raked the sandbags on the fire control tower, ripping some of them to shreds. As they spilled the sand, part of the protective wall collapsed. Bromhead was crouching behind the intact wall, watching as the assault crossed the killing ground, but realized the tower would soon be useless.

General Patterson leaned on the berm, his weapon resting on the top. He didn't fire until the first of the wave hit the concertina wire protecting the camp. There was enough light so that he could use the iron sights of his M-16. He aimed at the chests of the attackers. He didn't wait to see if he had hit the target, moving the sights to the next man and firing again. He kept at it until he emptied the magazine. He then reloaded, scanned the enemy lines and opened fire again.

Sergeant Major Stein was standing next to him. Stein believed his role in the fight was to protect the general and nothing more. He wasn't firing at the enemy but watching for threats to the general. There was no one close enough to injure the general, but Stein knew the principle of the Golden BB. A round that comes out of nowhere. It isn't aimed, it isn't planned, just a random shot that strikes the target. Stein couldn't stop the Golden BB, but he could make sure that none of the enemy soldiers got close enough to the general to kill him.

Gerber was at the berm on the north side of the camp. This

wasn't a single battalion coming at them. He saw that it was an entire regiment, possibly two. It was an overwhelming force designed to overrun the berm quickly. He didn't think they would be able to hold if they didn't get more air support.

He turned and ran toward the redoubt. He stopped there for a moment and then sprinted to the communications bunker. Inside, he found the commo sergeant and asked, "Who is standing by? We have a gun team nearby?"

"We have the Magicians about ten out. Heavy gun team."

"Armament?"

"Miniguns and two-point-seven-five rockets. There is a Super Spooky on the way but he's maybe thirty out. Maybe less."

"Okay," said Gerber. "Okay. We need to hold for ten minutes before we get more air support?"

"Yes, sir."

"Tay Ninh arty standing by?"

"They've been putting up the flares."

Gerber walked around the desk and grabbed the microphone. He said, "Magician Lead, this is Eagle Command."

There was a slight delay. "Eagle, this is Magician Five Six."

"Five Six, I'm shutting down Tay Ninh arty. There are no gun target lines to worry about. The north side is under heavy attack. They're in the wire and we need suppression there immediately."

"Roger that."

Gerber looked at the commo sergeant. "What freqs are they on?"

The sergeant consulted a small booklet. Before he could answer, there was an explosion that shook the dirt from overhead. He grinned and said, "That was close."

The communications sergeant flipped through the SOI. "I got it."

"Can we listen in?" asked Gerber.

The sergeant tuned one of the radios. There was a tuning squeal that lasted a few seconds and then the voice of Magician Five Six came through.

"Rolling over to one hundred knots."

"Got the camp in sight. We'll come in from the east, working to the west."

"Roger."

Gerber said, "They got here fast."

"Five Six is rolling in."

Gerber, in the bunker, couldn't hear any change in the noise from outside. It was just a continual roar punctuated by the detonation of a mortar round fired by the enemy. He turned, staring up at the northern side of the bunker. He couldn't see anything.

"Five Six, you're taking fire from your five. Looks like a fifty."

"Roger. Breaking left. Can you hit it?"

Then, from one of the other radios, "Eagle. Eagle. This is Bird Dog Four. We're five out."

"Roger. Say ordnance."

"We have napalm and fifties."

"We have a heavy gun team working the north side."

"Roger that."

From the first radio, "We're taking heavy fire."

"I see it. I'll get it."

"Crap," said Gerber. "That's more than a couple of regiments out there. Maybe a division."

"Can we hold?"

Gerber shrugged but said, "With the air support, especially if that Super Spooky can get here."

Fetterman stood just inside the tree line. The enemy didn't know that he was there. He watched the assault begin as the enemy ran across the killing field. When the enemy reached the wire, Fetterman ordered the strikers, "Be sure of your targets and open fire."

He didn't fire but stood behind the line, watching the enemy reaction. They were confused, first by the gunships attacking them and then by the strikers in the trees. Fetterman's main concern was that the enemy commander would attack his small force. Fetterman knew they were in a vulnerable position, but they had good cover. Even if the attack on them was large, they would be able to hold, continuing to cause trouble. Anything that caused the enemy to split his force was helpful to the defenders.

The enemy was in the wire. The gunships were creating gaps on the attacking wave, but they were taking heavy fire. One of the gunships broke his firing run early. His wingman didn't get turned in fast enough to cover the break. The enemy fire raked the bottom of the aircraft and Fetterman thought he saw flames near the rotor. If there was any fire there, it disappeared quickly.

The gunship aimed for the runway, near the wrecked helicopter. The gunship flared out, leveled the skids and dropped about ten feet to a hard landing. The rotor flexed down, and it looked as if it was going to cut off tail rotor.

As the blades stopped moving, the crew leaped out, running for the camp. The enemy attacking didn't see them. They reached the berm and scrambled over the top. They disappeared. They were safe for the moment.

"We have movement."

Fetterman turned his attention to his right. They were about to be attacked on their flank. Fetterman had prepared for that. He said, "When you have a target, take it."

There was only sporadic firing until the enemy was closer. They put out aimed rounds and turned back the assault, though it was more of a probe than an attack. The enemy attempting to learn the strength of the unit.

Fetterman stood behind the strikers, watching. He was searching for flaws in the defense, but the strikers stopped the assault. The enemy fell back, not in a rout, but in a disciplined retreat.

To those strikers, he said, "Hold your fire. Keep watch. If you have a target, take it."

He turned his attention back to the main force. They were still firing at the enemy attacking the camp. But now they were taking some fire themselves. It wasn't well aimed, most of it over their heads. There was no move to attack from that area. It was more like a suppressive fire than anything else. The enemy wanted the strikers to take cover.

Fetterman knelt by a large tree, his free hand on it. He held his M-16 in his right hand, holding onto the pistol grip. He didn't say anything. Lieutenant Nguyen had taken charge and Fetterman could find no fault with his orders.

Colonel Nguyen was confused by the firefight that had developed on his flank. His enemy was not moving toward him. They were holding their position. There others, firing into the flanks of his assault force but he didn't think they were inflicting many casualties. The trick now was to get over the berm. It was the only way to win the fight. They had to get into the camp.

The helicopters had slowed the attack, but they had shot down one of them and the other two had flown away. Nguyen didn't know why, only that they were gone. The firing from the camp had intensified, but his soldiers were continuing the attack. He knew they were taking heavy casualties, but the attack hadn't broken. His soldiers were about to storm the berm, and they should be able to overwhelm it in seconds.

One of the company commanders who was being held in reserve approached. "General, we have enemy on the flank."

"I know this."

"Do you want me to wipe them out?"

"No. You remain in reserve. They are not moving on us. We'll take care of them as soon as we have overrun the camp's outer defense."

"They are shooting our soldiers."

"They are a distraction. They are not overly dangerous." Nguyen fell silent and then glanced to the left. "Break off a platoon. They are not to overrun the position. They are to stay back but engage from a distance. I don't want them to advance on us and if they're busy with your platoon, they won't be a danger to the attacking force."

"Yes, sir." The officer jogged back to his company.

"Is that a good idea, sir?" asked the aide when the company commander was gone.

"Of course. Those puppet soldiers on our left are not a threat to us. We'll hold them in place and deal with them later. Much easier that way."

"Yes, sir."

His soldiers had penetrated to the third strand of concertina. Many were kneeling or laying prone, exchanging fire with the defenders. Mortars were still falling, but they were overshooting the main body and having little effect. He wished he could silence them but that would happen when they took the camp.

"Get the artillery officer over here."

The aide ran off, disappearing into the darkness, beyond the dying flames from the napalm. He returned in minutes with another officer.

Nguyen asked, "What can you do about the enemy mortars?"

The man looked at the camp. The mortar pits had to be in the redoubt. He said, "I can try to put some rounds into the area where their mortars are located."

"Do it and keep firing until our men have overrun the outer defense. I don't want our mortars to kill or injure our soldiers."

"Yes, sir. Not a problem." He ran back toward his own mortars.

Nguyen said, "These puppet soldiers are putting up a better fight than I expected. They usually run when hard-pressed."

"This is a Special Forces camp. They are better trained."

There was a rattling in the trees above them. The aide threw himself prone, but Nguyen just crouched, taking a knee. He wanted to watch as the fight developed as his men pushed their way through the wire.

Bromhead lost communications with the rest of the camp. His radio had taken two rounds through it and the wires to the field phone had been cut at some point. He was doing nothing useful in the fire control tower. He wanted to get to the north side where the real fight was developing. He knew Gerber would be there, but it was his camp. He needed to be there. He was in command.

He wanted to wait for a lull in the fighting, but the enemy was getting too close to the berm. There wouldn't be a lull. Instead, he pushed some of the sandbags out of the way, climbed over others, and then slid down the ladder. On the ground, he listened for a moment but couldn't hear any mortars firing. Bending over, like a man trying to run against a hurricane-force wind, he headed to the entrance of the redoubt. Beyond it, there was nothing to see other than a few bodies.

Glancing up, he noticed that the flares were burning out. Tay Ninh arty wouldn't fire any more unless he requested them. He ran toward the north side of the camp, dodging around wreckage and bodies. He reached the berm, leaned forward, and aimed over the top of it. There were almost too many enemy in the wire, working toward him, screaming, firing and dodging. More bugles and whistles. This was the final push.

He found Patterson kneeling between two bunkers, firing at the NVA on single shot. Patterson hit one soldier, turned slightly, and dropped another. Stein was next to him. Bromhead yelled, "What we got?"

"Too many of them. I don't think we're going to stop them this time."

"We only need to hold them a little longer."

Stein glanced at him and then at the top of the berm. A man stood there, aiming down at Patterson. Stein shot him and said, "That's one for me."

That was the last thing he said. A round caught him just below the helmet. Stein dropped and didn't move. Patterson looked down at him and said, "Dammit, Frank. You should have stayed in the bunker like I told you." There was little emotion in his voice.

Without thinking, Bromhead moved his thumb to the selector switch on his weapon. He switched from single shot to full auto. He aimed at the men in the wire and pulled the trigger.

In the communications bunker, Gerber kept working the radios. There were fast movers on standby, but Gerber wanted the Super Spooky. He'd use Bird Dog flight to mop up. He called the Spooky. "Spooky, this is Eagle. Where are you?"

"I have just arrived on station. Where do you want it?"

"Dump everything you can on the north side. They are about to overrun the berm."

"Roger."

Gerber wanted to go out to watch but he needed to stay on the radio. He heard the first run. It sounded like half a dozen giant buzz saws starting up. There would be a stream of ruby-colored tracers that looked like the red ray working the ground. If Super Spooky did his job, that could break the back of the assault. The miniguns were putting out thousands of rounds a minute. It was hard for enemy in the open to withstand that sort of an aerial assault.

Outside, the pilot of the Super Spooky, a C-130 aircraft that had been converted to a combat platform, held miniguns and even a 105mm howitzer, orbited to north of the camp. They were over the jungle, firing down at the enemy in the wire. The aircraft turned, keeping the guns on target, raking the enemy in the wire with a devastating fire.

He could see the green tracers from the enemy weapons firing up at him. They were huge, watermelon-sized rounds that looked closer than they were. Over the intercom, he heard, "We are taking fire on the right."

"Kill it."

"Consider it done."

Two of the miniguns on his aircraft engaged the antiaircraft guns. The stream of green disappeared. He didn't know if they had eliminated the threat, or if the enemy had stopped shooting up at him.

"We got him."

"Roger."

They completed an orbit and turned back. The miniguns worked the enemy on the ground. The pilot couldn't see much. He was keeping his eyes on the instruments.

"Getting low on ammo, sir."

"Roger."

He turned again, letting the other gunners take up the suppression. When he completed the orbit, he used the radio. "Eagle, this is Spooky, we are leaving the area."

"Thank you, Spooky."

Gerber didn't know what the situation was outside. He thought that Spooky would have broken the current assault, but he didn't know. There was still firing out there.

"Bird Dog, this is Eagle Command."

"Go."

"Situation is the same. Need the ordnance on the north side."

"Roger. We have that in sight. We'll be rolling in."

Fetterman, with his small blocking force, watched the destruction of the enemy assault force. As the enemy pressed forward, toward the berm, they were met with a wall of fire. The heavy machine guns in the bunkers were tearing gaps on the attacking force. There was little return fire as the enemy tried to reach the berm. Once there, they'd then be safe from the fifties in the bunkers.

Some of the enemy soldiers reached the berm and scrambled to the top. A few made it into the camp, but others were cut down immediately. The attack stalled and then fell apart. Those who survived the Super Spooky had turned and were fleeing. They were no longer a fighting force, but a mob trying to get out of the line of fire.

Those who had been sniping at his platoon stopped shooting. Fetterman was sure that they had been recalled. The enemy commander was trying to save what remained of his force. They had been badly mauled and had been unable to overrun the berm. That final attack had failed. The enemy commander knew that he must preserve what remained of his force.

Jets flashed over, raking the ground with machine-gun fire. The first pulled up into a spiraling climb while another dropped napalm. The clouds of flame erupted at the edge of the wire. Fetterman thought it was too close to the camp, but he was sure that the pilots knew what they were doing.

Firing from the camp had slowed and was now sporadic. The enemy was disappearing.

Colonel Nguyen watched the destruction of his attacking force. He had expected to overrun the camp quickly, but that had failed. He planned for the massive assault succeed, but the air support had turned the momentum. His soldiers couldn't stand up to the onslaught the Americans could throw at them.

He took a deep breath and told his aide, "We need to get out of here." He couldn't keep the sadness, the defeat, out of his voice.

"Yes, sir."

"The company on the far west will lead the maneuver to Cambodia so that we can connect with the other forces there."

"Where will you be, sir?"

Nguyen wanted to run down, across the open ground in a one-man assault, but that would do no good. The only way he could recover from this disaster was to lead what remained of his command out of Vietnam. He could recoup the loss, but he would have to lead a successful attack on the camp. He'd need a larger force, and they would have to plan the attack better.

The aide ran off, to give orders to the other officers. Nguyen watched him disappear into the jungle. He noticed that the sky was beginning to brighten. He knew that he had to win by dawn, or he would have to withdraw. That just wasn't going to happen now. The only move left for him was to flee to Cambodia.

Fetterman knew that the enemy was beginning to fade away. Those that had been near his platoon were gone. He found Lieutenant Nguyen and said, "We should shadow the enemy. We might be able to get more air support to follow up."

"There are many of them."

"Yes. We need to be careful. Send three squads back. We'll hang back and trail them. It will be easy to follow from a distance."

Nguyen almost said, "Yes, sir," then remembered that Fetterman was an NCO. Instead he said, "We don't need to follow. They will leave many sign."

"Yes. That's why we can hang back. We'll continue until Captain Bromhead recalls us."

"I give orders." Nguyen turned and ran off to give the orders.

Fetterman sat down on a thick log. He realized that it was slightly chilly and wondered about that. It was early morning, getting lighter rapidly. He wasn't sure how far he should follow the enemy. It might not even be necessary, but Fetterman thought he should ensure that the enemy was withdrawing.

*

Gerber left the communications bunker. Lieutenant Carson, Bromhead's exec, was now in the bunker. Gerber had told him, "We have several gun teams on standby. I don't think we'll need them."

"Yes, sir."

"Remain here. Answer their questions if they ask them. Either Captain Bromhead or I will let you know when you can release them. That shouldn't be long."

"I understand."

Gerber couldn't help grinning. "I think we critically damaged the better part of two, maybe three regiments. I suspect they are retreating to Cambodia. Sergeant Major Fetterman will let us know."

Carson, on his first tour, smiled back at Gerber. "Quite the fight."

"And we won. We hold the camp, and the enemy is leaving the field."

"Yes, sir."

CHAPTER 21

General Dekker was pacing his office. He was more than annoyed. He was flat-out angry. There had been no word from General Patterson who had critical information. Dekker knew that they should have used the LRRPs or the Special Forces and not a general who was in a midlife crisis and wanted to play soldier one last time. That job was for younger men who had not been tested by combat. Patterson had been through that in Korea. Now, he should be sitting in an air-conditioned office ordering those younger men into the field instead of going out there himself.

Dekker walked to the window and looked out. The sun was coming up and he didn't know where Patterson was but thought he was still at the Special Forces camp. He turned toward the door and yelled, "Sergeant Major!"

"Yes, sir."

"General Patterson?"

"The last word was that he was still at the Special Forces camp."

"Why is he still there?"

"They're under heavy attack. They've called for air support and there is a battalion of the First Cav standing by at Tay Ninh in case they need reinforcements."

Dekker glared at the man. "And you didn't bother to share this critical intelligence with me because...?"

"There was nothing that could be done, sir, and I was waiting for additional information."

"Okay," said Dekker. "Here's what I want. I want the latest communication for that camp. I want a C-123 standing by, no, I want it airborne and heading to that camp —"

The sergeant major, knowing that Dekker hated being interrupted, said, "Wouldn't a helicopter be faster? Could come from Tay Ninh?"

Dekker's voice turned icy. "If I need input from you, Sergeant Major, I will give you permission to speak."

"Yes, sir."

"The C-123 will be able to get from that camp faster than a Huey. That's why I want it in the air now."

"Yes, sir. I'll get with Colonel Evans to arrange the flight."

"Did I say anything about bringing the Air Force into this. Use Army assets."

"Yes, sir. But the Army doesn't have any C-123s. All those assets were passed on to the Air Force a while back."

"Just how in the hell do you know that, Sergeant Major?"

"It was one of those things that has been mentioned in the past. I remember I looked it up because it didn't sound right to me, but it was."

Dekker was about to make another suggestion but thought better of it. He needed more information. "The priority is this. Status of the fight and then orders to Evans for the C-123 support."

As the sergeant major turned to go, Dekker said, "And don't ever interrupt me like that again. If you do, you'll learn that a Sergeant First Class does not have the prestige of a Sergeant Major and many of them are stuck at fire-support bases living in sandbagged bunkers for their entire tours."

"Yes, sir."

Colonel Nguyen thought about a rear guard. He thought that

the Americans and the puppet soldiers might give chase. But he still commanded hundreds of NVA soldiers and that was a formidable force. His mission now was to get out of South Vietnam without any more losses. He believed that the enemy would not follow. They had been severely weakened by the attack but then, they still held the camp.

Nguyen was in the middle of his formation. They were scattered now, using what he had learned in his study of other guerrilla forces. The Native Americans would break their war party into two parts as they escaped. And then into four parts and continue that until they had fragmented to the point where the war parties were too small to chase and those giving chase gave up.

He was using that strategy. Regiments broken into companies and companies into platoons and then into squads. Each leader knew where the rally point was in Cambodia, and all were attempting to get there by separate routes.

There were very few wounded with them to slow them. He hadn't liked leaving his soldiers behind, but knew the Americans would not kill them. The strikers might, if the American leadership was weak, but the Americans would consider them intelligence assets. None of the men left knew the overall strategy, only that they had left Hanoi long ago and marched south to attack the camp.

As the sun came up, they shifted to trails deeper in the jungle. Now it was a question of making time. If they could reach the Cambodian border before any American aircraft spotted them, they would be safe. The Americans had a thing about crossing invisible lines on the ground.

Nguyen turned to his aide. "About two hours, if we hurry."

"Yes, sir."

Nguyen was sure that once they were at the border, where another division waited, they would be able to repel any attack by the Americans, as long as the Americans didn't have close air support. Air power changed the dynamics of the situation.

Carson left the commo bunker. In the growing daylight, he was surprised by the extent of the damage to the camp. Most of the striker's bodies had been carried to a makeshift morgue. The fires had either been extinguished or had died out after they burned all the fuel. Smoke hung close to the ground, but the morning breeze would blow it away quickly.

He hurried to the team house and found both Bromhead and Gerber sitting at a table. They looked tired and were just sitting there quietly. Neither of them moved when he entered. They didn't even look up.

"I've had a message from MACV…"

"Wondering where our after-action report is?"

"Telling us that a C-123 is coming in to evac General Patterson. Where is he?"

"He was at the dispensary. His sergeant major was badly wounded," said Bromhead.

"I think he was killed," said Gerber. "Looked like a head wound. Patterson insisted on taking him to the dispensary once the attack broke."

"I'll go alert him."

As Carson left, Bromhead asked, "Why are they sending a C-123 for him?"

"Because he's a general and they think he'll be able to give them the straight poop on what happened here."

"And what happened?"

"We survived a rather heavy attack."

"Where's Sergeant Major Fetterman?"

"Chasing the enemy with a squad. He's hanging back and aware that there might be an ambush waiting on the trail. I told him that once he has a sense of where they are going, to break off the pursuit." Gerber grinned. "Just the other day he was telling me he was too old for this and was thinking about retiring. Now, he's in the jungle chasing the enemy like he's twenty years old, not to mention that he'd been at it for more than twenty-four hours."

Fetterman was on point. He believed he understood the enemy better than the strikers with him even though they were Vietnamese. Fetterman was an experienced combat soldier and those he was chasing were also experienced. Fetterman understood asymmetrical warfare better than most because of his training and experience. And he understood that a retreating force would have a rear guard. Fetterman didn't want to run into that rear guard because he would be outnumbered.

The trail left by the enemy had diverged three times, but the main force was the one he was following. He moved slowly, listening to the jungle around him. If he was getting close to the enemy, there would be clues. It was his job to make sure they didn't walk into an ambush.

He thought he saw a flash of metal in front of him. He held up a closed fist, telling the strikers to halt in place. He dropped to a knee and turned his head right and left, letting his peripheral vision pick up on the movement. There was a shadow fifty or sixty meters in front of him that didn't look natural. It almost blended with the environment but not quite. Good camouflage could do that, but the shadow had a human look to it.

Slowly, watching for other movement, he slipped the safety off his M-16 and raised his weapon. He drew a bead, aiming carefully, and squeezed the trigger. An instant later the shape disappeared. Fetterman was sure that he had hit it.

Firing erupted as a dozen or more AK-47s opened up on full auto. It was poorly aimed and missed completely. The rounds snapped overhead, striking trees. Leaves fell and birds took off, screeching.

The strikers held their fire, waiting for good targets, but there were none to see. Muzzle flashes sparkled but didn't reveal much. Then suddenly there were men crashing through the jungle, running at them. Without an order, the strikers opened fire. That surprised the enemy, and they dropped behind the cover available. If they knew what they were doing, they'd try to flank Fetterman's tiny force.

Using hand signals, Fetterman ordered the strikers to fall back. He didn't want to get into an extended firefight with a superior enemy force. Quietly, they withdrew a hundred meters and waited. Lieutenant Nguyen leading them.

Fetterman saw an NVA soldier, dressed in khaki, moving toward him. Fetterman kept an eye on him and when he kept coming, aimed at the enemy's chest. The man was big for a Vietnamese and Fetterman wondered if he might be a Chinese advisor. There was intelligence value in capturing him, but that was impossible, given the circumstances. Of course, insignia from his uniform and any papers or documents he had on him would be of intelligence value. Fetterman didn't expect to find any of that. An experienced soldier would not carry that into combat. Special Forces soldiers often removed all their insignia before they entered the field.

When the man was thirty meters away, Fetterman fired. He saw dust fly off the uniform as the man fell. Fetterman didn't wait. He waved to the strikers, telling them to retreat. Now, Fetterman became their rear guard.

But there was no pursuit. The enemy rear guard had done its job, halting Fetterman's tiny band. Fetterman had learned what he wanted to know. He wished he could have checked the body of the man in khaki, but the risk was too great.

He caught up to the strikers, took the point, and began leading them back to their camp. Then he fell back. He knelt near a thick tree, watching and waiting. He wanted to set a mechanical ambush, but didn't have the time. He only had a single grenade and not much line for a trip wire. It would be a difficult task and would end up as a danger to the local farmers and not the VC or NVA.

Instead, he waited and when he sensed the enemy was near, fired a long burst, spraying the trees like a man watering his shrubs. He didn't expect to hit anyone, he just wanted to slow them down.

He stood and backed up several feet. He didn't see any of the enemy and was sure they were working to flank him. He turned and fled into the jungle, hurrying after the rest of the strikers. He knew that the enemy wouldn't follow much longer. Their job was to protect the rear of the formation and not chase others through the jungle.

Fifteen minutes later, he caught the strikers. They had stopped for a quick rest and to wait for him. He told Lieutenant Nguyen, "We're in the clear. Let's get back to the camp."

Bromhead found Becker and his flight crew on the eastern side of the berm. In the wire beyond them, and along the runway, there were a few scattered bodies. The enemy had not made a big push toward that area. Fetterman's force in the jungle had discouraged them. It was more like a diversionary attack to keep them where they were so they couldn't reinforce the north side of the camp, but it had never developed.

As he approached, Becker stood. There was a smear of black on his face, near his right eye. He had lost his cap and wasn't wearing a steel pot, but had on his chicken plate. "There is a C-123 coming in soon. I thought you and your crew might like a ride out of here," Bromhead said without preamble.

"Okay. Yes, sir. Okay. We would be grateful for the lift."

"Might not be able to take you to your base, but they can get you to a place where you can arrange transport."

Becker thought that over. "Might be easier to get a Huey in here, sir."

"I'm not sure, considering the circumstances. You and your crew are welcome in the team house for breakfast."

"Okay. I thought I might go to the commo bunker to see if I can get in touch with our operations."

"If that fails, let me know. There is space on the C-123 if you want to take that option."

Becker nodded and then asked, "What about the wounded?"

"We'll get the critical wounded out on Medevac helicopters. We can treat the others here. I think we've got a doctor coming in to assist." Bromhead grinned. "Well, the doctor will take over."

"Yes, sir."

Gerber found General Patterson in the dispensary with the body of Sergeant Major Stein. He was just sitting there; the body bag was on the gurney but it was zipped closed. Patterson didn't look up when Gerber entered.

"There is a C-123 coming in for you, General. I have assumed that you'll want to get those flight crews out along with some of the wounded."

Patterson didn't move. Finally, he said, "He was a good man. He was a good friend, or as good a friend as he could be given the differences in our ranks. Sergeant majors are at the top of the enlisted grades. Made it easier."

Gerber stood quietly but then said, "We're in a dangerous occupation."

"Yes, but Stein didn't have to come out with me. I lost my aide and now my friend. He could have stayed in Saigon, but he insisted on coming. Saved my life here."

"I think that we all can say that. We have all lost friends who saved our lives."

"I knew him a long time, Major. This just isn't right."

"Yes, sir."

Finally, Patterson looked up at Gerber. "I want him to go out with me. I need to take him home."

"The aircraft can accommodate him without a problem. Why don't you come over to the team house?"

"No. I'll stay with Franklin."

"I'll have someone tell you when the aircraft is inbound. We'll want to get it off the ground as quickly as we can."

"I'll be here."

Gerber understood the emotion. The battle was over and there was now time to reflect. He'd been through it himself. Without another word, he turned and left the dispensary and wondered where Fetterman was.

Bromhead found Cornett in the team house, sitting with his flight crew, eating Cheerios. He pulled a chair around and sat down. "We have a C-123 coming in and it can take your crew out of here."

"Won't be soon enough," said Owens.

Cornett gave Owens a dirty look but said, "Is it always like this?"

"It's been a bit more exciting than usual. We take a few mortars, and the strikers sometimes run into the enemy, but mostly they don't throw human wave attacks at us."

"I would have thought, by now, they would have learned that they have to fight more than just the people in the camp."

Bromhead was going to respond but then didn't. Instead, he said, "You'll be on your way in about an hour or so. You can arrange for transport back to your unit when you get to Saigon."

"That won't be a problem," said Cornett. "I just hope they don't charge me for losing the aircraft."

"They can do that?"

Cornett smiled. "I suppose they can, but the loss was combat-related. I think that if I had lost it through negligence, they might try that. Probably get a flight evaluation board and if the accident was my fault, they might remove me from flight status. That really doesn't happen much."

"I should look into that. I'm signed for all the equipment here. Wonder what losses they might try to stick me with."

"Loss due to combat. You should be clear, Captain."

"I'll just pass the buck up to Major Gerber. Let him deal with the paperwork."

"There you go," said Cornett.

"If you'll excuse me, I need to go arrange for some patrols. We need to make sure that there are no enemy lingering around to cause trouble and I need to alert the gun team they can get out with you."

"After all that, you need to patrol the area? Why not just get a Huey or two to look around?"

"Now that you mention it, I'll do that too. Thanks for the idea."

Cornett shrugged as if it was no big deal.

Kendall Stacy, who had stayed in the dispensary during the height of the attack, finally moved to the team house when it was evident that the attack was over. He hadn't heard a shot fired in fifteen minutes and had noticed a change in the attitude of the soldiers. They knew the attack was over.

In the team house he found one of the flight crews and the senior Green Berets eating breakfast. He wasn't sure why they were eating. He had no appetite himself. The events of the night, the utter fright he had felt, was still too fresh in his mind.

One of the sergeants, he didn't know which one, said, "Well, look what the cat dragged in."

"Where have you been?" asked Bromhead.

"In the dispensary. I saw General Patterson there —"

"And what were you doing in the dispensary?"

"Whatever I could," said Stacy. The statement covered much. He hadn't been helping, but he had been staying out of the way, which was what he could do.

He realized that he was still a reporter and pulled out a small notebook and a pen that had survived the night with him. He looked at Bromhead and asked, "What did you see last night?"

"Everything."

"That's not much of an answer."

"It's as complete as the one you just provided. I'm not in the mood to talk about last night with you."

Stacy suddenly understood what was happening. These men had been involved in the defense, and he hadn't even done his job as a reporter. He had been hiding in the dispensary during the fight. They weren't going to answer his questions. It didn't matter to him. He could deduce enough that he could write a convincing story. One that none of the men here would ever see and therefore couldn't contradict. He'd just walk around the camp, see what he could see and talk to those who would talk. Then he'd get out, back to Saigon. He'd be able to write a good story there.

He closed his notebook and stood up. "I'll see you later." He left the team house and made his way to the runway where he found Becker and his flight crew. He approached them and found them far less reluctant to talk. They'd make his story for him.

Captain Cooper, who hadn't done much during the fight, was in the communications bunker. He was trying to get through to Saigon. His job — to learn what he could about Patterson — had been completed hours earlier when Patterson was brought to the camp. He hadn't been able to communicate that information to Colonel Evans then and had been with Becker and his crew on the east side of the camp near the runway. There hadn't been much action there, but he had engaged the enemy with his revolver. He didn't think he had inflicted any damage or hit anyone, but he had been there and had been shooting.

But with the sun coming up, it was clear that the camp had repelled the attacks. Given that things had slowed, he thought he now had his chance to contact Saigon. He walked over to the communications bunker and passed the damage to the camp and a few bodies of enemy soldiers. He hadn't known that any of them had penetrated the berm. That surprised him.

When he asked about contacting Saigon, the communications NCO said, "Radio contact with Saigon is weak, right now, sir. I can keep trying. You have permission from Captain Bromhead?"

"I haven't seen him this morning," said Cooper. "I just want to report that General Patterson is here and is safe."

"Yes, sir. I'll check with Captain Bromhead."

Cooper, about to lose his temper, said, "I'll check with Captain Bromhead. Do you know where he is?"

"Probably in the team house."

"Thanks."

He did find Bromhead in the team house. When Bromhead saw him, he asked, "Where have you been?"

"With that helicopter crew by the runway."

"You see much there?"

"There was a weak feint toward us, but we were able to beat it back. I don't think anyone there was hurt."

Bromhead waved at one of the empty chairs. "Have a seat and join us for a little breakfast."

"I'd like to get in touch with Colonel Evans and let him know that we have General Patterson here."

"I think they already know that."

"Still, I'd like to report that. Your NCO said that I needed your permission."

"Well, he's technically correct on that point. You tell him that I have no objection to you reporting to your boss. Don't talk about the assault here last night and do suggest that General Patterson is gone."

"Is that true?"

"He's in the dispensary with his sergeant major who was killed in the fighting. He'll be flying out of here as soon as the 123 gets here. I don't want to let anyone know that he's still on the camp."

Cooper shook his head as if he didn't understand. "I'll just report he's been recovered and is in good health."

"Tell the sergeant that I said you could pass along your message."

"Thanks."

Gerber was waiting at the gate when Fetterman and the strikers returned. The C-123 had been in and gone. Hueys had taken out some of the critically wounded and there had been a couple of reconnaissance flights around the camp looking for any of the enemy who might be close. None had been found. The patrols had been out and returned. Some of the strikers had been checking the bodies out in the field, looking for items of intelligence value, looking for wounded that might be saved with medical attention, and counting the dead. And more than one of them was taking anything of value from the bodies that they could find.

Fetterman was the last of his patrol to enter the camp. Lieutenant Nguyen had led them in. He had stopped near Gerber, who just waved him on so that he could report to his superior officer.

When Fetterman was close, Gerber said, "I thought you were getting too old for this?"

"I did too, and I was right. This is a young man's game."

"You look tired, Tony. Tired and dirty."

Fetterman ignored the comment. "How close was it in here?"

"A little closer than I cared for. We had good artillery support, and the gunships did a fine job. Super Spooky broke their back with his miniguns. I'm not sure we could have held without Spooky, but he sure put an exclamation point of the defense. Let's head to the team house and I'll buy you a beer."

"Yes, sir. Thought you'd never ask." As they began toward the team house, Fetterman added, "I was certainly glad Spooky was here. I watched him work. That is an awesome sight."

"That it is. How were things in the jungle?"

"I think we surprised them. They didn't know what to do about us and the fight for the camp distracted them. I think we distracted them, too. Confused them and split their command, which was the whole point."

"What'd you find chasing after them?"

"Fairly good command and control in the retreat, but they weren't practicing noise discipline. They were losing equipment which made following them easy. They were making a beeline for Cambodia. They did have a rear guard that we ran into, but I got us out of there as quickly as I could. No one was hit. I hoped we could get a blocking force in there to engage them."

"Not enough time but if General Patterson has his way, I think they might be engaged by the Air Force."

"We can't cross that imaginary line on the ground, but the Air Force can?"

"I don't think they can see it. If the enemy is close to the border, regardless of which side he is on, I think the Air Force will engage."

They entered the team house and Fetterman dropped his web gear near the door but kept his weapon with him.

Gerber said, "Get the sergeant major a beer before he collapses from dehydration."

Bromhead opened the refrigerator, grabbed a can and tossed it to Fetterman. He caught it, popped the top and said, "I needed that."

EPILOGUE

General Dekker was not in the habit of traveling to the offices of his subordinates. He made them come to him, but this was a different circumstance. Although he outranked Brigadier General Patterson, he tapped on the door but then entered without waiting for a reply. "You have a moment, General?" he said.

Patterson looked up and then stood up. "Certainly, General. I could have come to your office. I'm just thinking about the next report I need to write."

Dekker waved a hand, dismissing the comment. "I'm sorry to hear about your aide and especially Sergeant Major Stein."

"Stein was old school. A pure and tough soldier. A great loss to me and to the Army."

"Of course. Have you considered a decoration for either of them?"

"Purple Hearts, certainly. Maybe the Bronze Star Medal for heroism, seems appropriate. I'm thinking of something higher for Stein. He had no reason to be caught in the circumstances he found himself in. He was there because he thought himself responsible for my safety. He was guarding me."

Dekker nodded and pulled out a chair to sit down. "Silver Star for certain. I'm not sure that a Distinguished Service Cross is appropriate."

"Let's try for that. His family would think it appropriate for his sacrifice."

"If you prepare the citation and I sign it, then it should be approved. The regulation on the approval authority is a little vague. Calls for a major general, but he might have to be the commanding officer. I can talk to General Abrams about it. As the theater commander he certainly has the authority."

"That would be kind of you."

"What about the pilots? Have you thought about them?"

Patterson shook his head. "Not in my chain of command. I guess most people don't think about them. The warrant officer, Cornett, should get something. A Silver Star or a DFC. The rest of the crew needs something. I'll think on it."

"And the pilot and crew who pulled you out?"

"I suspect the Green Berets will get them something."

Dekker changed the subject. "What about this Captain Cooper? He seems to have dropped the ball."

Patterson closed his eyes for a moment, as if in deep thought. "That's a tough call. He was there, at the camp, when we landed. I don't think the commander there let him use the radio."

"Why not?"

"I think it had to do with OPSEC. The commander, Bromhead, was worried about the VC learning I was there. He wanted to get me out."

Dekker was silent. "I don't like this. Cooper failed. Let's find him something else to do for the rest of his tour."

"I'm not sure that is completely fair. He was involved in the defense of the camp."

"Let's find him a place somewhere else. Maybe he would fit in better at Nha Trang."

Patterson didn't respond.

Dekker waved his hand again, wiping the slate clean. "Your initial after-action report, from both your observations during the recon flight and later at the Special Forces camp, have found its way to higher authority."

"Yes, sir."

"Further recon suggests there is a large contingent of North Vietnamese just on the other side of the Cambodia border. Later, high-altitude recon suggests they have not dispersed, but are preparing for a large-scale operation in Vietnam, possibly targeting Saigon."

"Are we going to intercept them as they cross the border?"

Dekker picked at a spot on his pressed jungle fatigues. "No. Time isn't right for that. The best thing would be to engage them in Cambodia, but you know how the press would greet that. An expansion of the war. Something that we must avoid at all costs."

"So, we just allow them to assemble their force and take heavy casualties as we repel this because the press would complain?"

"Not at all, General. Arc Light."

"We're going to use B-52s to drop bombs on them?"

"Flying above thirty-three thousand feet, where their antiaircraft won't be able to engage them and where they have no fighter support to intercept them. If we hit the target right, it will disable them to the point where they'll have to call off their plans."

Patterson laughed. "And the world press won't be in up in arms about that because no American soldier crossed the border."

"I think of this as a better tribute to Sergeant Major Stein. He helped gather the intelligence that provides this opportunity."

"There is no better tribute."

Kendall Stacy, having rested for a couple of days after the ordeal with the Special Forces, sat down to write his account of the attack. He sat staring at the paper and typewriter, but inspiration didn't hit. He couldn't think of a good opening for the story. He didn't know if it should be directed at a newspaper or a magazine. He didn't know how much he should report because he didn't want to give away any secrets. He needed some guidance.

He got up, poured himself a drink, and thought about the Public Affairs Officers. Maybe one of them could help him design the story. He walked over to the main headquarters, found the office of the PAO, and asked to talk with him. Instead, he found himself sitting in the office of a captain who looked as if he hadn't been in Vietnam long. His fatigues were bright green, and his nose was badly sunburned.

"What can I do for you?" the captain asked.

"I'm trying to put together a story about an assault on a Special Forces camp a couple of days ago. I fear that I might be violating some of the rules here. I don't want to write anything that is going to endanger the men in the field."

"Got it. Show me what you have."

Kendall smiled. "I'm having a little trouble starting."

"Okay, let's see what we can do."

Stacy told him what he had seen and what he had heard and didn't mention where he had been during the fight. He made it sound as if he was in the middle of the battle, which wasn't accurate, but it was true. After three hours, they had a rough draft of a four-thousand-word analysis of the fight. Stacy nodded his approval.

"You'll just need to polish it. There is nothing there that would be useful for an enemy. We've left out enough detail that the story, when published, will have little intelligence value."

Stacy took the pages, straightened the edges and said, "Thanks. You've been a big help."

The captain grinned. "Just doing my job. Let me know how it goes later."

"Of course." Stacy had no intention of ever seeing the captain again.

Colonel Nguyen, of the People's Army of Vietnam had left his command in Cambodia for Hanoi. General Giap wanted his personal observations of the attack on the Special Forces camp and why it had failed so spectacularly. Giap wanted to be able to counter the strength of the levels of support the Americans brought to the defense of their camps and bases throughout Vietnam. Not only the defenses of the camps themselves, but the interlocking artillery from fire support bases, helicopter gunships and jet fighters.

Nguyen was twelve miles from his advanced headquarters when he heard a distant rumbling. He turned in the seat, looking out the rear window of the truck. At first, he saw nothing, but then he spied a line of dirty clouds hugging the horizon and growing rapidly.

The driver slowed. "Don't slow down, you idiot," said Nguyen. "Find a place with good cover and pull over."

They entered a patch of thick, triple-canopy jungle where the road became a muddy track that required a four-wheel-drive vehicle. As soon as the truck stopped, Nguyen jumped out. He couldn't see much more than the rising clouds of smoke and dirt in the distance.

He climbed up onto the bed of the truck. "Binoculars!" he shouted. "I need binoculars."

The driver found the binoculars and hurried around. He handed them up to Nguyen.

Now, from the raised platform and through the binoculars, he caught a flash of silver. He couldn't quite make out what he was seeing, but that made no difference. He knew what it was. B-52 bombers were attacking his unit.

The rumbling stopped and he thought it was over. But then, from a different place, it started again. This was a coordinated attack. He jumped down and handed the binoculars back to the driver. "I need to return to the unit."

The driver stood as if rooted to the ground. Finally, he turned and walked back to the cab of the truck. There was one thing that he didn't want to do and that was drive back. Not with that part of Cambodia under attack by enemy bombers.

Nguyen climbed back into the cab. "Hurry up. Let's go."

The driver worked slowly. "If you don't get moving right now," said Nguyen, "you'll be leading the next human wave attack on an enemy installation."

By the time he got back to the unit, the attack was over. The disaster was complete. There were long lines from deep craters and men stumbling around, injured by the overpressure of the bombs. There were so many bodies and so many pieces of bodies that Nguyen knew there were men who had just disappeared in a flash of fire. He doubted he had many more than a hundred or two hundred men who were uninjured. It was an effective attack.

The plan that had been laid out in Hanoi so many months ago was now ruined. Nguyen believed that when he returned to Hanoi, he would be arrested. The blame would be placed directly on his head because he had failed to overrun the American camp and then lead the enemy back to his base in Cambodia.

For an hour, he walked around viewing the damage and looking for survivors. He just couldn't believe what he was seeing. He knew his career was over and he wondered how he could recover. He just knew he wouldn't be part of the war from now on. He wasn't sure that he would survive the trip to Hanoi.

Gerber was sitting in his office at Nha Trang and drinking Pepsi. He was looking at a classified report provided by the Air Force. Fetterman entered the office. Gerber held up the report. "The Air Force apparently just finished the job. I've got the BDA."

"How bad is it, or rather, how good?"

"According to this, there had been a division or two that had traveled down from the north. The Air Force claims the B-52s destroyed them. I think they're being a little optimistic, but I'm sure the NVA felt the attack."

"Let me see that assessment when you have finished with it."

"They don't mention the intelligence you gathered about the location of the enemy, if that's what you're looking for."

"No, Major. I just want to see how badly they were mauled."

"They won't be able to mount an effective attack from that area for quite a while."

"Then our job here is done."

GLOSSARY

AC — Aircraft commander. The pilot in charge of the aircraft.

ACP — Automatic Colt Pistol.

AFVN — American Forces Vietnam Network.

AIT — Advanced Individual Training. The school soldiers were sent to after basic training.

AK-47 — Assault rifle normally used by the North Vietnamese and the Viet Cong.

ANGRY-109 — AN-109, the radio used by the Special Forces for long-range communications.

AN/PRR9 and **AN/PRT4** — Intrasquad radio receiver and transmitter used for short-range communications. The range is something under a mile.

AO — Area of Operations.

AP — Air Police. The old designation for the guards on Air Force bases. Now referred to as security police.

AP ROUNDS — Armor-piercing ammunition.

APU — Auxiliary Power Unit. An outside source of power used to start aircraft engines.

ARC LIGHT — Term used for a B-52 bombing mission. Also known as heavy arty.

ARVN — Army of the Republic of Vietnam. A South Vietnamese soldier.

ASA — Army Security Agency.

ASH AND TRASH — Refers to helicopter support missions that didn't involve a direct combat role. They hauled supplies, equipment, mail and all sorts of ash and trash.

AST — Control officer between the men in isolation and the outside world. Responsible for taking care of all the problems.

AUTOVON — Army phone system that allows soldiers on one base to call another base, bypassing the civilian phone system.

BDA — Bomb Damage Assessment.

BODY COUNT — Number of enemy killed, wounded or captured during an operation. Used by Saigon and Washington as a means of measuring the progress of the war.

BOONDOGGLE — Any military operation that hasn't been completely thought out. An operation that is ridiculous.

BOONIE HATS — Soft cap worn by a grunt in the field when not wearing his steel pot.

BROWNING M-2 — Fifty-caliber machine gun manufactured by Browning.

BROWNING M-35 — The 9mm automatic pistol that became the favorite of the Special Forces.

C AND C — Command and Control aircraft that circled overhead to direct combined air and ground operations.

CARIBOU — Cargo transport plane.

CHECKRIDE — Flight in which one pilot checks the proficiency of another. It can be an informal review of the various techniques or a very formal test of a pilot's knowledge.

CHINOOK — Army aviation twin-engine helicopter. A CH-47.

CHOCK — Refers to the number of the aircraft in the flight. Chock Three is the third, Chock Six is the sixth.

CLAYMORE — Antipersonnel mine that fires 750 steel balls with a lethal range of 50 meters.

CLOSE AIR SUPPORT — Use of airplanes and helicopters to fire on enemy units near friendly troops.

COLT — Soviet-built small transport plane. The NATO code name for Soviet and Warsaw Pact transports all begin with the letter C.

CONEX — Steel container about 10 feet high, 10 feet long and 10 feet deep, used to haul equipment and supplies.

C-RATS — C-rations.

DAI UY — Vietnamese Army rank equivalent to U.S. Army Captain.

DEROS — Date of Estimated Return from Overseas Service.

DIRNSA — Director, National Security Agency.

DZ — Drop Zone.

E AND E — Escape and Evasion.

FEET WET — Term used by pilots to describe flight over water.

FIELD GRADE — Refers to officers above the rank of Captain but under Brigadier General. In other words, Majors, Lieutenant-Colonels and Colonels.

FIRECRACKER — Special artillery shell that explodes into a number of small bomblets that detonate later. The artillery version of the cluster bomb, it was employed as a secret weapon tactically for the first time at Khe Sanh.

FIREFLY — Helicopter with a battery of bright lights mounted in or on it. The aircraft is designed to draw enemy fire at night so that gunships orbiting close by can attack the target.

FIRST SHIRT — Military term referring to the First Sergeant.

FIVE — Radio call sign for the Executive Officer of a unit.

FNG — Fucking New Guy.

FOB — Forward Operating Base.

FOX MIKE — FM radio.

FREEDOM BIRD — Name given to any aircraft that took troops out of Vietnam. Usually referred to the commercial jet flights that took men back to the World.

GARAND — The M-1 rifle that was replaced by the M-14. Issued to the South Vietnamese early in the war.

GRAIL — NATO name for the shoulder-fired SA-7 surface-to-air missile.

GUARD THE RADIO — Stand by in the commo bunker and listen for messages.

GUIDELINE — NATO name for the SA-2 surface-to-air missile.

GUNSHIP — Armed helicopter or cargo plane that carries weapons instead of cargo.

HALO — High Altitude, Low Opening.

HE — High-explosive ammunition.

HOOTCH — Almost any shelter, from temporary to long-term.

HORN — Term that referred to a specific kind of radio operations that used satellites to rebroadcast the messages.

HOTEL THREE — Helicopter landing area at Saigon's Tan Son Nhut Airport.

HUEY — UH-1 helicopter.

HUMINT — Human Intelligence Resource.

ICS — Intercom system in an aircraft.

IN-COUNTRY — Term used to refer to American troops operating in South Vietnam. They were all in-country.

INTELLIGENCE — Any information about enemy operations that would be useful in planning a mission.

KIA — Killed in Action.

KLICK — Thousand meters; a kilometer.

LIMA LIMA — Land line. Refers to telephone communications between two points on the ground.

LLDB — Luc Luong Dac Biet. The South Vietnamese Special Forces.

LP — Listening Post. A position outside the perimeter manned by a couple of soldiers to give advance warning of enemy activity.

LRRP — Long-Range Reconnaissance Patrol.

LSA — Lubricant used by soldiers on their weapons to ensure they will continue to operate properly.

LZ — Landing Zone.

M-3A1 — Also known as a grease gun. A .45-caliber submachine gun favored in World War Two by GIs because its slow rate of fire meant that the barrel didn't rise and they didn't burn through their ammo as fast as they did with some other weapons.

M-14 — Standard rifle of the U.S. Army, eventually replaced by the M-16. It fired the standard 7.62mm NATO round.

M-16 — Became the standard infantry weapon of the Vietnam War. It fired 5.56mm ammunition.

M-79 — Short-barreled, shoulder-fired weapon that fired a 40mm grenade. These could be high explosives, white phosphorus or canister.

M-113 — Armored personnel carrier.

MACV — Military Assistance Command, Vietnam. Replaced MAAG in 1964.

MEDEVAC — Medical Evacuation. Also called Dust-Off. A helicopter used to take the wounded to medical facilities.

MI — Military Intelligence.

MIA — Missing in Action.

MONOPOLY MONEY — Term used by the servicemen in Vietnam to describe the MPC handed out in lieu of regular U.S. currency.

MOS — Military Occupation Specialty.

MPC — Military Payment Certificates. The Monopoly money used instead of real cash by the U.S. Army.

NCO — A noncommissioned officer. A noncom. A sergeant.

NCOIC — NCO in Charge. The senior NCO in a unit, detachment or patrol.

NDB — Nondirectional Beacon. A radio beacon that can be used for homing.

NEXT — The man who said it was his turn to be rotated home.

NINETEEN — Average age of the combat soldier in Vietnam, as opposed to twenty-six in World War Two.

NVA — North Vietnamese Army. Also used to designate a soldier from North Vietnam.

ONTOS — Marine weapon that consists of six 106mm recoilless rifles mounted on a tracked vehicle.

OPORD — Operations Order.

OPSEC — Operations Security.

ORDER OF BATTLE — Listing of units available and to be used during a battle.

P (PIASTER) — Basic monetary unit in South Vietnam worth slightly less than a U.S. penny.

PETA-PRIME — Tar-like substance that melted in the heat of the day to become a sticky nightmare that clung to boots, clothes and equipment. It was used to hold down the dust during the dry season.

PETER PILOT — Copilot in a helicopter.

PLF — Parachute Landing Fall. The roll used by parachutists on landing.

POL — Petroleum, Oil and Lubricants. The refueling point on many military bases.

POW — Prisoner of War.

PRC-10 — Portable radio.

PRC-25 — A lighter portable radio that replaced the PRC-10. Sometimes called Prick-25.

PULL PITCH — Term used by helicopter pilots to mean they are going to take off.

PUNJI STAKE — Sharpened bamboo hidden to penetrate the foot.

PUZZLE PALACE — The Pentagon. It was called the Puzzle Palace because no one knew what was going on there. Puzzle Palace East referred to MACV or USARV headquarters in Saigon.

RLO — Real Live Officer. Term used by warrant officers to refer to officers who were commissioned.

RON — Remain Over Night. Term used by flight crews to indicate a flight that would last longer than a day.

RPD — Soviet-made 7.62mm light machine gun.

RTO — Radio Telephone Operator. The radioman of a unit.

RUFF-PUFFS — Term applied to the RF-PFs, the Regional Forces and Popular Forces. Militia drawn from the local population.

S-3 — Company-level operations officer.

SA-2 — Surface-to-air missile fired from a fixed site. A radar-guided missile nearly 35 feet long.

SA-7 — Surface-to-air missile that is shoulder-fired and has infrared homing.

SACSA — Special Assistant for Counterinsurgency and Special Activities.

SAFE AREA — Selected Area For Evasion. It doesn't mean that the area is safe from the enemy, only that the terrain, location or local population make the area a good place for escape and evasion.

SAM TWO — Refers to the SA-2 Guideline.

SAR — Search and Rescue.

SECDEF — Secretary of Defense.

SHORT-TIMER — Person who had been in Vietnam for nearly a year and who would be rotated back to the World soon. When the DEROS was the shortest in the unit, the person was said to be *Next*.

SIX — Radio call sign for the unit commander.

SKS — Soviet-made carbine.

SMG — Submachine gun.

SOI — Signal Operating Instructions. The booklet that contained the call signs and radio frequencies of the units in Vietnam.

SOP — Standard Operating Procedure.

SPIKE TEAM — Special Forces team made up for a direct-action mission.

STEEL POT — Standard U.S. Army helmet. The steel pot was the outer metal cover.

TAOR — Tactical Area of Operational Responsibility.

TDY — Temporary duty, temporary assignment.

TEAM UNIFORM OR COMPANY UNIFORM — UHF radio frequency on which the team or the company communicates. Frequencies were changed periodically in an attempt to confuse the enemy.

THE WORLD — The United States.

THREE — Radio call sign of the Operations Officer.

THREE CORPS — Military area around Saigon. Vietnam was divided into four corps areas.

TO&E — Table of Organization and Equipment. A detailed listing of all the men and equipment assigned to a unit.

TOC — Tactical Operations Center.

TOT — Time Over Target. Refers to the time the aircraft are supposed to be over the drop zone with the parachutists, or the target if the planes are bombers.

TRIPLE A — Antiaircraft Artillery or AAA. Anything used to shoot at airplanes and helicopters.

TWO — Radio call sign of the Intelligence Officer.

TWO-OH-ONE (201) FILE — Military records file that listed all of a soldier's qualifications, training, experience and abilities. It was passed from unit to unit so that a new commander would have some idea about the capabilities of an incoming soldier.

UMZ — Ultramilitarized Zone. Name GIs gave to the DMZ (Demilitarized Zone).

UNIFORM — Refers to the UHF radio. Company Uniform would be the frequency assigned to that company.

USARV — United States Army, Vietnam.

VC — Viet Cong, called Victor Charlie (phonetic alphabet) or just Charlie.

VIET CONG — Contraction of Vietnam Cong San (Vietnamese Communist).

VIET CONG SAN — Vietnamese communists. A term in use since 1956.

WHITE MICE — South Vietnamese military police who all wore white helmets.

WIA — Wounded in Action.

WILLY PETE — WP, white phosphorus. Called smoke rounds. Also used as antipersonnel weapons.

WOBBLY ONE — Refers to a W-1, the lowest of Warrant Officer grade. Helicopter pilots who weren't commissioned started out as Wobbly Ones.

WSO — Weapons System Officer.

XM-21 — Name given to the Army's sniper rifle. An M-14 mounted with a special ART scope.

XO — Executive Officer of a unit.

X-RAY — Term that refers to an engineer assigned to a unit.

A NOTE TO THE READER

Dear Reader,
If you have enjoyed this novel enough to leave a review on **Amazon** and **Goodreads**, then we would be truly grateful.
Sapere Books

Sapere Books is an exciting new publisher of brilliant fiction and popular history.

To find out more about our latest releases and our monthly bargain books visit our website:
saperebooks.com